CHAINSAW JANE

a novel by

Marie-Jo Fortis

For Pierre and Maïa

Acknowledgments

My gratitude to the c.i.a. (clarion irrepressible authors), my talented writers group, for all their support and suggestions that went from substance to semicolon and back. Any writer knows that such contribution is invaluable. It adds an essential tool to our toolbox—humility. So merci beaucoup to all, especially to Loretta McNaughton, who is an intrinsic part of my life; Melissa Downes, Joseph Occhipinti, Judy Rock and Vincent Spina. Writing is everything to me, even more so since this not-so-shy bunch started adding their grain of salt to my prose. Salt here is the key word.

My thoughts also go to Lynda Bennett de Valladares, just for being Lynda, a poet and mi amiga.

I also want to thank my epistolary friend Jason Ellis— whom I consider the first real reader of Chainsaw Jane.

Note from the author

Although Pennsylvania is real, the town of Noliar is not. The witty among you will retort: of course, Noliar couldn't possibly exist. In any case, if the place is imaginary, this means so are the characters. So if you find there someone who reminds you of your Uncle Bobby or your Grandma Paula, it's just a coincidence. I know some think there is no such a thing as a coincidence. But if you look in the dictionary, you will find it.

PART I

■1■

THEY WOULDN'T FIND HER.

And even if they did, they wouldn't find him. He was dead.
Dead, smiling, and e-reading the paper.

May 10. Oblivious of the breakfast remnants scattered around the
rustic kitchen table, of the buzz of a couple of satisfied flies, or of the
odor of dishes that now formed a dirty Tower of Pisa in the sink, he sat
behind his laptop. He had moved away crumbles with his forearm to
nest his computer on an arguably clean spot. Now he took a swallow
from his coffee mug before gliding down toward the Classifieds of *The
New York Times* website. He loved *The New York Times*. Nostalgia—was
it? He always started with the Personals, as they always cracked him up.

"Here we are," he mumbled to himself as he started reading.

EASY GOING AND EDUCATED Petite, athletic blond, 27, seeks
sweet, sexy, successful man, 70-82, to share best of life with.
Box 13699600.

That's one legal way to kill a guy and inherit in a jiffy, the man
thought. Not bad. The gal probably looks like Paris Hilton, minus

the wealth, plus the brains. She sounded yummy but a bit dangerous. He tapped his beer belly. He'd pass. He ruffled his gray mane. He was a bit too young for this praying mantis, anyway.

He glided through a few boring ads then stopped at this one:

OPEN-MINDED REPUBLICAN Sexy, well-built, 69-year-old man...

Yeah, right.

...seeks pretty, well put together, warm 30-year-old woman. Intelligence not a requirement. Box 15423198.

Why, sure! Better find a dumb one who believes in open-minded Republicans. Let's move on.

He went on perusing. Blah, blah, blah. Yeah, yeah, yeah. They all want to fuck but are not honest enough to say in what position.

And then he found what he was looking for.

HAVE YOU SEEN MY FRIEND? Urgent. Dorothea Sishy, owner of Open Page bookstore-cafe on East Side 66VANCE\u3th St. Missing since May 4. Box 5473908.

Yep, he knew exactly where Open Page was. At the corner of 66th and 1st Avenue. A few steps away from Rockefeller University and the Cornell Medical Center. Smart location, successful business. Students and faculty came for lunch there and often bought books at the same time. There were used books that kids and stingy profs could buy for a buck or two; there were new editions, rare editions, you name it. There were page markers, souvenirs, T-shirts, and statuettes caricaturing authors and politicians—stuff for all kinds of budgets and all sorts of brains. There were readings and book signings. There were bistro tables where one could eat and drink this and that, you name it: espressos, lattes, frosties, even plain coffee; muffins, dough-nuts, the soup du jour (Soup *du jour*! Well excuse me! Like, soup of the day was not good enough!). So people could have a plate on one side and a book on the other, 'magine that! They could wander around the store all day long if they wished. Sofas and chairs were placed at strategic points, so customers could relax while scanning various volumes, and make their choices or no choice at all. No pressure. Talk about fancy. So-phis-ti-ca-ted. But he knew that out of guilt for invading the place, they would buy a thing or two. How come he hadn't thought of that? How come that bitch had? How come she had been able to start all over again, without money in the bank?

Unless, unbeknownst to him, she had put money somewhere under the mattress. With her pointy little face, she might have been a sly thing. Well, no more.

He produced a twisted grin. They won't find her. He would bet his brand new pickup truck on it. It would be nothing short of a miracle if they found her. He quit the Classifieds and went to the big titles. It was all about war, the economy, same old shit, but let's face it, the writing was way better than the soporific stuff he found in *The Noliar Call*.

■ ■

ON MAY 15, HE didn't go to the Classifieds. One of *The New York Times* big headlines caught his attention first.

OWNER OF OPEN PAGE BOOKSTORE DISAPPEARS, POLICE INVESTIGATING

He banged his desk with his coffee mug, and coffee splashed all over his face. What the—what the fuck! He wiped the coffee stains off his face with the back of his hand. Why so big a title for this type of news? Why not just a paragraph lost somewhere in the crowd of words?

Could it be that the bitch had connections?

He scratched his head. The NYPD had that detective with the weird mustache—Leek, the name was. The guy gave him the creeps. He looked everywhere, at places no one thought of. No mystery unsolved with that moron. Well, that was not entirely true. There was that one thing he had never figured out. He had been outsmarted, for once.

He thought Mr. Mustache would be retired by now. But no.

To top it all, there was that Russian woman. Jane Coogashvillain. Or Dugosh...Dugosh-somethin'—a cock-and-bull name he could never remember. Chainsaw Jane, everyone called her. Wrinkled like a garment forgotten in the dryer, but able to drink like a tribe of Cossacks. For some reason, she was in contact with them. Pff...What was it—the KGB and the NPYD were pals now?

He sneered. Why, sure! And he would enter a monastery next week, too. He looked at his cup. It was time for more coffee.

They wouldn't find the bitch. They couldn't.

He rose slowly, and the wooden floor cracked and hissed in agony. Most of the time people hardly noticed his limp; he could control it just fine. But today, his walk produced a thump. It was as if his legs were two sticks playing on a gigantic drum, with a slow, uneven beat. Boom-boom-puhm, puhm-puhm, boomm...puuhm...puhm.

Boom. It had a rhythm from hell, and it hurt like hell.

The birds—those damn birds—were at it again. Singing, chirping, with the same fury. As if mocking him. He promised himself to slash off those woods behind his house and have a real backyard once and for all.

◼ 2 ◼

EVERYONE IN NOLIAR LOVED Chainsaw Jane.

The exceptions to that rule were the few xenophobes who would have loved to reinvent the KKK. This time, the burning of crosses would have occurred on Russian ground —Jane's lawn to be exact. But then they were reminded of another organization born in the old USSR whose name also started with the letter "K." If the USSR was now dead, the KGB was very much alive, they realized. So they reasoned themselves to a standstill and expressed grouchiness only when they were sure they were out of Jane's earshot.

Nobody knew how and why Chainsaw Jane had landed into Noliar. She suddenly was there, small and wrinkled like a Russian bad seed, and she rooted herself into the old PA town like a stubborn vine. Her real name was Yana Dzhugashvili. The few scholars who managed to survive in the community were well aware that Dzhugashvili was the real last name of Joseph Stalin, and they passed on the info to the ones whose only intellectual stimuli were the beery debates at the local bars or the readings of tabloid titles at grocery stores checkouts. In any case, this was another reason for the xenophobes or, as they would be ultimately called, the Foreigners Allergy and Rash

Tension Sufferers (the FARTS), to take their pain like men, in silence. After all, the woman could be a descendant of the communist dictator. When asked, she didn't confirm it. But she didn't deny it, either. She just said, "I have interesting family tree." And that was it.

Noliar natives had tremendous trouble pronouncing the Russian woman's name. So in time Yana Dzhugashvili became Jane Dugash. Before acquiring the final nickname of Chainsaw Jane, the name Dugash got transformed into "Docash," and it was for a reason. No one knew the source of Jane's income. How she made a living was a mystery. Members of the FARTS declared that "money must grow on Jane's fucking trees."

Jane had reformed the English language by primarily using the principle of decapitation. This meant that all the articles, be they definite or indefinite, were guillotined without a second thought, so that a sentence like "I went to the city with a pickup truck" became "I went to city with pickup truck." To this, our Robespierre of linguistics added a second reform that she unwittingly shared with the FARTS—her irrepressible penchant for the word "fuck." But she managed her difference by making it rhyme with "hook." In Jane's verbal territory "fook" and "fooking" were used liberally. So now the sentence became "I went to fooking city with fooking pickup truck." But her common sense made her add, "Who wants to go to fooking city with fooking truck unless one wants to rob bank or something and look like fooking country fool?"

"Fook," therefore, was Jane's breathing device which attained yogic proportions when it came to her love-hate relationship with the trees in her yard. She loved the shade they created and hated the branches that the squirrels used as highways to access her attic. So it was "fooking trees, fooking squirrels" until one day she couldn't stand it anymore and called DOOGY TREE SERVICES.

Shawn Doogy, sturdy, late fifties, raucous voice, came to evaluate the work a few days after Jane's initial call. He found her in the backyard, planting tomatoes. With her staccato gestures, mud-covered baggy jeans and clodhoppers, she looked like a barrel drunk with its own wine.

"You cut fooking branches, Mr. Doogy, so that fooking squirrels can't reach roof and attic. Can you do that?" Jane looked at Doogy with eyes that had become slits thanks to aging, myopia, and excessive smoking.

Doogy had bought his landscape and tree-cutting business from old Joe Smith, who had decided to retire and devote what was left of his life to boozing, women, and maybe church, at least once a month.

How long had Shawn Doogy lived in Noliar? Two, three years, maybe. Well, for a relative newcomer, he had adapted well to the community. He didn't talk much about himself, but it didn't take him long to become a member of the FARTS. So hiring a man secretly dreaming of a KKK against Russians secretly amused Jane.

"I can, but—" Doogy responded.

"I'll give you four hundred bucks, how is that?"

Doogy acquiesced.

Money talked, even to Nazis, Jane reflected, then said, "Very well. When can you come?"

"Saturday."

Jane slipped her hand into the front pocket of her decrepit 501s and removed a pack of Marlboros. She extracted a cigarette and planted it in her mouth. Doogy waited for an answer. Instead, Jane lit her cigarette, took a deep drag, and only produced a dismissive gesture as she let the smoke out of her nose and mouth.

"Saturday it is. You can go now." She duplicated the dismissive gesture with her free hand and looked in Doogy's direction as he went toward his pickup. The man was still fairly attractive, with some leftover mane that kept amidst the gray a bit of reddish coloring. He walked funny, though, at least not like men around here. She put the Marlboro pack back in her pocket, mumbled something in the order of "fooking asshole," finished her cigarette, and went back to her tomatoes.

A few raindrops fell on her neck. She kept working. She liked the feel of rain much more than she liked the sun.

■ ■

On the following Friday morning, the sun was throning big and wide in the sky and Jane was in her kitchen having coffee and her eleventh cigarette when she heard loud and strident sounds in the vicinity. Chainsaws, she figured. Looked like one of her next door neighbors was doing some pruning. Between two drags, she mentally cursed the damn neighbor, for the cacophony was close and nearly unbearable. If trees had a history of massacres, this certainly sounded Stalinian, like the Katyn episode against the Poles. It was almost as if it came from her own backyard. She suddenly got up, looked through the window. The sun was not the only thing drawing patterns on her grass. "What fook!" she exclaimed.

She rushed outside and saw that three of Doogy's men were in her yard. She ignored the two young and shirtless Adonises and went directly to the older guy, a man of sixty built as wiry as a Giacometti statue and still able to climb trees like a chimp. He was on top of her maple tree when she yelled, "Ed, come down now! This fooking instant!"

Ed didn't seem to hear. The competition was a chainsaw after all, so she screamed her lungs out. "Come down now, I said!" She now picked up some cut branches and started throwing them upward. At last she caught Ed's attention.

The older man turned off his chainsaw, mumbled an "Oh, boy!" and descended.

"What are you doing here?" Jane asked as soon as Ed was on the ground.

Ed, otherwise known as Ed Reed or simply "Monkey" because of his aforementioned climbing abilities, removed his cap and scratched his head. "Cutting your branches, Jane. Isn't that what you wanted?"

"You were supposed to come tomorrow!"

Ed scratched his head again. "Tomorrow?"

"Are you fooking stupid or what? Yes, tomorrow! Saturday! Your boss and I had agreement. He said Saturday, and I agreed."

"He never said no Saturday to us, Jane. He just told us today to come to your place, do some trimmin', and that was it."

"Did he tell you about taking care of fooking squirrels that go to attic?"

"Well, Jane, see, I don't know if by just cutting branches we..."

"Okay. Your boss said he could get rid of squirrels. So you better do it."

"Jane, if you really want to get rid of squirrels, you have to shoot them. If you want..."

"There will be no killing of fooking squirrels. Just make them go away! You hear that? And, here is five fooking bucks!"

"What for, Jane?"

"Buy calendar for your boss. Maybe dictionary. Asshole don't know difference between Friday and Saturday."

■ ■

SOME OF JANE'S BRANCHES were trimmed, and some others were left alone. The two shirtless Adonises had spent a quarter of their time dragging a few of the cut branches to a corner in her backyard, and the rest of it flirting with the bikinied girls next door. Monkey had done most of the work, but being sixty-something and seldom sober, his view of a completed job differed widely from the norm. To top it all, Doogy never came to supervise his men's work. As a result, squirrels kept having parties in Jane's attic.

"Fooking squirrels fooking in my attic!" Jane kept yelling as she hit the ceiling with a walking stick in an unsuccessful attempt to make them shut up.

■ ■

A FEW DAYS LATER, on a sunny June day, neighbors saw Jane on her roof with a camera.

"What are you doing, Jane?" asked Cruz Mojada.

Cruz, who lived across the street from Jane, worked at the Noliar Public Library. An abundant looking, fifty-something divorcee of Cuban origin, she was addicted to miniskirts and convinced that she bore a strong resemblance with sexy singer-actress Jennifer Lopez. She bore the burden of that conviction alone, however.

"Put some clothes on, Cruz, and I'll tell you," retorted Jane.

"Come on, Jane!"

Jane thought for a moment. Cruz didn't know how to dress, that was a fact. On the other hand, she happened to be an excellent gossip. Almost as good as Lara Clement, Noliar's Gossip-in-Chief.

"I'll tell you, Cruz. But just between us, okay?"

Cruz twisted her upper and lower lips between her right thumb and index and said, "My lips are sealed."

Jane knew what that shit meant, and that was fine with her.

"What are you waiting for? Climb to roof and you'll know everything."

Cruz looked at her tight miniskirt and pondered. She finally crossed the street, went to Jane's ladder, and began her ascension. During the process, a couple of older guys were passing by, walking their dogs. The face of one the men expressed shock, then just plain panic. The other guy almost fainted.

"What's matter with you?" Jane said. "Do you know that old Dick Carson and George Mutant almost had heart attacks when they saw your pink panties? And they're gays!"

"Fuchsia, I have you know."

"What?"

"The panties, they're fuchsia."

"It's not your age to wear that kind of clothes."

"I still have my period, you know."

Jane rolled her eyes. "When? Every time February decides to give us extra day?"

"How people can love you when you are such a bitch is beyond me, Jane. But now, tell me! Why the pictures?"

"Look," Jane replied. "I can touch tip of branches from roof."

"And?"

"And? And? Where were you when Doogy's men came?"

Silence.

"Oh, I get it. You watched shirtless young men. Did you wear bikini too, like girls next door?"

Silence again. Jane slapped her friend on the thigh.

"Cruz, what fook! Don't you know it's high time to hide cellulite?"

"I got distracted by the beautiful view, is all."

"Well, here is other view. Fooking squirrels can jump on roof and dance troika in my attic because beautiful view didn't do good job."

"What do you plan to do with the pictures?" asked Cruz.

"Show them to judge."

"What do you mean?"

"I didn't want to pay Doogy, so he's taking me to court."

"But, Jane—"

"Doogy didn't do job; Doogy shouldn't get money. Period."

Cruz acquiesced, then looked at her watch.

"Are you in hurry?" Jane asked.

"Well, Jane, as a matter of fact, there are things I need to do."

"Good-bye, then," Jane said.

"Bye, Jane."

Jane knew the cause of Cruz' hurry. In less time than it takes the overstressed mother to microwave processed foods, the whole neighborhood would know about Jane's tree trouble. The old Russian woman admired the efficiency of Cruz' gossip. "She's really very good. Maybe because her parents are from Cuba," she thought. "She knows all the fooking right moves. Her mouth can cha-cha-cha like no one else's."

■■

WHEN JANE ARRIVED AT District Judge Nora Cadence's court, she was dressed in her Sunday clothes. Since she never went to church, the dress was old, outmoded, and inconsiderate of the fact that Jane had gained a few pounds. This only could underline her barrel-like figure. But Jane was happy that it still fit somehow and that she wouldn't have to go to the local Wal-Mart to buy something new. Strangely enough, she had never been to court before and had managed once or twice to evade jury duties, but now she was resolute and convinced that justice would prevail. She had pictures and she had affidavits from neighbors who had undergone similar experiences with SHAWN DOOGY TREE SERVICES.

And she had Cruz' gossips.

Not to mention that she had lived in Noliar longer than the Doogy man.

What could go wrong?

When she saw Doogy drag himself to court, unshaven and in dirty work clothes, she knew that she was going to win. She argued her points with a mix of passion and minutia while Doogy barely babbled. It dawned on Jane that the man talked like he walked, with uncertainty. Judge Cadence, a thin woman with curly bleached hair, listened impassively, but Jane knew, she just knew, what side she was on. When she exited the District Court, she was proud of herself.

The following week, a letter from Judge Cadence arrived. Jane opened it with a wide grin. But the smile soon disappeared. That overpermed bitch was ordering her to pay Shawn Doogy the sum of four hundred dollars, plus court expenses.

Jane threw the letter on the floor and stepped on it. "I bet Judge and Doogy are fooking!" she yelled. She lit a cigarette and filled a water glass with Russian Standard, her favorite vodka.

The next day, she was walking downtown Main Street. When she reached the True Value store, she explained to Bill Carey, a jolly older man and the owner of the store, what she needed. Minutes later, locals saw Jane carrying a big package.

"What's that in there, Jane?" some of them asked.

"Chainsaw, that's what in there," Jane responded. "Best chainsaw Bill has too."

And she kept on walking.

At home, she carefully read the instructions. The rest of the day, she was up in her trees, cutting every branch she could reach. She finally stepped down and looked at her work. Her trees now looked like columns conceived by some drunk Corinthian architect.

"Who needs SHAWN DOOGY TREE SERVICES?" Jane told herself.

Of course her back hurt some, but it was nothing that a few glasses of vodka couldn't remedy.

From that day on, Jane Docash, formerly known as Jane Dugash, formerly known as Yana Dzhugashvili, simply became known as Chainsaw Jane. After that, members of the FARTS started smiling at Jane. They didn't want the self-made landscapist to apply her new-found skills on them. And the political debates on immigration that went on at the Moisol, Jane's bar of choice, only referred to the Polish and the Ukrainians. Her voice warmed up by a few Smirnoffs (that's all the fooking vodka that stupid bar carried), she expressed the view that no Ukrainian should be allowed anywhere and that Polish sausage should be made illegal, like any other dangerous drug. Only the passing tourist dared to disagree. Otherwise, Jane declared with pride that there was no prejudiced bone in her body and that any bigot should sit as far from her as possible, or else.

■ 3 ■

ERITAGE LANE WAS CLEAN, neat, and mainly inhabited by retirees who had little to do besides mowing their lawns and spying on each other. As a consequence, curtains and drapes were always moving one way or another. People hungry for the next local scandal rearranged their window covers as discreetly as their arthritis allowed. Some had added binoculars to their equipment and claimed to be bird-watchers. To the brave soul that occasionally confronted them by indicating that bird-watching was an outdoor activity, they gave a glance that told the foolhardy creature that she didn't know anything, and would she please move away from their damn curtains so they could go on with their mission. Gossip-in-Chief Lara Clement was more skillful. She had see-through curtains that needed no lifting. Her glasses, which looked like portholes hanging miraculously on her small, triangular face, gave her a twenty-twenty vision. And she had binoculars as well. She, too, was a bird-watcher.

That first Monday of June, Lara Clement and the less professional gossips saw two people knock on Jane's door. They didn't dress like the locals or like the young Mormon missionaries who came to harass neighborhoods every summer. They came from another species yet.

Neighbors had seen them before on Heritage Lane and knew for a fact that they came from the NYPD. Why were they so sure? Because one of them was Julie Hoffman, who had been a police officer in Noliar for a few years before going to the Big Apple where she now worked as a detective. She came with an older man who wore a three-piece suit, sometimes a hat, and always a spectacular mustache. They assumed he was her partner. After all, they watched *Law & Order, Law & Order: SVU, Law & Order: Criminal Intent,* and the whole freaking family of cop shows, so what they couldn't learn from Noliar Chief of Police Johnny Dumasky or their local paper, *The Noliar Call,* they learned from the box. They had to admit, though, that Julie's partner looked rather odd, but what could you expect from city cops.

Last time they had seen these two was April. They were at Jane's place in the middle of winter before that. And last year, it had been at least a couple of times. What did Chainsaw Jane have to do with the NYPD?

Lara Clement had brought homemade cookies time and again to try to cajole Jane into a confession. Cruz Mojada had promised her friend to give her the ten best of her porn flick collection. "And I know a wonderful website that sells la creme de la creme among dildos. I can give you the address if you want." Under the condition, of course, that Jane would tell her everything about the New York cops.

To no avail.

And it wasn't for lack of trying. For Cruz kept on questioning her friend, asking if Zoe Zimmerman, a Noliar native now living in the Big Apple, was in trouble. All Jane would answer was this: "You know what, Dildo Woman? What makes you think I don't know about dildos? Maybe I know more about dildos than you. I have lived in many countries before coming here. And I had number of husbands of various sizes and nationalities—some two-termers, some one-termers, and one impeached in middle of term. And between husbands, I have used transitional objects. Matter of fact, I am living through long, long transition now. And I may make transition permanent, why not? So perhaps I have impressive international dildo collection. What do you say to that?"

And that cut Cruz right off. The faux Jennifer Lopez walked out indignantly. How could Jane say disgusting things like that! No one knew about dildos as much as Cruz. No one! Different sizes, different colors, different noises, she had them all!

Watching her friend rush to Lara Clement's house, Jane rubbed her hands and said, "And then there were none!"

"Well, at least for two or three days," she added philosophically.

■ ■

"STILL FOOKING GIRLS, JULIE?" Jane said to the short-haired, blond athletic woman facing her.

That was Jane's form of hello every time she saw Julie Hoffman. She had seen her grow; she had witnessed her troubled teenage years and, later, her beginnings as a cop. She had seen her cope with being gay in a town that had trouble coping with anything that wasn't macho-centric. Julie and Zoe Zimmerman had come to her house many times when they were kids, played together, fought each other, then played again. Jane had never meddled. She had let them self-regulate. And that was why, she thought, they kept coming back to her. They had grown into two alpha females of sorts. One blond, the other a redhead. One straight, one gay. Although, when it came to brains, it was Julie who was the straight one. This said, Zoe's somewhat twisted mind echoed Jane's in more ways than one.

Julie smiled. "Still *fooking* girls."

Jane picked a cigarette from a pack of Marlboros that had seen better days and planted it in her mouth. She lit it and took a drag with obvious pleasure.

At that moment, the mustached man scratched his throat.

"You remember Detective Leek," Julie said.

"What do you think I am, Julie, old degenerate woman?" Jane puffed smoke right into Julie's face. "Of course I remember! First name, too. Hercules, right?"

Leek's appreciation was manifest in his smile and the way he bowed his head.

"Mrs. Dzhugashvili, your memory is marvelous."

Jane wanted to respond that if her memory was occasionally deficient, what helped in Leek's case was the absurd contrast between the appearance of the man and his mythological counterpart. Had he come from a younger generation, Jane would have bet that LSD had been the main influence on parents when choosing such a name. What she was sure of was that God had not yet invented musculature when the detective was born. Hercules, what fook! She had never met a Hercules *with* a three-piece suit, a potbelly, and a weird mustache until now. She had to admit, though, that like so many Russians and so few Americans, he had good manners. And for a New York cop, he was downright exceptional. Matter of fact, he was a bit like a character that had jumped out of a novel from more civil times and landed in the here and now by accident. Every time she saw Detective Leek, she couldn't help it: she wondered if he was for real.

"Thank you, Mr. Leek. Now, sit and tell me purpose of visit."

Jane's living room was an unnerving ode to eclecticism, with a contemporary sofa, a country-style armchair, and a battered Pennsylvania Dutch coffee table. The Queen Anne armoire contained Russian Standard, Jewel of Russia, and Sputnik—in other words, Russia's finest vodka. To this collection Jane had added the Swedish Absolut because she liked its mix of intensity and sweet almond flavor and Citadelle simply because it was French vodka and that simple fact somehow cracked her up. That and the aggressive, almost satiric citrus aftertaste. The American Smirnoff, she kept in a back corner for drunkies who didn't know a thing about vodka. All these bottles had something in common: they were all capable of altering consciousness and had put many of Jane's friends on the floor and snoring, while she stood proud and victorious and holding a refill.

On the walls, the faded reproductions of paintings by major French Impressionists had a blasé air about them; the framed comics from old newspapers had refrained their satire and declared their ennui; and the painted plates and wooden spoons from old Russia hung at their own risk, like senile Bolshoi ballet dancers.

Julie looked out of the window. "First, tell me one thing, Jane."

"Tell you what thing?"

"What happened to your trees?"

"You like? I cut branches myself."

There was a brief silence, after which Julie decided to change the subject. "How about some Tarot?"

"It looks, Mrs. Dzhugashvili, like we need your expertise again."

"Tell me why."

"A woman has disappeared, Jane."

"How old?"

"Fifty-one."

"Maybe she went to other state, or even other country. Sometimes women do that. They're tired and they want to see something else, something new. Maybe new men. Or women. Maybe she needed vacation from Americans."

"I don't think that's what happened, ma'am."

"Have you heard of menopause, Mr. Leek? Women do crazy things when they get menopause."

"Why don't you just get your Tarot cards, Jane? You know why the NYPD uses you."

"Although NYPD keeps it big secret, right? They're ashamed of old Russian woman finding clues with Fool or Devil."

"Maybe we're ashamed *because* you find clues with cards," Leek gallantly said.

"Maybe I should charge NYPD more, then."

Julie was drumming her lap with the palms of her hands. "Jane, please!"

But Jane was on a roll. "Or I could send Five of Wands to hit them on head."

Absolute silence. Stern masks plastered on the two cops.

"All right, all right! Let me finish cigarette first." Jane took three more inhales and pressed her cigarette butt into a large ashtray.

She now got up and dragged her feet across the living room. As she disappeared into her bedroom, Julie whispered to her partner: "Remember not to try to explain things to Jane. That's an incentive for her to start her little arguments. A favorite pastime of hers, you should know that by now."

Leek's wide green eyes went still and dreamy all of a sudden, as if seeing the invisible. Julie had grown accustomed to that gaze. Somewhat. But it did manage at times to give her the chills. Like right now.

"You're right. I keep forgetting. Sorry," he finally said, his voice as gentle as Mr. Rogers'.

You're so fucking creepy sometimes, my dear feline partner, Julie thought. And then she got up, picked up the ashtray, and went to empty it in the kitchen trash can.

"Stop fooling around with ashtray," Jane told Julie when she returned.

"It was full of butts. And stinking. How can you smoke all that shit!" Julie replied.

Jane shrugged. Lesbians, she thought. Then, looking at Detective Leek, she said, "Come to dining room. It's easier to read on big table."

If Jane's dining room furniture was not exactly harmonious, it was fairly uniform. Only two of the six chairs had arthritic legs. A third one was as reliable as a drunken sailor.

"Don't sit there," Jane told Leek. "Take chair next to that one."

"One of us is safe," Julie said. "Okay. Deep breath. Now, my turn. Where do I go, Jane?"

Jane did not necessarily appreciate the sarcasm. "Go where you want. Fall on ass and see if I care."

■ ■

"Now, TELL ME WHEN woman disappeared."

Detective Leek adjusted his mustache. "May 4. A month ago."

Jane was about to shuffle her cards when Leek touched her arm, and asked, "You're going to deal with the Major and Minor Arcanas, right?"

"Yes, it's more complete that way."

"Would you mind reminding us the difference between the two, Jane?" Julie said.

"Major Arcana reflects major turning points, big patterns in life. Minor Arcana is for details. Sometimes it acts like detective for Major Arcana. Can I start now?" Jane was getting impatient.

The two detectives acquiesced.

"I'll start with Romany Spread. Row One, seven cards. It's woman's past. She lost husband nine, maybe ten years ago. Then, started having sex. Lots of fooking with many men. Happy widow. See the Queens? Queen of Wands. Also Queen of Cups. And then, from Major Arcana, Devil and Lovers. Look at other cards. No Hermit there. Fooking, fooking, and more fooking. Although woman doesn't look at all like Playboy bunny. More like librarian. Or someone associated with books. I see lots of books surrounding her."

"How on earth do you know that, Jane?" asked Julie.

Jane looked at Julie as if she were an annoying bug, then shrugged and continued. "Now, Row Two, seven cards also. It's her present. Let's see, Tower, from Major Arcana. That's big mess. Big, big mess. And Three of Swords. That's broken heart. She had sex, but she found love. Too bad. Love is no good for her. Not this one. Seven of Staves here. She's brave woman. Trying to cope, to get up. But she can't. All other cards go against her. "And now, Row Three, seven...Oh, no!"

"What, Jane? Why did you stop?"

"I was wrong! I made mistake!"

"A mistake? What kind?" asked Leek.

"Maybe about past. But surely about present."

"Well, Jane, redo Row Two. You can correct the mistake, right?"

"No, I can't correct mistake. It's impossible."

"For Chrissake, Jane! Why do you say that?"

"Because there's no present."

"No present? What do you mean?"

"What I mean is that present is gone because woman is dead."

Detectives Hoffman and Leek looked at each other.

"Can you tell us how?" asked Leek.

"Let me do other spread. Celtic Cross Spread. Give me name of woman."

"Can't guess that one, Jane?" Julie said.

Julie managed to control her smart-ass attitude most of the time. Obviously, today was not one of those times. As a result she was now the target of a fiery Russian glance.

"Her name is...was Dorothea Sishy," Julie added contritely.

Leek scratched his mustache.

"Very well. Dorothea, tell me something. Tell me who you are."

"Were," Leek corrected.

Had Jane's eyes been bullets, Leek would have been dead on the spot.

"Now listen to me, you two! I don't give shit whether or not you're cops. I like peace and quiet when I do readings for dead people. Dead people tell me things. Now, since dead people don't tell you things, shut fook up!"

Two cops suddenly on pins and needles echoing each other: "Yes, ma'am!"

"Very well. Now, here is first card for Dorothea. Come on, tell me something. Confusing. Maybe Dorothea was confused person. Bipolar or something."

"What makes you say that?"

"The Tower. It's back. It's what defines her. Let's see next card. Possibilities, or problems. The Moon. Another Card from Major Arcana. Not good. Things not being what they seem. Now, card three. This one should tell how Dorothea tried to get out of mess. Ten of Wands. Ten not so good in Minor Arcana. Means possibility of change, but resistance to change as well. And Dorothea tried to get out of problems, but not hard enough. Card four is influence from past. Ace of Cups. Beautiful Card. Means Dorothea was happy with her husband. But husband died or—"

Jane suddenly stopped. The two detectives looked at each other.

"Or?" asked Leek.

"Death of husband is strange," Jane commented.

"Sishy. The name brings bad memories," Detective Leek mumbled. Julie and Jane looked at him.

"Sorry," Leek said as he adjusted his mustache. "I was talking to myself. Please go on."

Jane took a deep breath and shook her head. "Ace of Cups is weak influence here. I said before she was happy widow. I was wrong. She fooked a lot but used fooking as compensation for loss."

"No Death card yet?" asked Leek.

"It's cliché to think Death card means death. Don't watch shit on TV, Mr. Leek."

Julie produced a one-sided smile. "Yeah, Leek. Don't watch shit on TV."

"I don't own a TV, Mrs. Dzhugashvili."

"Then where does Death shit come from?"

"Being a cop, Jane, that's where it comes from. To us, death means death."

Detective Leek scratched his throat.

"So what does the Death card mean?" Julie continued.

"Regeneration. Rebirth. Getting rid of old to give room to new. Spring cleaning of mind."

Detective Leek looked at the Death card. "I see."

"Card number five is current atmosphere—Page of Wands. That's you, detectives, trying to gather information. Card number six is short-term future. Not Dorothea's future, obviously. But finding out how she died. Ten of Swords, reversed. Dorothea died painful death. Murdered by someone she trusted. Or...maybe not trusted, but knew. Card number seven is present state of situation. It will tell us if you will be able to move on with your investigation. Ouch! Hanged Man from Major Arcana. This guy is major pain in ass. It means you will have to wait. Things will be static for while."

Jane remained silent for what seemed like a long time. The detectives observed her, but said nothing.

"We have other investigations we can work on while things unravel a bit," Leek finally said. "Although this is now a murder investigation. And waiting may not be a good idea."

"Right. Waiting is no good here. See card eight. That's outside influences. King of Swords, reversed. It means people will lead you astray. No, not people. Just man. I see one man. Or two. Twins? There is something confusing here. Either twins, or double personality, or someone pretending to be someone else. Card nine tells about how Dorothea felt before she died. Not quite happy, but content enough. Eight of Cups. Was in bad relationship and thought she had got rid of him. Dorothea finally understood man was no good. But it was too late. She felt very insecure. See card ten, Queen of Cups, reversed? Lots of reversed cards in this spread. Card eleven is for investigation. Long-term future. Ah, good card! Strength, from sign of Leo. Not easy card, but good card. Things will go around in circle for while, but truth will come out!"

"Thanks, Jane."

"You're welcome."

"Is there something you wish to add to your reading?"

"You mean, besides bill?"

"Yes, besides a bill. You kept silent a moment ago. I feel you saw something."

"Yes, I saw something. But I am not sure."

"Tell us," Julie insisted.

"Perhaps not yet."

"Jane!"

Leek changed the subject. "Can you tell us where the body is?"

Silence.

"That's what you saw, isn't it?" Julie said after a while. "The body."

"Yes. More or less."

"What does that mean?"

"The body," Jane mumbled. "It's everywhere."

Silence.

"What do you mean, everywhere?" Julie finally asked.

"Exactly that."

"But a body cannot be everywhere," stated Leek. "Unless—"

Julie swallowed hard. "Unless—unless someone cut up her body into pieces. Is that it, Jane?"

"Yes."

"Do you know more about the locations of Dorothea's remains?"

"I'm telling you, Julie. I am not sure."

"Are her remains everywhere in New York City, or are they elsewhere?"

"I am not sure."

"What if we show you a map?" Leek suggested.

"Maybe."

Julie went outside. A few seconds later, car doors were slammed. Julie returned with a wrinkled map of New York.

"Characters are too small. Give me magnifying glass, Julie. In kitchen—second drawer by sink."

Julie did as Jane asked.

There were sounds of objects clashing against each other.

"Have you started World War III in drawer, Julie? Or can't you find fooking magnifying glass?"

"How can one find anything in that mess? All these keys! What are they for?"

"There must be one to lock your mouth there," Jane said as she dragged her feet to the kitchen. "Lock mouth, and open eyes. Magnifying glass is right here."

■ ■

DETECTIVE LEEK SCRATCHED HIS throat.

Jane examined the map.

Julie looked out of the window and saw that the sky was in a mixed mood, with the sun occasionally managing to pierce through thick clouds. Beneath stood Jane's amputated trees.

Silence blanketed the room. Jane, magnifying glass in hand, stopped moving. A sun ray landed now on her wrinkled face, tracing twisted roads around her mouth and eyes. She suddenly became aware of the summer light on her features and produced a dismissive gesture, then bent her head toward the map once more. She shook her head.

"Looks like murderer is also artist," she said at last.

Julie turned to Jane. "What do you mean?"

"Or else, he likes symmetry."

Leek dusted the collar of his blazer with the back of his hand. "I don't quite follow."

"Head was placed in Central Park North. Left arm, in Upper West Side; right, in Upper East Side. Right leg is in East Village and left leg is in West Village. Torso is in lake."

"What lake, Jane?"

"Central Park lake."

"Belvedere Lake?" asked Leek.

"No. Just lake."

"I think she means The Lake," said Julie.

"Can't you tell us more, Jane?"

"More?"

"Upper West Side, East Village, and the rest. Those are big areas. It may take a long time to search—"

"You won't find body parts there anymore."

"When was Dorothea killed? Do you know?" asked Julie.

"About two, maybe three weeks ago," Jane replied before getting up. "Excuse me," she said as she walked away.

The sound of a flushing toilet. When Jane returned, she was drying her mouth. She went to the armoire, opened it, and asked, "Who wants vodka?"

"You do, Jane. Although it might not be good for your stomach right now."

"Vodka is best remedy for stomach upset." Jane returned with a water glass filled to the rim.

Julie grabbed the glass and tasted the liquid. "Hot and bitter. So today's choice is Sputnik."

Jane grabbed the glass back and took a big gulp. "What makes you fooking connoisseur? It's not for American palates. And certainly not for working cops."

"As opposed to working mediums," Julie muttered.

Detective Leek tapped his chin, knit his brows, and remained deep in thought for a while. "When you said we wouldn't find Dorothea's body parts in the locations you mentioned, Mrs. Dzhugashvili, do you mean that the murderer put the body parts in garbage bags? Is that it?"

Jane acquiesced and swallowed a big gulp of liquor.

"Leek, how—?"

"How did I guess, Julie?"

"Well, yeah."

"I had a couple of cases like this in the past."

Julie stared at her partner and frowned.

Leek got up and paced around the living room, then returned. "So if the body parts have been picked up with the garbage, it will be almost impossible to find them."

"Almost, Leek? Gee, you're an optimist. The damn Big Apple produces 12,000 tons of garbage a day, and you think it's *almost* impossible? It's worse than a needle in a haystack, if you ask me. But what about The Lake, Jane?"

"Torso is still in lake."

"Then that's where we'll start," Leek said as he got up. "It's always a pleasure, Mrs. Dzhugashvili."

Julie hugged Jane. "Don't drink all the vodka. Keep some for my next visit."

Jane frowned. "And when will that be?"

The Russian medium watched the NYPD Crown Vic glide away and then her attention turned to a scene across the street. Two people were walking by, having some kind of a discussion. She went near the living room window, squinted. She saw a flashy mini-dress. Okay, Cruz. Cruz with some guy. Probably another lover. All these gestures, most of them coming from her friend. Cruz needed her stage. She needed to show the neighborhood her new conquests.

She grabbed her glass, swallowed what was left of the vodka, went for a refill, raised her glass, and said, "Here's to your fooking, Cruz."

Later that night, she called Cruz. "I saw you with what looked like new dress and new beau."

"What is it to you?" Cruz' voice was on the aggressive mode.

"What's with you? I was just teasing you."

Silence.

"Jane, frankly, it's none of your business."

Jane raised her eyebrows. "Well, excuse me! I'll call when you're in fooking better mood, okay?"

"You do that."

"Actually, *you* call me when you feel better."

Cruz hung up without saying a word.

Something was wrong. In her friend's voice. In her manner. Cruz was very seldom rude.

She had not acted like herself tonight.

As a matter of fact, Cruz and Jane had been friends for years. And Cruz had never acted like this.

■ 4 ■

JANE WAS IN DANGER. Aunt Jane, in danger.

Julie had said that much on the phone.

Zoe looked through the car window at the unfolding land-scape. The rain had stopped but night had begun its covering-up job. Bridges, lights, small roads branching off God knows where, appeared disembodied, nonsensical. New York City was far behind, and what she saw now were ghosts of the occasional farm, trees drilling up the ground like risen dead, expanses of land slowly but surely abandoned by color.

Why Julie had wanted Zoe to pick Jane up was still a puzzle. Zoe knew Jane to be a stubborn mule. She had strong doubts that the Russian woman could be persuaded to come with her to New York City, even if once Jane had lived in Queens. Did she want to save Jane? Hell, yes! But she was afraid to mess up. Zoe's life had been total chaos up to, well, recently, and she still couldn't figure out how she had managed to emerge in one piece. She grabbed her hair. Still short, too short, but growing. Chemo was over, cancer was gone, and her boobs were miraculously intact. But her heart had been broken, and when she had worked on putting the pieces together, it had felt like a strange mosaic at first. More like a kaleidoscope, with pieces moving in incessant deconstruction. If she was such a klutz at self-rescue, how efficient could she be with someone else? Someone like Jane. Someone she loved like a mother.

"You know I live with Marc," Zoe had told Julie.

"Hell-o-o-o! A doctor. That's good. Maybe he can regulate Jane's booze and smoke intake."

Zoe had made a face at the phone, despite the fact that she knew her friend couldn't see it, and then taken a deep breath to soothe her irritation. "Right. You ask me to take Jane in my home. Fine. I'd have Jane over any time. But Jane and Marc clash. I tell you, Julie, with these two, cohabitation is dangerous. It will be the Cold War all over again."

"Stop the shit, Zoe. It's fear talking. Usually, you punch that thing right in the face. What's happening to you?"

Julie and Zoe had been raised in Noliar, PA, in part by their own respective parents, mostly by Jane, "Aunt Jane," at whose place they interacted like authentic sisters. In other words, by pulling each other's hair, figuratively or physically speaking, and at any chance they could get. "Be a couple of bald heads and see if I care," Jane would interject every now and then, a cigarette in one hand and vodka in the other. The girls would send Aunt Jane a surprised gaze. "Think I haven't seen Mongols before? Do you realize where I come from? If you want to look like them, be my guests!" Jane would add, lifting her brows. Zoe and Julie had no idea what she was talking about, but it sounded frightening enough to sober them up. And in the end, Julie had kept her sleek blond mane basically intact and it was chemo, not any attempt at mutual depluming, that had momentarily removed Zoe's red curls, now since returned, still short but as indomitable as ever. If Jane loved both girls, Julie was some-how convinced that Jane had a slight preference for Zoe.

"You must go and pick her up. She listens to you," Julie continued.

"Why can't you? You're a cop. You have the authority."

"I am investigating here. Can't leave, Zoe. Leek and I might be on to something. Come on, Zoe! What the hell is the matter with you?"

"Don't know. What you're asking. What if I mess up?"

"You just have to convince Jane to come with you. She loves you. I would suggest you leave your rat at home, though." Zoe's special pet was a spoiled rat named after her brother Zieg.

Where Zoe went the rat went. After a moment of silence, Zoe added, "Okay, when do I pack?"

"How about tonight?"

"Now?"

"Yeah!"

"What—"

"Are you in your living room?"

"Uh-uh."

"Look out the window. See the white Crown Vic illegally parked?" Zoe went and saw. The car was unmarked. No visible sirens or logos.

Still, Crown Vic. Cops liked their Crown Vics.

"Yeah."

"Well, that's your ride to PA. He's waiting for you."

"You mean I am going with a NYPD cop? Why didn't you say so before?"

"Well."

"Well, what?"

"Mm. Actually, you know the cop. Pretty well."

Zoe's jaws tensed up. "Aimé. Tell me you didn't send Aimé!"

Aimé Rippon and Zoe had a story together. He had come into her life when she thought it was all over between her and Marc. A gorgeous cab driver from Guadeloupe who had spent his childhood in Paris, he had brought the right dose of fun and exoticism. It was the right happening at the right time thing. If it had not saved her, it certainly had made survival more bearable. Survival, yes, that was the word. Her life was a mess, and it had gotten messier yet. She was working as an editor at that time, and when her boss had been found stabbed in her office, Zoe had been one of the murder suspects. Little did she know then that Aimé was an undercover cop working on that case. Apparently he had taken his job a little too literally, for he had been under *her* covers too many times. And these days, the last person she wanted to see was Aimé Rippon.

"Surely you got over that?" Julie said.

"Got over that? You two played me like a fiddle!"

Silence, followed by: "You don't get it, Zoe."

"And you thought me capable of murder?"

"I am a cop. I have to put my feelings aside. And you were very incoherent at that time."

"Marc had left me; I had cancer. My boss got murdered. Almost all at once. How would you have felt?"

"OK, Zoe. You were incoherent. Now you're just high maintenance. The problem is that I need you. Jane is in danger, in real danger. I think we've got a three-day timetable. No more. That means, within three days you must have Jane here in the city. So please, deal with the Aimé issue within the next few minutes. For your information, he did fall for you. I don't know if he played you like a fiddle, but you dropped him like an old sock. Now, go pack and do it quick!"

And Julie had hung up.

And Zoe had packed.

And left a note on the kitchen counter for Marc.

■ ■

"WHAT'S THAT?" AIMÉ SAID after he placed Zoe's small suitcase in the trunk and looked at the carrier she was holding. And then he burst into a deep, sexy laughter and said, "I forgot, your rat!" He bent toward the pet carrier—a time during which Zoe was able to admire that part of Aimé's anatomy that was as admirable as ever—and talked to the rat: "Salut, Zieg. Comment ça va?"

And now they were on the road, Aimé at the wheel.

■ ■

NIGHT HAD COMPLETELY ESTABLISHED its dominion now. From gray to dark to nothingness. The occasional light on the road burst out now here and there like one of the magician's tricks.

"So who told you that Jane was in danger?" Zoe finally asked.

Silence.

"Julie wouldn't tell me, either. I don't get it. You want me to help you, but you don't tell me shit."

Aimé tapped his temple. "It was an anonymous phone call."

"Yeah? How many anonymous phone calls do you cops get? Why take this one seriously?"

"Details. Details this caller seemed to know about Jane. Plus, when it comes to Jane, we take everything seriously. Specially with the case we're working on. It seems almost unbreakable, and without Jane, I don't even know if we got a chance."

"What's that case about?"

"Disappearance. Murder."

Zoe did her valley girl act, wrapping a lock of hair around her finger and pretending to chew gum. "No-o-o-o! You've got to be

kidding! I mean, like, you're criminal investigators and you're working on, like, murder? Oh-my-God! Oh-my-Go-o-d!"

"Cut the crap, Zee-Zee."

Aimé was one of the rare persons who called Zoe "Zee-Zee," after
her Zoe Zimmerman initials. She swallowed—hard. Bittersweet
memories, with the bitter still going stronger than the sweet.

"You'll know soon enough in the paper," Aimé continued.

"Thanks for the vote of confidence."

"You're a writer."

"A novelist, not a journalist. Suppose for a second you tell me all
your little NYPD top secrets about the case. What happens then? I
take notes and write my novel. Do you think it's gonna be published
tomorrow before the next edition of *The New York Times*? Do you
know how long it takes to write a fucking novel in the first place?"

Aimé's brakes screeched. The Crown Vic hiccupped and stopped.

"What—" Zoe started. And then she saw. Illuminated by the car
lights on this deserted PA road, a family of deer was gliding across the
night. A mother and her fawns. Strangely enough, they were followed
a few steps behind by a buck. Instead of sleeping? Or did deer like
the occasional paseo? Had they been chased after? Had there been a
nocturnal hunter?

Another fuckhead who mistook his gun for his dick?

Zoe and Aimé remained in awe for an instant, silent, almost
comfortable. Zoe had seen deer all her life, but she couldn't help it:
she remained fascinated by how they managed to combine grace,
demureness, and mystery. She didn't know a single PA native—not
even those fuckhead hunters—who ever grew tired of watching this
animal, perhaps because more than anything it symbolized the forest,
its depth, its secrets. And its precariousness, too. The buck closed the
march and before melting into the woods, he stood still with only his

head slowly rotating toward them, as if wondering whether or not to charge the car. His antlers, which were beyond the velvet stage but not quite fully grown just yet, were at an incline, arched like pride, like the promise of a new genesis. Aimé tensed up, grasped the wheel. Zoe clenched her teeth, waited. Man, woman, and animal remained in a triangle of hush for elastic, interminable seconds.

The Crown Vic roared.

On the back seat, shuffling, nervous sounds.

"What's that?" Aimé whispered, his gaze still on the buck.

"Zieg II," Zoe mumbled.

"Your rat? Shouldn't he be asleep?"

"Yes. I guess he's sensing something unusual."

The buck was still there.

The Crown Vic engine growled.

"What if you backed up just a bit and then went around him?" Zoe suggested.

"Do you know one of those attacked my car once and destroyed the whole right side? Better wait."

The buck started moving. Very slowly.

"Still wait?" Zoe asked.

Aimé did not answer.

The buck drew a step closer to the car.

Absolute silence in the Crown Vic—front seats and back.

The buck approached Zoe's side.

Aimé grabbed her arm in a protective gesture. With a small yet swift move, Zoe shook it out of the grasp, straightened her back, her chest forward like a rooster, and in this posture she let her gaze travel toward the buck. They were now fixing each other, woman and animal immobile but for the scrutinizing eyes. The buck took one step closer. Aimé tightened his jaw. Zoe inhaled and exhaled deeply, her glance still locked on the male deer. A thin crescent moon, like the beginning of a road penciled in by some absentminded cartographer, made a detour around the buck's head. She couldn't help but notice that its top antlers duplicated tonight's lunar shape. So did the wheel, the part of it that received some light. Black eyes remained on her. They seemed bigger by the second. Shiny, dark planets.

All of a sudden it was all that mattered: the eyes of a deer and the eyes of a woman. The universe had shrunk—or expanded—all of a sudden. It had become a connection between glances, between two worlds that civilization had uselessly separated. Perhaps it was an illusion, but she didn't care. What she knew was that she was part of a *now*. And that she felt her pulse. Very distinctly, she felt her pulse. A pulse. A rhythm. Some secret drum. She was not fearless, but she went with it.

And then her whole body relaxed, her face blended into the car seat and she smiled. The buck bowed his head as in a salute, his antlers tracing complicated patterns on the foggy car window, like stained glass, like possibilities. Now the animal resumed his regal progression before blending into the night.

Aimé started breathing again and finally said with a tight smile, "Well, Zee-Zee, looks like you attract all sorts."

Zoe replied with a silent stare.

He stared away as he let the Crown Vic glide back on the road, its engine back to the purring mode.

■ ■

NIGHT WAS LOSING ITS density, and from a coarse linen it was evaporating now into a dull silk, grayish, with darker spots here and there. What was still shallow would soon gain definition. What was still immaterial would silently solidify. Dawn was around the corner, ready to sculpt a new day. And Zoe was exhausted. Aimé had finally decided to reveal the main lines of the case he, Julie, and Leek were investigating. It would soon come out in the press anyway. "Okay, okay. There's this woman who disappeared. We couldn't find her, so Julie and Leek went to visit Jane. Jane let them know that the woman is now dead."

"Murdered, of course. Did you find the body?" Zoe asked.

"No. Not yet."

"Didn't Jane help you locate it?"

"Yes...yes. She did. Sort of."

"What do you mean, 'sort of'?"

"Well, it appears that the body has been sliced up like pepperoni and then rearranged."

"What do you mean, rearranged?"

"Each part of her body was thrown in a different part of the city. One went to the north, one went to the east, one to the south, one to the west. That's what Jane said. In any case, it was all very methodical. If New York had been a dinner table, well, that damn butcher would have sort of set the freaking table."

Zoe swallowed. "You're as sick as this guy, you know that?"

Aimé turned to her. "You wanted to know."

Zoe took a deep breath, swallowed again. "So you're looking for a killer and a sicko."

"Yeah."

Zoe frowned. "The anonymous call you got about Jane being in danger. Do you think it is connected to the case?"

Silence.

"Well? There was an anonymous phone call, wasn't there?" Zoe insisted.

"It came a day after Leek and Julie went to visit Jane." Aimé cleared his throat. "On June 5."

"Yesterday."

"Yes."

"What? I don't get is this. The crime apparently took place in New York City, right?"

"That's what we're trying to find out."

"But Jane told you the victim's body was scattered in the city."

"Scattered, yes. We don't know where she was killed."

"Still. Jane lives hours away from New York. In a small PA town. If her life is in danger because of the case, it means there is a connection between Noliar and New York City."

"And you think that's far fetched." Aimé grimaced.

"A bit."

"Why? Didn't Jane live in Queens once?"

"I guess. But that would mean that—" Zoe massaged her forehead. "It could mean that the murderer knows exactly who Jane is. And has known so for a long time. And is aware she's good at what she does."

"Right. Could be someone she knew in Queens who is aware that she now lives in Noliar, PA."

"Someone who knows about her psychic powers as well. Takes them seriously." Zoe wondered if there was someone in Noliar who would fit the bill. Most people she knew there thought Jane's Tarot and psychic readings were part of Russian folklore. She made money out of it. In other words, out of people's gullibility. Noliarites didn't blame people who made a buck or two out of fools. They got what they deserved. So that made Jane totally acceptable in the community. But as far as her gifts being real, they didn't buy it.

Well, someone in Noliar had to. Someone who knew what she was into. If this was indeed linked to that woman's murder. It was someone who knew Jane, who knew Noliar, who knew either Julie or Leek. Or both. Someone who was scared of being found out and who took Jane's ultra-sensory abilities very, very seriously. Someone who didn't want to be caught.

But who? The murderer-slash-butcher, that's who. The chainsaw operator, that's who. Zoe shook. Was there a possibility that he lived in Noliar? But he had to know New York as well. Was he somehow organizing his life between New York and Noliar, PA? Two residences, maybe? Two lives?

Zoe's imagination assailed her and she tried to shut it out.

Aimé's hands tensed up on the wheel, but he said nothing. At some point, he released his right arm and patted Zoe's leg, to which she responded with a sad smile, eyes forward on the awakening landscape.

Silence unfolded as the Crown Vic finally snaked into I-80 West and sped through the next thirty miles until the Noliar exit. Taking the scenic route had been interesting, but anguishing at times, Zoe thought. Not that she had mentally painted the landscape with her own anguish. Of course not. They passed the local Wal-Mart. She observed the entrance of her native town. More lights, more fast food restaurants than when she last remembered. She knew those had been there for a while, but after she had left she had somehow fossilized her memory, transformed Noliar into what it used to be when she was a kid. These days, it looked like the pretense of a city—something a child asked to design a big metropolis would have come up with. Illuminated, commercial, yet too small to be taken seriously.

Or was she becoming a fucking snob because she was living in The City?

No, that wasn't it. She had nothing against small towns. Nothing against Main Street as the main story, the stage of comedies, dramas, little sagas in the making. But she liked small towns that assumed their identity as small towns. And Noliar had been charming once. What with its little antique stores and shoe stores and clothing stores and candy stores and food stores. And bookstores! And the local gossip on the sidewalk, the adding of comments on the latest real or pseudo-scandal. Fiction and fact in the Cuisinart. Was that the root of her calling as a writer? As a kid she had enjoyed the Main Street life. A Mr. Roger's neighborhood of sorts. Please won't you be my neighbor, 'specially if you're able to tell me some salacious stuff about other neighbors. But now, the socializing occurred at Wal-Mart, between underwear and artichokes. It was not the same flavor anymore.

"At what time does Jane get up?"

Zoe jumped out of her reverie. "What?"

Aimé was parallel parking in front of AM EYE, the only breakfast place in Noliar that opened at around five a.m.

"Have you been here before?" Zoe asked.

"No, but it's the only restaurant in town with lights on."

"We could have gone to a fast food."

Aimé grabbed the car key. "We could have. I know how much you like those." He smiled. "You hungry?"

"Me sleepy. So fucking, fucking sleepy."

"Do they make strong coffee in that place?"

"They make flavored water in that place. But their pancakes ain't bad."

"Where is their Starbucks?"

Zoe burst into laughter. "You've gotta be kidding!"

"You mean, they've got all these fast food places and no Starbucks?"

Zoe shrugged and grabbed his arm. "Let's get in."

AM EYE (you could either pronounce it "a.m. eye" or "am I," but of course the natives created a senseless and very nasal hybrid out of it, calling the joint "ehmaye") had about twenty habitués at this ungodly hour. Sausages were half-eaten, egg yolks were traveling on plates, mouths were mumbling or blabbering; *The Noliar Call* pages, with today's or yesterday's news (the paper came out biweekly), were making crackling sounds and building walls for patrons who wanted to begin their day amidst people without having to talk to them. The white linoleum was still fairly clean, and the banquettes had been re-upholstered, this time with bright red faux leather. A couple of waitresses Zoe knew from high school came to hug her and give Aimé a close examination. Had they come any closer, Zoe reflected, they would have been handed their urology degree on the spot. Before they resumed their serving duties, they gave Zoe serious nods of approval.

Pancakes, coffee, good old Noliar—bathing into what seemed at once strange and familiar—had totally reawakened Zoe.

That, and what Aimé called "the plan."

"That's what Julie concocted?" Zoe poured a generous dose of maple syrup on what was left of her pancake.

Aimé smiled. "It will be like old times."

"Don't count on it." Zoe took a few paper napkins from the metallic distributor on the table and dried her sticky hands. "I could have come up with something better. I am not sure Jane will believe it."

"Ah, have faith, Zee-Zee. You can make anything believable."

"Ha! Look who's talking."

They got up. Aimé left a generous tip on the table. "That's for the way your friend looked at my ass," he said with a sparkling grin.

Zoe rolled her eyes.

"By the way," she asked as they got into the car, "what was the name of the victim again?"

"Again?" he responded as he smoothed the Crown Vic into Main Street. "I am not sure I gave you a name in the first place."

"Why not? It's gonna be in the papers soon, right? Has Julie given you instructions about that too?"

Silence.

"She has, hasn't she?" Zoe insisted.

"Look, Zee-Zee. It's just another murder. The name that matters for now is Jane. Jane Dzhugashvili. Jeez! Where did she get that name?"

"She's Russian, duh!"

"Da."

"Well, aren't you the funny one?"

"Okay, tell me when to turn."

"Second light, make a right."

"Okay."

"Now turn left. Right here."

"Voilà."

"And another left. See the Heritage Lane sign. There. Now, it will be the fifth house on the right."

"Cute little street. Looks like everybody's up. Lights are on. Wow! What's that? The trees on that property. Looks like they underwent some kind of severe amputation."

Zoe shook her head. "That's Jane's place. We have arrived."

5

VALERIAN HAD NOT HELPED. Sleeping pills had not helped. Jane had never been a sound sleeper. Not since her childhood in Russia, anyway. But she managed a few scattered hours of slumber every night. And that was enough. Squirrels had done their act; she had done hers, hitting the bedroom ceiling with her stick and telling them to shut the fook up, but that was routine. Eventually the attic grew quiet and so did she.

Last night however, she had not slept a wink.

The full moon would not come until ten days from now, so that couldn't be it.

Yet, there was something unnerving. She could feel it. A burning energy ran through her palms until the pain became nearly unbearable. It felt explosive, radioactive. Like some electrical stigmata.

It couldn't be that trivial thing she had seen last night, could it?

Heard it first, then seen, to be precise.

Cruz. Always Cruz. For her the world had to be a fooking stage.

She was quietly inhaling her Marlboros and sipping a glass of Sputnik in her living room. There was nothing on TV, so she had turned it off and was thinking about taking her cigarette and vodka to the porch when she heard voices. One man, one woman. At first she thought it was the newlyweds two houses down. These two fought every other day at about the same time. Warm-up time for more serious business between the sheets. Give them a few years and silence would conquer both living room and bedroom.

No, these voices were different. Older. Soon she recognized one of them. Cruz. Prelude to a kiss? She wondered, when she heard her friend's passionate discourse.

Passionate discourse, my ass, was what came to Jane as an afterthought when she heard Cruz' pitch getting more strident by the second. She couldn't make out what she was saying, but she could tell Cruz was upset. The man's voice came out muted, like a tired drum. She knew that voice too. The fact that she couldn't put a name to it vexed her.

She looked through the window. She could make out two silhouettes, but it was dark. She was sure about Cruz. Stilettos and a dress that made boobs and butt stick out confirmed this. But the man, dammit! She knew it was someone she didn't care for, for some reason. Why couldn't she remember his name? Was she getting senile? Too many vodkas?

She abandoned her smoke and drink and stepped out on the porch.

"I know what you did!" Cruz kept yelling. "I know what you did!"

"Oh, yeah?" The guy was saying. "Can you prove it?"

Jane shrugged. So Cruz' new lover is cheating on her. For once the roles were reversed. Her Cuban friend collected men the way philatelists collected stamps. Once she found a better looking one, she said adios, amor mío to the current paramour without forgetting to add his photo to her special album on Facebook. The special album that she called "My Trophy Book" that she was happy to share with her Internet friends, the ones she didn't really know and the ones she would never meet. The other special feature on Cruz Facebook page was the list of books she had read. Cruz was an avid reader, and the fact that she was a librarian certainly contributed to that hunger. But how the woman could gulp that many volumes when she did so much fooking left Jane perplexed and, to some degree at least, respectful.

Still, Cruz sounded more upset than usual. It was beyond disquiet, Jane felt. Was she in love with the guy? Truly, truly in love? "They'll find out about you!" Cruz was yelling. "Like I did! They will! And it will be over!"

Should Jane pretend to go for a walk and see for herself what was going on?

As soon as she resolved to do just that the two parted. She finally identified the man. The tree man. Shawn Doogy.

So that motherfooker had many mistresses, that was it, she deducted as Doogy left. The man sure had a funny walk. Tonight, it seemed worse than usual. He had a definite limp.

Jane could have told Cruz that, at last, she had found her match. But it was obvious that Cruz was humorless tonight. More than that, she was distressed. Crying, it seemed.

Should she go to her?

With most people, this would have been the easiest question to answer. Rush to the friend who's upset, hug her, tell her they'll both get drunk and curse all the men on the planet and, mañana, things would be better, not perfect, not even good for that matter, but better. For a while, the head would take over. That's what she would have to tell a friend. Trust the head for a while. For the head would bandage the heart, look daily at its chart until the heart was ready to feel and give again. And she would be there anyway, to help the friend's head, and the friend's heart.

Well, that strategy worked with most of Jane's friends.

But Cruz was proud like a matador. So Jane retraced her steps in silence and let her friend and her tears go back home.

Five minutes later, Jane grabbed her cell phone. "That you, Cruz? Hope I didn't interrupt anything?...Oh, I did? What's the name of your current fooking interest?...Oh...Listen...Why don't you let him snore and come have game of chess with me?...You can't? You sure? Listen, I won't go to bed 'til two or three...That's right, as usual. So if you feel like telling me about your guys, dildos, whatever, I'll be here. Okay?"

But Cruz had not come. And Jane had not slept. It was six a.m., not her usual wake up time, but there was no use staying in bed.

Jane made her bed distractedly, dragged her steps to the kitchen, started Mr. Coffee, and lit her first cigarette of the day.

She suddenly realized that the guy she saw with Cruz two nights ago was probably Doogy too. Not that this was significant. Her friend had been capable of keeping lovers several weeks at a time. So why did she feel uneasy about this? Of course, there was the fact that between Shawn Doogy and Chainsaw Jane there was no love lost. That fookhead had taken her to a judge, and it would take time and quite a few bottles of vodka to forget about that.

When she heard her doorbell, she rushed to open it. She was about to say, "Cruz!" when she saw instead a tall black man and Zoe carrying a box.

So instead, she said, "What fook!"

Zoe frowned. "Nice welcome, Aunt Jane!"

Aimé went to shake hands with the Russian woman. "Hello, Mrs. Dzhugashvili. I am Aimé Rippon. It's a pleasure to meet you at last."

"I know who you are," said Jane as she forwarded Zoe an interrogating glance. "What's that in box?"

■ ■

AIMÉ HAD GONE FOR a walk in Jane's neighborhood, and the two women were having coffee in Jane's kitchen with "the box."

"So you've got rat in box. Can rat get rid of squirrels?"

Zoe shrugged.

"What's matter?"

"I don't know what to do, Aunt Jane. That's why I came to see you."

"You're cheating on Marc?"

Zoe nodded.

"Marc is doctor and Aimé is...?"

"I told you before. He is a taxi driver."

Jane frowned. "He is? Yes, that's what you told me. So, you're torn between two lovers, feeling like fool."

"Yes. I'm in a mess again."

"Mess is your specialty, Zoe."

"What should I do?"

Jane lit a Marlboro. "What fook, Zoe! You've got health and transportation covered. And you came all way here to complain about that!"

Something was wrong. Not only was Julie's "plan" shit, but Jane's level of irritability was particularly high this morning. Zoe looked at her watch. It was seven thirty in the morning. No wonder.

"Did we wake you up? I'm sorry, Aunt Jane."

"No, you didn't. I didn't sleep wink. Something's wrong."

Jane got up, crushed her cigarette in the ashtray, and said, "I'll be back in while." Zoe heard her slam the door. She went to the living room window and saw Jane walking down the street in the direction of Cruz' house.

■ ■

JANE RANG CRUZ' BELL. No answer. She rang it again. Nothing. She knocked. No one came. She knocked harder. Still no response. She was about to give the door a serious beating, but decided against it. Cruz would have responded by now. She finally used the spare key Cruz had given her to water her houseplants when she was away, and entered the house.

"Cruz!" She called. "Cruz! It's Jane! Are you there?"

Silence.

Jane walked slowly from room to room. Cruz had a pleasant home decorated with bright colors. There was a bit of disarray: a T-shirt thrown on the yellow sofa of her living room, high heels abandoned on the floor, some dirty dishes in the sink, a bra hanging from a picture frame near her bedroom door, an open bathroom drawer with a few sex toys and batteries. None of this surprised Jane. She now entered Cruz' bedroom. The bed, with its satin sheets and red cover, was perfectly made. The entire bedroom was neat, with no hairbrush, perfume, or jewelry out of place. No surprise there, either. "That's my love temple," Cruz liked to tell her friends when they compared the state of that room with the rest of her home. "*Ici, tout n'est qu'ordre et beauté, luxe, calme et volupté,*" she inevitably added.

"Ugh, fook Baudelaire," Jane inevitably commented.

But now she wished she could hear her friend quoting the French poet one more time. As annoying as it was, Jane wanted to hear it. Her throat knotted tight and she could hardly breathe. She swallowed, steadied herself.

Perhaps it was just nerves, fatigue, lack of sleep. For everything in her friend's house appeared normal. Cruz was not here, true, but she might have gone to work early today. It might be inventory day at the Noliar Library; or, there might be some meeting.

She retraced her steps and was about to leave when she saw a shape on one of the kitchen chairs that caught her eyes. Cruz' purse. She went to open it and saw that her wallet and car keys were there. She unlocked the kitchen door that gave access to the garage. Cruz' crimson Corvette sat there. Jane remembered when Cruz had bought the car—a used one that needed to be repaired time and again but that was as flashy as its owner. Jane twitched her nose, sniffed, but didn't smell any gas. She walked to the car. No one was inside. Jane tapped the car. "Do you know where she is?"

Then she tapped her own head. "Jane, you are fooking crazy! Talking to car!"

Perhaps Cruz walked to the library. This would also explain her leaving early, even if leaving without her bag seemed a bit strange. Jane locked Cruz' house. A few minutes later, she was driving her own car. She did so slowly, looking here and there for an ambulating mini skirt with accompanying heels. But the only creatures on foot she saw that morning were a three-legged dog, a jogger, two bunnies, and a few squirrels. It was a little after eight when she parked at the Noliar Library. The lights were on.

Cruz' colleagues had not seen Cruz since the day before, they told her, but it was still early. Jane could wait and surely Cruz would show up any time. Jane sat on an armchair at the magazines corner and picked up the latest issue of *Vanity Fair*. Johnny Depp was on the cover, dark eyed, mustached, bearded, and with a black skull tattooed on his right arm. Inside there were pieces on Jackie O; on a doctor gone the route from healing to murder; and on the pharmaceutical industry who tested its new drugs on destitute Indians, Argentinians, Romanians, Ukrainians, Russians (Russians! What fook!)—places where the already overwhelmed FDA would have trouble investigating. Ladies and gentlemen, please meet the new rats. International rats, all ages, baby rats. Dying anonymously.

Jane slapped the magazine shut. She walked around the library, but Cruz had not yet arrived.

On the library clock she read 9:22.

The other librarians didn't seem worried about Cruz' absence when she went to talk to them. When Cruz arrived late, and that happened once in a while, she would also stay after hours, put books, CDs and DVDs back in their shelves, straighten chairs around tables, put computers in sleep or hibernation mode, and make sure that the library would be operational for the next day. It was a tacit understanding that worked for everyone, and that could only function in a small town.

Jane went back to the magazine corner and picked up a copy of *Photography,* a special issue on famous photographer Steve Knight, who shot war scenes like no one else. Ugh. Good at death. She didn't want to look at that. She did take a peek at the photographer's face, however. Although she had never met him in person, the face looked somehow familiar. She shook her head, trying to shake the idea away at the same time. This was absurd.

The closed, silent space of the library gave her an oppressing feeling. She needed some air.

As she got up and walked away, she reflected. Cruz' house looked normal. Cruz' colleagues weren't worried. She shouldn't be, either.

Then why was she?

What was this nagging concern that refused to go away? It was like a hair caught between tongue and throat. It was a leaking faucet with nagging drops. If she didn't do anything, she would go nuts. But do what? Read Tarot? Not in that mood of hers. She could go visit Cruz' friends. She knew where they lived and where they worked.

Sounded like a plan.

■ ■

"AUNT JANE!" ZOE LOOKED at the haggard Russian woman coming home.

Jane let her body drop on her armchair. "Ah, yes. I forgot. You're here for visit."

"Perhaps you would like some tea?" said Aimé who had just come from the kitchen. "I hope you don't mind, but I took the liberty of cooking dinner."

"French dinner, too!" added Zoe. "Aimé was raised in Paris, remember?"

"I thought he was from...uh...Guadeloupe," mumbled Jane.

"That's correct, Madame. That's my country of origin. But I spent most of my childhood in Paris."

"So you're a *Parisien*...whoopsie fooking doo."

"Jane! That's rude! Even for you!"

"Sorry. I actually like French food. And Paris. And Parisians too, I suppose."

"So you know Paris, eh, ma'am?"

Jane closed her eyes. "What did I just say? But that was in other life." She took a deep breath, then turned to Zoe. "Give me vodka. Any vodka. But big, big glass."

"Something wrong, Aunt Jane?"

Jane lit a cigarette. "Where's ashtray?"

Aimé rushed to the kitchen and brought a spotless ashtray.

"What are you, cleaning specialist?" She squeezed her eyes. "What I know is that you're not cab driver. Not real one."

"What are you talking about, Aunt Jane?"

"Oh, stop shit, Zoe, will you?"

Aimé and Zoe exchanged glances.

Jane shrugged. "Cruz disappeared. I looked everywhere."

She then went on to explain her day, the exploration of Cruz' house, the wait at her workplace, the visit at friends', the phone calls that she and other friends made. She even had a small conversation with Shawn Doogy.

"Shawn Doogy? The landscapist? Why?" asked Zoe.

"I think Cruz and that asshole are having affair," answered Jane. "They were having fight in street last night."

"Are you sure?" asked Aimé.

"She was upset, saying something like 'It's over! They'll find out about you!'"

"Looks like maybe they were breaking up," said Zoe.

Aimé grabbed a chair, saw that it was none too stable, so decided to stay up. "So what did this Shawn Doogy tell you when you talked to him?"

"Said he had not seen Cruz since last night." Jane opened her eyes wide as if suddenly a brilliant idea had invaded her head. Vodka in hand, she looked straight at Aimé. "Since you're cop, you can help me find Cruz."

Zoe and the guy formerly known as cab driver stood aghast for a second.

"Yup," mumbled Zoe to herself. "The plan. Julie's plan. It's really working."

6

NOLIAR CHIEF OF POLICE Jonnhy Dumasky had what Aimé liked to call embonpoint, but what most Noliarites preferred to define as a nasty beer belly. To be frank, the stomach told stories of doughnuts as well. A blond, thin, and receding hairline haloed a face that contained shrewd baby blues and a swollen red nose that, besides ale, had smelled quite a few bourbons before the mouth decided to swallow them whole. When Dumasky rose from his desk to shake hands with the NYPD cop, the whole room shrank. If Aimé was tall, Dumasky was huge. And in such a contained space with yellowed walls and papers in disarray, the Noliar cop looked like a mountain of a man.

Metaphorically speaking, skyscraper versus Mount Everest, thought the city man, half-amused, half-frowning.

Besides competitive handshakes, no pleasantries were exchanged. Instead, the city cop told a brief story with few details.

"If I understand correctly, Detective Rippon, you think that something happened to Cruz Mojada," Dumasky mumbled after hearing Aimé's narrative.

"That's a possibility." The NYPD cop sat across from the Noliar Chief of Police, trying to figure out whether or not he would get reliable help from this rural end. Dumasky's face had no more expression than a cow's. That could mean two things: either the Chief was dumb, or he played dumb.

For now, the detective wasn't ready to place a bet.

"Mm. No one saw her yesterday, you say?"

"She didn't show up for work."

"And she wasn't home, either, eh? Chainsaw Jane...uh...I mean, Jane, went to Cruz' place and there was no one there." The Chief frowned. "Well, maybe there was some kind of family emergency. She might have had to leave precipitously."

"Except that her bag was there, with her wallet, credit cards and IDs."

"That's right, that's right. You mentioned that. Couldn't have gone very far without that."

Aimé didn't respond.

The Chief looked at his notes. "Well, Jane went to Cruz' yesterday morning. Did she check last night as well?"

"Yes, Chief, she did."

"How 'bout this mornin'?"

"This morning we went together. I checked every room. Everything looks normal. Too normal."

"What do you mean, Detective?"

"The aforementioned bag, for one. It's there, as if she had left for a few moments. Are you married, Chief?"

"Yup. A wife, plus two daughters."

"Then you know as well as I do—better than I do, in fact—that a woman's whole life is in her bag."

The Chief belched out a brief laughter. "Couldn't have said it better myself." He scratched the scarce rows of yellow hair on his scarlet cranium. "Jeeweez. Who would want to hurt Cruz? She's about as popular as Chainsaw Jane 'round here. More popular with men, actually. Kinda exotic, because she's originally from Cuba. Her parents were, at least. Cruz, she was born in this country." His lower chin stuck out in bovine reflection. "I'll keep her house under surveillance for a while."

"That might be a good idea. You said Ms. Mojada was born in this country."

"Yeah. Unlike you."

Xenophobic punch. Well, fuck you, Chief. Or, as we say in my country, va te faire foutre. Aimé addressed a radiant smile to Dumasky. "Unlike me. Is she a Noliar native?"

"Nope. Not even a PA native. Lemme see. I think she told me once she came from New York." Dumasky frowned and tapped his desk with his notepad. "No, that ain't right. Jersey. Yeah, I think the wife told me she came from Jersey. Newark. That's it."

"Your wife is friends with Cruz Mojada?"

"Yeah. Cruz is friends with many people. She's a very friendly woman. Best friend is Chainsaw Jane, though. A Cuban and a Russian, go figure."

Aimé felt like answering, "Fidel Castro, the former Soviet Union, hey, why not, there was some sort of logic to it." Instead he asked, "When did she come to Noliar?"

"Who? Jane? Cruz?"

"Cruz."

"That one is easier. For Jane, I wouldn't know. Seems that one has always been around." Dumasky stretched his arm toward his trousers' back pocket. Wallet in hand, he fished for a crumbled piece of cardboard.

"What's that?" Aimé asked.

"Library card."

"And that's your clue?"

Chief Dumasky bowed his head. "I guess it's confession time. Most local men started to become Noliar Library regulars when they heard Cruz was hired as librarian there." He looked at his card. "And that was eleven years ago."

Aimé smiled the complicit smile he ordinarily used while talking to suspects while undercover. This helped loosen the Chief's tongue a bit more. "Most librarians dress, well, you know. Like librarians. Not Cruz. She's like this tropical bird. Nice hair and brightly colored clothes."

"And not very long, right?" Aimé's eyes lit.

"Say what?"

"The clothes. Above the knees, right?"

The Chief grinned. "You can say that."

"I bet Noliar is the town in the US that has the most male readers. And they say nobody reads anymore!"

"Well, they sure read 'round here!"

The two men chuckled.

Smile still on, Aimé suddenly said, "Did you have an affair with Cruz Mojada, Chief Dumasky?"

Dumasky sobered up. "Yeah, sure. Have you met my wife?" After a moment, he added. "It's not because guys look that they collect." He frowned. "Although quite a few did. Collect, I mean. Most of them single or divorced. The married ones, well, I don't know. Oh, I am sure there are some. But in such a small place, they have to be discreet. The weird thing is no one holds a grudge against Cruz."

"Perhaps until now, Chief."

And then the office narrowed again as silence circled around them. The space was almost too oppressive for these two large men, one on a mission, the other apparently at a loss.

Un ange passe, that's the French expression that came to Aimé's mind just now. Un ange passe, an angel goes by.

With overwhelming wings.

What kind of an angel?

When the Chief scratched his throat, it cracked up the silence like a step on thin ice. And then he talked. "Somethin's wrong, isn't it? Somethin's definitely wrong."

The NYPD cop nodded.

"You know, Detective, Noliar used to be a quiet little town. Used to complain 'bout it. Not much to do but give speeding tickets. And then over the years things got, oh, I don't know, less friendly. We've got more battered women, battered young women, go figure. You'd think this young generation would be more evolved. Drugs don't help, I guess. Trafficking went from big cities to small ones. Oh, it's not Chicago, no, but it's gettin' organized, real organized. We keep arresting sellers, but there's some kind of mafia behind it. There's a network all right. Only we don't know who. No one was ever killed 'round here. I mean, murdered. A hunting accident or two, maybe."

How convenient, thought Aimé.

"But with the heroin and cocaine getting more accessible," Dumasky continued, "and all the money people make from that. Oh, I don't know. People can still leave their doors open during the day-time, I guess, but for how long? With all that's happening, and now Cruz disappearing. Sure, it's less boring to be a cop in Noliar these days. But I am not sure I wouldn't trade all this mess for a little more boredom. At least things were a little more innocent before."

Little House on the Prairie had long been abandoned on dusty library shelves and its TV adaptation only came up on the Hallmark Channel. And who watched the Hallmark Channel, Aimé reflected.

Apparently, *he* did. On occasion. It reminded him of his childhood in Paris, when they would broadcast *La petite maison dans la prairie* on the *télé* and the whole family would watch together.

Fucking nostalgia. Now was not the time.

"Maybe not, eh?" The Chief said as if he had read Aimé's mind.

The detective eyed his rural colleague. "Listen, Chief Dumasky. Perhaps it's time I leveled with you. Thing is, I haven't exactly told you everything."

The Chief's baby blues squinted and his mouth twisted. "Oh, I figured that one out."

"You did?"

"Am a small town cop. But I am a cop. Cruz disappeared, and you're interested. Why would some NYPD cop be interested otherwise? You probably think it's connected with some stuff going on in New York City. How's Julie, by the way?"

"Mm."

"You work with her, don't ya?"

"Yes."

"And with that funny guy with the big mustache."

"So you know."

"I told you. Noliar's a small place. People talk. They see Julie with that guy—"

"Detective Leek."

"I know Julie's a cop. Worked here for a while. Didn't like it. Thought I didn't treat her right because of her sexual preferences. Maybe I didn't. Or maybe I should have told the other cops around here who teased her nonstop to cut it out. I didn't. But she was a good cop, and I was sorry when she left."

Aimé took a deep breath.

"In any case, when Julie comes to see Chainsaw Jane with that Leek guy, I figure it's not a courtesy visit. Jane works for you guys, doesn't she?"

"How many people know this?"

The Chief shrugged. "It's not because I figured it out that I talked about it."

"So you didn't share it with anyone."

"Not even the wife." The Chief smiled. "Particularly not the wife." He sighed. "That doesn't mean some other people haven't put stuff together, either."

Few things were neglected in little towns, Aimé realized. What New Yorkers would see as insignificant would go under the radar in Noliar.

The rural cop and the urban cop got engaged in a duel of glances for stretchy seconds.

The Chief rose. "I'll be right back."

He came back five minutes later with two cups of coffee and an assortment of doughnuts. "Now we can talk."

■ ■

THE CHIEF LOOKED AT his notes. "Okay. Cruz disappears on June 6 or 7. This comes shortly after the NYPD gets an anonymous phone call...uh...June 5, right?"

"Pardon?" said Aimé.

"The anonymous call saying that Jane's life is in danger. It was on June 5, you said?"

"Hm. Yes, yes. June 5."

"And so far, you have not been able to trace the call. You think it might have come from one of those disposable cell phones. But logically, the caller should be someone who knows Jane well and who lives in the area. Otherwise, how would he know? The voice sounded like a man's voice, but it could have been disguised."

"Right," said Aimé. He looked at the cup of coffee that Dumasky had placed before him and hesitantly took a sip. *Dégueulasse. Du jus de chaussettes.* Socks' juice. He produced a grimace, which he quickly converted into a tight smile. Now was not the time to offend local sensibilities, even about coffee.

"The reason why you think Jane is in danger is because she works for you." Dumasky continued. "And it is probably linked to the case you're working on right now. The Dorothea Sishy case."

"That's a possibility, yes."

"This woman was murdered and became cut grass that blew in the wind. At least that's what you're sayin'. Have you found the body parts yet?"

"We have people on the ground searching. But no proof yet."

"But that's what Jane says."

"Yes."

"And when Chainsaw Jane says somethin', she's pretty damn sure, am I right?"

"You're right, Chief."

Dumasky swallowed the last of a sugar doughnut. "Has she been wrong before?"

"Not that I know of."

"Yeah. So the guy who knows Jane is in danger probably knows the person who wants to harm Jane."

The city cop nodded

"And that person could be our guy—the murderer."

"We're not sure it's a guy."

"Come on, Detective. It takes a lot of physical strength to chop up a whole anatomy like that."

"Agreed. But some women are as strong as men. This is rural PA. You have women who hunt in these parts, don't you? I bet they can kill a deer and then cut up the animal and cook their venison without so much as the blink of an eye."

"Oh, sure! I know a couple of gals like that 'round here. I see them during hunting season. But they have never set foot in New York City for one. Have no intention to go there, for two. For them, all these sky-scrapers and high traffic and noise and all that is hell on earth. Now, why would they want to kill this Dorothea Sishy? A bookstore owner from a city that, frankly, scares them shitless? 'S'cuse my French."

Aimé smiled. He had to admit, the guy had a point.

"And all they read is the Bible and *The Inquirer*. We can find that right here in Noliar. In my opinion, Detective, our guy probably knows both Noliar and New York. He may not be a native but—"

"He could be a member of a Noliar family who moved to the city. Like Julie did. Like Zoe Zimmerman did. Like Dr. Trenton did."

"Marc Trenton, you mean?"

"Yeah, you know him? He left his wife and followed Zoe to New York."

Aimé made a face and when he tried to recover his cool he was half a second too late.

"You don't like the guy much, eh?" The Chief continued. "In any case, it'd have to be someone who's familiar with both places, don't ya think? Someone who visits here regularly."

"Mm. Someone who knows who Jane works for, that's for sure."

"Someone with strong feelings for Ms. Sishy."

"I'd say. It's as if this guy wanted to erase her, deny her the fact that she ever existed."

"Oh, I dunno if I'd unpack the whole psychological blah-blah-blah. The guy's simply a sicko, is all. Maybe it's drugs. But as I was sayin', I wouldn't push it with the whole psychological stuff. Although, I must admit, there's lots of anger in that sicko's action."

Silence.

"What about Cruz?" Dumasky went on. "Where does she come in all this?"

"We don't know." Aimé gave Dumasky a half-grin. "Any idea, Chief?"

"Maybe Jane confided in her. That's why she disappeared. She knew too much."

"So you believe Cruz' disappearance and Dorothea Sishy's murder are linked, is that what you're telling me?"

"Well, ain't that why you came to see me?"

"I came primarily to advise you of Cruz Mojada's disappearance, Chief Dumasky."

"But—"

"But your theory is an interesting theory."

"Ah, see—"

"That's why we wouldn't mind getting your help. We would like you to work with the NYPD."

Dumasky's torso swelled up like a rooster's. "What can I do, Detective?"

"Well, you can ask people around about Cruz, for one. And take it from there. Jane tells me—and you confirm this— that she was—"

"Was? Is there something I don't know? She's not dead, is she?"

"I am sorry, Chief. No. At least, I hope not. What I meant to say is that Cruz is a very talkative person and that she probably told stories to many people around here. There might be clues there."

Dumasky acquiesced.

"And you tell me she likes men. So they can be a good source as well. Sometimes people know things, but they don't know that they know."

"You mean they hold a real important piece of the puzzle and don't realize it?"

"Yes, that's one way to put it. By the way, there was one guy Jane saw her with on the night of June 6. She said they were having a fight." Aimé retrieved a small notepad from his shirt pocket. "The name is Shawn Doogy."

"Doogy? The tree guy? Cruz was sleeping with him?"

"You seem surprised, Chief."

"I am. As I told you, most men like Cruz. Doogy was about the only one who didn't. Never figured out why."

Aimé looked at his watch, rose, and handed a card to Dumasky. "If you find out anything—anything—about Cruz Mojada, here's the number. Day or night, anytime. I'll be your NYPD liaison, if that's okay. So we can count on you, Chief?"

"You bet."

"And thanks for the coffee. It was really good."

"Funny. You hardly touched it."

"Oh, you know us city guys. We're kinda nervous. We've gotta be real careful with caffeine."

The two cops shook hands and parted on neutral terms.

■ ■

CHIEF DUMASKY STUDIED HIS notes on June 8, then bolstered himself up after verifying that the magazine of his Glock 22 was properly loaded into its chamber and stepped out. He shook his head. City cops thought they knew better, it never failed. And this black guy, all polite and with his little French accent, and pretendin' to be an equal, was even worse.

He knew how the French liked their coffee. Real strong. He had gone to the station area front desk and asked the receptionist to make a fresh brew with their ten-year-old Mr. Coffee. She had complied the only way she knew how: by producing something that tasted like hot water. And he had brought two cups of that excuse for bean juice to his office.

He wondered if Detective Rippon had seen the little espresso machine seating on a corner table near the office door when he left.

Ah, a guy got to have fun once in a while. He petted his pistol and left. He had some patrollin' to do, some questions to ask.

■ ■

"JULIE. OKAY, I TALKED to the guy. He asked about you, by the way... Yeah, I did like you said. Made him feel real important. Made him think Cruz' disappearance was linked to our case. May very well be, you never know...Anything is possible at this point...Where am I? Driving around town. Just in case Cruz fell in a ditch somewhere. Although something tells me this is dead serious. Something happened to the woman. That's why I had to have Dumasky take the case seriously. Otherwise, there is no way we could take Jane out of here. As it is, your plan failed miserably...What do you mean, because Zoe and I couldn't act it out? No, that wasn't it! It's because your plan sucked. Period! She saw right through me, knew I was a cop from the start. What do you think she is, chopped liver? Come on, Julie! You should know better! A psychic working for the NY fucking PD!

"Mm...That's right, that's right. Yeah, we'll do it tonight. Although I don't know how. I know you need her over there for the Sishy case! You've got a list of suspects...Who are they? Lovers. Sishy was a widow, right? But she had quite a few lovers afterward. Well, God bless her! Although, maybe not, if this is a crime of passion.

"You're not buying the Cruz Mojada–Dorothea connection, are you...You're noncommittal about that. Okay, that's fine. What does Leek say about it? The mustache guy...What does he have to say?...A theory. Well, theories are all we have right now.

"Oh, fuck!...No, nothing! I almost hit a cat. Maybe I should pick it up and present it to Zoe's rat. Ha, ha!

"Mm...I know, I know. But Jane is worried sick about Cruz. I'll have to convince her that Chief Dumasky will do everything he can on this end to find her. You believe he will too? How come, Julie? Didn't you tell me he was a fuckhead?... Okay, fuckhead, as in sexist pig, but a good cop. Okay, I can add that to my arguments when I try to convince Jane to come with us...Ah, convincing her is not my job, you say. It's Zoe's? But, ma chère, with your fucking plan, Zoe needs all the help she can get.

"Dumasky. Yeah, what about him? You want to change the subject. He may be a good cop, yeah. But I prefer your fuckhead version, quite frankly. Why? Because I can confirm it! Hear this: the guy had an espresso machine in his office and instead of offering me decent brain juice, he gave me socks' juice. Fucking *jus de chaussettes*!

"Don't laugh, Julie! That's not funny!"

■7■

"**N**o! I WILL NOT go! You two go back! I'll stay here!"

Jane's face appeared to have shrunk, like a rag assailed by rain and then dried up by a brutal sun. The woman had been crying, Zoe could tell from the bloodshot eyes and the hastily powdered skin. Jane never touched makeup unless she cried or attended some funeral, which didn't necessarily amount to the same thing. "Aunt Jane, it will be good for you to see New York again. And Queens, where you used to live, remember?"

"I must find Cruz first." Jane sat in her armchair and had a bottle of Smirnoff in front of her on the coffee table. She had gone to her liquor cabinet and grabbed a bottle indifferently. That she drank the vodka brand she most despised and reserved for amateurs and/or personal enemies was a sign that she was not well. That the bottle was now almost empty showed that Jane sensed something grave, something that she had no power over.

"Mrs. Dzhugashvili," said Aimé. "I think I told you already that both the Noliar Police and the NYPD are working on finding your friend."

"I drew cards. Cruz is in fooking danger. I'll stay here."

"But they need you in New York, ma'am."

"Fook you, you damn lying cop."

Zoe and Aimé looked at each other.

"You came here under fooking false pretense, you asshole!" Jane swallowed a whole glass of Smirnoff and poured herself another one. "And you, Zoe, go to fooking hell. You fooking accomplice! You both fooking liars!"

Today, Jane's rudeness was not of the routine kind, Zoe thought. Plus, she was right. They had lied to her.

"Okay, we're both fucking liars. If Julie had let me do things my way, maybe you would not have called us fucking liars."

Jane swallowed liquid, then smoke. "But you would have fooking lied nonethefookingless."

"With a better lie." Zoe admitted as she took hold of the Smirnoff.

"Gimme that!" Jane's voice was now draggy.

"Maybe you've had enough, Aunt Jane!"

"Give that back! Give..." Jane's voice went from slur to snore.

"I am going to pack Jane's bag," Zoe told Aimé.

"So we're leaving now?" asked the cop. "I'll carry Jane to the car."

"Not so fast! Jane will be up and aggressive like a wild boar in about half an hour. And what will we do with a wild boar in a car? No, I have a plan."

A plan! Another one of those! Oh, boy! thought Aimé.

■ ■

"YOUR BORSH IS WONDERFUL, ma'am."

After half an hour, just like Zoe had said, Jane had risen from the dead. There was no sign of drunkenness, just clues of belligerence. After a few cigarettes, Zoe had cajoled her into cooking dinner. Jane always felt better after cooking, no matter the situation. And her borsh was "fooking fantastic." No question about it.

But resentment on the Russian front was not totally gone, and the conversation was scattered, at best. Zoe noticed that Jane's hands were trembling and that her complexion was redder than usual. "Aunt Jane, come with us to New York. Come on, it will do you good!"

"When hell fooking freezes over. You, your rat and your cop go. I'll stay."

"But—"

Jane lit a cigarette, took a couple of drags, and let the cigarette fall. Her eyes were lost in space for a moment.

The feeble speech made Zoe jump on her seat. Jane opened her mouth again, but no sound came. She sat there, immobile, her glance expressionless.

And then her head fell in her soup and she collapsed.

Aimé and Zoe got up. Aimé straightened Jane up. Zoe slapped her as hard as she could. "Jane! Jane!"

"What are you doing?" Aimé said.

Zoe fixed her eyes on him for a brief moment, then rushed to the bathroom where she opened the medicine cabinet.

"Was that part of your plan?" Aimé asked when Zoe returned with a couple of medicine bottles.

"Not exactly. But it may work." Zoe said, feeling Jane's pulse.

■■

"WE SHOULD HAVE TAKEN her to the hospital," Aimé said.

"Should have, but we can't. Not here anyway," Zoe answered.

After a moment of silence, she added, "She's had high blood pressure forever."

"And I'm sure her intake of nicotine is really helping."

"Right. And don't forget vodka. The woman is convinced that it is a remedy for everything."

Aimé was clenching the wheel as if his life depended on it. "Are you sure she's going to be all right?"

"Stop being so tense. I gave her her med. A sleeping pill too."

Great! Aimé thought. Zoe was playing doctor. And not the way he would have liked.

"Is it a good idea to give a sleeping pill with a high blood pressure pill?" Aimé asked.

Zoe shrugged. "If you hold the wheel any tighter, you're gonna pull it out of the car," Zoe continued. "Let me drive."

Yeah, right! Aimé thought. He had seen Zoe drive and was in no mood for a thrill ride. He took a deep breath and loosened his grasp of the wheel. "I'll let you drive *your* car, how is that?"

They were on I-80 East and would stay there for at least two more hours, until they found the I-80 Express Lane in New Jersey. From there, they would merge onto I-280 East and would stay there for seventeen miles or so. And then, ten miles and a few turns later, they would be downtown New York. Zoe knew the road by heart. Christ! Did that mean she had gone back to Noliar more times than she cared to admit?

It was night, and all the landscape had melted. The trees had become a massive dropping of black ink. Road lights were scattered. There was little traffic, and the lights from distant trucks looked like curious eyes from extraterrestrials. Slightly fuller than three nights ago when they had been on their way to Noliar, the crescent moon curled up in the darkness, like a cozy teaser. When Zoe looked at it, she saw a white smile, a white twisted smile.

What the hell!

Once more, she was in the middle of a mess.

A loud snore was heard from behind.

Zoe tapped Aimé's leg. "Reassured? I mean, when someone snores like a regiment of marines, things must be a-okay, right?"

Aimé smiled. He let his right hand travel away from the wheel and placed it on Zoe's lap. Zoe picked up the hand and talked to it. "Hey, go back where you came from!"

"It's really good to see you again," Aimé said.

"Good to see you too. But keep your hands for your current girlfriend."

"I am not totally over you, Zee-Zee."

"That makes two of us. I am still not over the fact that you were an undercover cop and that you never bothered to tell me."

"That's why we are called undercover cops."

"But we slept together."

"And it was good, wasn't it? Could be good again."

"Really? Your girlfriend likes to share?"

Zoe unbuckled, then reached toward her left shoulder. "Okay, buddy, back to your house."

"You had that rat on your shoulder for two whole hours?"

"And?" Zoe turned toward the back of the car and then grabbed Zieg II. The pet carrier was stable on the floor between her seat and the backseat.

She reached toward it, and Zieg II chose that moment to jump on Jane. "Shit!"

The rat ran on Jane's body as if it were the ultimate roller coaster. Zoe tried to catch him, but Zieg II was having a field day of it. He came toward Zoe's hand as if he were ready to be caught. Then, as soon as he would feel a finger on his fur, he would escape and do another sprint on Jane.

And Jane was still snoring.

"How many sleeping pills did you give the woman?" Aimé said after assessing the situation.

Zoe scratched her head. "I wanted to avoid her making a scene in the car."

"Yeah. So how many?"

Zoe shrugged.

"You don't wanna say, hm?"

"Don't feel like talkin' just now."

"I see. She's gonna wake up when we least expect it. And then realize we've taken her against her will. Tell you something. I'm not looking forward to it. It's gonna be World War III."

"So how about pressing on that gas pedal, so we can reach my place before she wakes up?"

Aimé slowed down and parked on the side of the road. "How about grabbing that rat first?"

■ ■

ZOE SAW THAT THEY had just left the New Jersey Turnpike and had taken Exit 16E toward NJ-495 E and the Lincoln Tunnel. They were just a couple of miles away from Zoe and Marc's place. Since Marc had come to live with her, they had remained in the same building on 72nd Street but had moved to a larger and, let's face it, better kept apartment. Zieg II had to get used to the new space and it had not taken that long. With Marc, it had been another story. Although he had been the one insisting on moving away from Zoe's claustrophobic quarters, seeing the rat run at every corner and at any time of day had taken some getting used to. The rodent and human males had finally reached a level of mutual tolerance, but it was not a love story just yet. They both competed for Zoe's attention, and Zoe had had to establish boundaries. There would be so much time for the man and so much time for the rat. The system worked 50 percent of the time.

Dealing with males gave Zoe the occasional headache.

"We have arrived," Aimé said as he parked in front of Zoe's building.

Zoe looked at her watch. 5:05 a.m. She saw lights across the blinds of Jack Liu's flower shop. Even immigrants got up at the same crazy hours as natives. What the hell!

Zoe went to pick up Zieg II's carrier. "You'll have to carry Jane up to the apartment," she told Aimé. "We'll get the bags later."

Aimé mumbled something indistinguishable. Grouchy mode, Zoe diagnosed. Then she raised her eyebrows toward him in a see-if-I-care fashion.

Aimé had Jane now, still snoring, in his arms. "Open the door, will you?"

"What fook!"

God, she's up! Zoe took a deep breath.

Then the snoring resumed.

Zoe relaxed with a grin. Apparently, clean language didn't belong in Jane's dreams, either.

Aimé looked at his load and made a face. "Feels nothing like when I carried you. You didn't snore and you saved swearwords for the right occasion."

■ 8 ■

"SHE WILL BE ALL right," Marc said after having examined Jane. "Show me her pills, will you?"

Zoe handed him a couple of bottles.

They were in the apartment guest room. Filled with a single bed from which Zoe had removed a number of orange and ochre cushions to make room for Jane, a chair, a desk by the window, and a chest of drawers, it was longer than wide, and the mimosa walls and dark furniture gave it a feeling of nesting intimacy. Soothing, comforting, sunny, it was the perfect recovery room.

Oh, shit! Zoe thought. Yellow. Jane hated yellow.

Marc was rotating the pill containers between his fingers. "Beta blockers, diuretics, good." He then observed Jane, checked her pulse once more, frowned, and turned to Zoe. "The woman is still sleeping. How many sleeping pills did you give her?"

"One or two?"

"Well, Zoe, which one is it? One, or two?"

"Uh…two. Two is good, right?"

He faced her, squinted, and adjusted his glasses. Why can't he keep his doctor's mode for his fucking patients? she thought.

"More like three or four, huh, Zoe?"

Okay, let's go for that. She gave him a half-smile.

"What kind?"

She handed him another bottle of pills.

He delivered a medical stare, a mouth twist, the lift of one eyebrow.

She looked away. Fuck doctors.

"Ramelteon, okay. You gave her a fairly unsafe dosage of what is usually a pretty safe med. Ah, Zoe! You're lucky this one is as tough as Rasputin. And let's face it, she won't be able to smoke or swallow her favored Russian Standard for the next twenty-four hours."

"See?" Zoe produced a sassy-victorious grin.

Marc grabbed her elbow.

"Oh, that's the lover's touch!" she grumbled. "Take your doctor's paw away from me. I have been here half an hour, and you didn't even kiss me once!"

He knit his brows, then leaned toward her and kissed her on the cheek.

"What are you? A distant cousin from Wisconsin or my fucking partner?"

"Let's go to the living room. We need to talk."

■ ■

A CHOCOLATE-COLORED SOFA WITH vermillion cushions drew a thick colorful line against the brick wall of the living room. An imperial red armchair with silk brown and white striped cushions elbowed it on its left. On the right, an unkempt rubber plant stood like a gangrenous articulation. Marc was so pedantic about every freaking thing, Zoe thought, except for plants. She rushed to the kitchen, went to the faucet with a tall glass, filled it, and watered the plant. After giving Marc that special glance she reserved for plant murderers, Zoe suddenly grew tired. She threw her legs on the sofa, let her head drop on one arm rest, hugged one cushion, and closed her eyes. Marc threw the armchair cushions on the floor and sat—another atypical behavior. He usually picked the cushions as if they were newborns and placed them delicately on a side table. "Actually, these are the pills I prescribed to her before—"

"Before?"

"Before she fired me."

"Aunt Jane fired you? What do you mean?"

Zoe was enjoying this line of conversation—at least more than the one she suspected Marc would soon undertake. So she would try to keep this one as long as possible. She knew damn well why Jane had "fired" Marc.

Marc looked suspicious. "She never told you?"

"No. I don't think so. In fact, I know so. She didn't tell me. Nope! Never! No sirree Bob!"

"Well, I advised her to quit smoking."

"She didn't mind that."

"I thought she never told you."

"Simple deduction," Zoe answered, eyes still closed. "All doctors tell Jane to quit smoking. I mean, the doctors she has been seeing after she got rid of you. Well, getting rid of you is not the right expression, exactly, but I am fucking dead tired, too tired for the right expressions anyway, but you get my drift. One doctor at a time, though. She only fired the ones who said bad things about her good friend Smirnoff. I mean, vodka. She's got no respect for Smirnoff. Well, you know what I mean. The doctor she has now drinks vodka, aged Russian vodka if I remember correctly, so of course she's a keeper. Although she too tells her, 'Quit smoking, quit smoking.' Jane doesn't take it personally, 'specially from another vodka addict."

"You need sleep, Zoe. You're not making much sense."

Yeah, sleep was good! Better than this stupid conversation. She yawned.

Zoe slowly sat up and opened her eyes halfway. Facing her was a large window that framed portions of tall buildings and skyscrapers across the street. Lights popped up from windows in random fashion. Somehow, they reminded her of the truck lights on I-80 a while ago. They looked like eyes too. Only the ones on the buildings seemed accusatory, as if they were ready to frame her, once more, for a crime she didn't commit. Fatigue was making her feel paranoid. New York is waking up, is all. Except that the city never slept, as the song said. It just roared slower when night came, with the exception of the strident sounds of police sirens and the nagging laments of ambulances that seemed louder during the night. "You're right," she finally told Marc. "I think I am going to turn in. It's almost six. If I don't sleep, I'll go insane."

"Not so fast!"

"Can't whatever you need to tell me wait? Don't you have to go and operate on someone or something?"

"It's my day off."

"Yeah. So you should relax. We could relax together when I'm done sleeping." Zoe winked at Marc. Only her drowsy state made the wink look like the grimace of a man who had not seen the sun for twenty years and was not exactly impressed by what he was seeing.

Marc observed that the femme fatale had gone to bed before Zoe's body and wondered if indeed he should let the rest of her join her. But he knew how Zoe would be after a few hours of sleep. She would answer his questions with jokes—some of them questionable, of course—and try every strategy—and she knew a few—to dodge his inquiries. The femme fatale would be awake then, at least Zoe's version of the femme fatale. But that very version, the saucy version where her wink would be right on target, he could never resist. He would take her into his arms and forget everything. So he had to take advantage of her present tiredness, for he needed to know. It seemed that, once more, she was involved in some impossible imbroglio. So he ignored the current weary wink. It was a miss anyway.

"And on my day off," he continued, "what do you do? You wake me up at five a.m., bring a Russian woman who, despite a lethargic state induced by dosage-challenged *You-Know-Who*, manages to swear every fifteen minutes or so. This woman I have known most of my life and treated with respect told me during one consultation that I was nuts, and after another she pulled a Donald Trump on me.

"A what?"

"Well, she told me, 'You're fired!' And with relish, mind you. All this because I told her alcohol shouldn't be part of her diet. On top of this, Jane makes her grand snoring entrance in the arms of one of your former boyfriends. So, Zoe, tell me, what the hell is going on?"

"I can explain...later." Zoe said.

"And a few days ago, you cancel a book signing and leave all of a sudden. You give me the cockamamie excuse that your mom is going crazy because your father, an atheist formerly known as a Jew, is no longer shaving and looks now like a prophet who has stepped right out of the Tora." Marc twisted his mouth in frustration. "I tell you something, Zoe, for a fiction writer, you could do a little better."

"You know my mom. She goes crazy for just about anything."

†† *Na-na-na-na-na-na, na-na-na-na-na-na, na-na-na-na-na-na, na-nana-na-na-na, na*

Saved by the cell. Zoe looked around, trying to remember where she had left her purse. Ah, it was on top of Zieg's carrier, ten feet away. Zoe dragged her steps in that direction. When her hands foraged into her bag, most of its content fell on the wood floor, but ultimately she found her cell phone.

Marc removed his glasses and rubbed his eyes. Zoe turned to him. His beard was in need of a shave, and he had been too busy lately to go and get a haircut. She loved that disheveled look. His doctor-gone-rebel look, his Che Guevara look—here devoid of masculine cockiness. And now that his glasses were off, she could see the veiled gaze. The doctor lost into uncertainties—a state of mind that Marc hated. He was used to finding solutions for his patients, and when he lost one on the operating table, he would come home sad and unapproachable for a while. Still, he could handle death better than he could handle incertitude. Zoe promised herself to show him how to love these moments when nothing is sure, when it's the Sahara Desert and you don't know if what comes ahead is a village or a mirage. Many times, Marc had told Zoe he would like to go into research, but didn't really know whether or not he could handle it. Zoe wanted to tell him that research was not unlike writing. In both cases you've got to learn to love the Sahara.

That's why she was a writer. People assumed writers knew more. But good writers know they don't know shit, and they're okay with that.

Ah, Marc, the scientist in love with the tangible. And yet.

Yet.

There was something that had not made too much sense lately. Or maybe it was the lack of sleep that made her half-delirious and overly imaginative. Impossible combo.

Yet.

Still.

When Marc left his old life and his Noliar office, he went to work at the Fontaine Clinic, where Zoe's breast cancer had been treated. Dr. Fontaine, a brilliant gynecologist full of himself and of Botox, had gone to study plastic surgery and taken Marc with him. From breast reconstruction to the resculpting of a face, there was only one step. To Zoe's chagrin, Marc had embraced it with a strange fervor. What was so great about this business of vanities? It only made the conceit of the rich more exacerbated. "You don't understand; it's more than that, Zoe. Much more," Marc said. What was there to understand about a procedure that erased human expressions as effectively as it erased wrinkles? There were roads and maps on a wrinkled face. Take Jane, for instance. A whole atlas was traced around her eyes. What was there to understand about people who refused to keep the itinerary of their own life?

And yet, somewhere, she feared she could become one of them.

What was odd about the whole business was money. Marc was doing very well, for sure, but with all the plastic surgeries he performed, he should be rich by now. A millionaire, or close. But that wasn't the case. There was something he was not telling her.

What was he hiding from her?

One or two gray streaks had snuck into Marc's dark mane. That was new. His eyes, dark blue on good days, were gray at the moment. Marc was worried.

He got up now, went to the purse and started to put back every fallen object into it: compact, lipstick, small notebook, tampons, mints, hairbrush, perfume, the whole array of female necessities. He held a small rectangular box. Damn! He had found her cigarettes. She had started to smoke again, he knew that now, so she would hear about it. Well, fuck that, she had to answer the damn phone.

She saw the number on her cell screen. Julie. "Hey, bitch!" Zoe said with a draggy voice. "Calling me past my bedtime? What's up?"

"Zoe, I am afraid I have bad news."

Zoe moved slowly toward the sofa and let her body collapse. "What—"

"Just talked to Aimé, who just got a call from Dumasky. There has been a fire."

"Where?"

"Jane's house. We don't know what caused it yet. Apparently started in the garage. It's gonna take a while to find what caused the fire. Could be Jane's half-defunct Oldsmobile. Could be Jane's electric system. She's got wiring that's at least fifty years old. Dinosaurs wouldn't want it."

After a pause, Julie continued. "Could be something else entirely."

"Well, you said that Jane was in danger, didn't you?"

Silence.

"Looks like we left in the nick of time. Had we decided to spend another night there, you would have three deaths on your conscience by now."

Zoe was shaking. Marc rushed toward her and held her.

■9■

"**C**AN YOU MAKE SOME coffee?" Zoe asked Marc after a while. "I guess I won't be going to bed any time soon."

Marc went to the kitchen and after fifteen minutes he had breakfast ready.

■ ■

ZOE CLEANED UP HER plate. She was either hungry or the eggs Marc had prepared for her were delicious. She was now drinking her third cup of coffee. When she lit a cigarette, Marc said nothing. She started by telling Marc about the fire.

"You say Julie and Leek got some anonymous call?" he asked Zoe.

"Yeah. Some caller told them that Jane was in danger."

"And Julie sent *you* to save Jane?"

Zoe tapped her cigarette with her index finger and watched the ash fall in the ashtray. "How should I interpret this remark? Protective? Insulting? Both?"

"Come on, Zoe! You're not a cop! You could have been killed! As it is, I have murderous feelings. I am ready to kill Julie."

Zoe took a deep breath. Ah, that felt good! If Marc could kill that bitch. She started fantasizing, imagining Julie dead, flattened and buried, her grave picked and *ha-ha-ha-HAA-ha*-ed by Woody Woodpecker.

Another *ha-ha-ha-HAA-ha—ha-ha-ha-HAA-ha!* That felt pretty good. The cartoon version of Julie, kaput.

Now the real one could stay alive.

"I bet it's easy for a doctor to be a murderer, especially if that doctor can perform surgery," Zoe deadpanned.

Okay, Zoe was not ready to forgive Julie this very minute.

"There was a cop with me, though," she added. "An undercover cop."

"Once under your covers."

Zoe swallowed. "What?"

"You think I didn't recognize the guy who carried Jane here?"

"We're not going there again, are we? Don't make that shitty face. You'll catch wrinkles in the wrong places. You know I never really loved Aimé. He just was there when I thought I was over you."

"Well, you were once over him, and I much prefer it when you are over me!"

"Ha, ha! That's a good one. Now, stop your shit." Zoe went to sit on his lap and gave him a big French one. "I'll give you more later, but I am dead tired. I need to tell you something else." Zoe left his lap and went back to her chair.

"Okay." He looked disappointed. He wanted something besides a conversation at the moment.

"Cruz Mojada."

"What about her?"

"She disappeared."

"What do you mean, disappeared?"

"Just that. She cannot be found."

"She didn't take a leave of absence? Visit a lover of hers, maybe? What about family?"

"She packed no bags. And her purse is in her house."

"A car accident?"

"Her car's in the garage."

"She could have gone somewhere with a friend."

"Without her purse? Besides, if that had been the case, she would have shown up by now."

"A walk in the woods? She could have fallen somewhere."

"Cruz and her stilettos? A walk in the woods?"

"True. But with the right guy, she would wear flats, wouldn't she?"

"And with the wrong guy...Oh God! What if..."

"What are you trying to say, Zoe?"

"I don't know what the hell I am saying. I know that Jane may need tranquillizers when she wakes up. She's convinced something bad happened to her."

"Who would want to arm Cruz?"

"That's what I have been asking myself. Who? You were her doctor in Noliar. Maybe she told you something about a jealous lover? Or maybe some jealous wife?"

"I was her gynecologist, not her psychologist."

"I know, but Cruz is a talker."

"And I, as a doctor, am supposed to be a non-talker. Professional secrecy, remember?"

"Did I ever ask you any kind of patient private detail? It's just that I am worried. And we are talking about Cruz, for Crissake."

"Noliar is a safe place, Zoe."

"Is it?" Silence. That she finally broke. "Julie and Leek are working on a murder case. And there is the theory that Cruz' disappearance and that murder are somehow connected."

"That's a bit far-fetched, don't you think? Is that a theory you have concocted yourself? Tell you what. Maybe, you should put it in your novels."

"Tell you what. Fuck you, Dr. Trenton. Matter of fact, it isn't my theory. It's Aimé's theory."

Marc had a long, long face. She took pity on him, smiled, and teased his hair. "I said something about theory, nothing about practice."

"Mm." He felt his messed up hair. "You could touch something else."

"Seriously," she went on after a few yawns. "I hope you're right. About the theory, I mean. I hope it doesn't stick. In the end, Jane will get it. I bet she will."

"Jane, Chainsaw Jane the psychic will get it, is that what you mean?"

"Yup."

"Those are Jane's shenanigans, trickeries she uses to make a living."

"Have you ever seen her clients?"

"No, but she must make a living somehow, and I assume...Anyway, Zoe, why do you believe in that shit?"

"And why do scientific minds have such a limited vision?"

"Reason, facts, those are not so limited."

"Pff. You don't believe in intuition? Don't you need a little bit of that for the tough diagnosis that surely must come your way once in a while, although now that you're in cosmetic—" She stopped. "Never mind. I'm too tired for a fucking philosophical discussion. But you'll be happy to know that you were right about Jane having clients."

"See?" He grinned.

"Guess who her main client is."

"Maybe it's a secret. Maybe I shouldn't know."

"Well, guess."

"How about the NYPD?"

"You knew all along, you s.o.b."

Marc chuckled. "Not for long."

"Who told you?"

"Julie."

"Why?"

"She had to prepare me to the events, didn't she? Tell me we would have a visitor? When I asked her why we needed to be the hosts of Catherine III of Russia, she had to give me some info. She was very succinct, however. Perhaps you could fill in the blanks."

And so Zoe went on to explain Jane's interactions with the NYPD, her Tarot, her abilities. Marc the Noliar native knew about Jane's reputation as a Russian witch and took it like everyone else as part of the town mythology. But Marc the man of science had trouble believing in extrasensory phenomenons, even if he knew for a fact that the police did use mediums and such. And he had to admit that if it didn't work all the time, it did work often enough to take these people seriously. All the same, he believed they were not guided by visions or intuitions. They were simply gifted with acute reasoning, heightened cerebral activities. In other words, it was reason and only reason that led them to crime resolution. They were "mentalists" of sorts, like the guy on the TV series. But if they admitted that, they might receive less remuneration. And in these days and age—in these New Age days, rather—successful psychics buttered their bread more abundantly than, say, successful professors. The right brain pocketed what the left brain claimed to do. So Jane was certainly very clever.

Zoe had hardly finished telling her story when sleep took over. Her head dropped on her chest, then on the kitchen table, like a rag doll. Marc lifted her and carried her to their bedroom. He undressed her, placed her under the sheets, kissed her forehead, and gently closed the door.

In his home office, he pressed a key on his Blackberry. "Yes, it's me. Yes, they're both asleep now. So what do you have? Photos? Jeez! That's the second far-fetched theory of the day. But I'll look at them."

PART II

■ 10 ■

WOMAN'S TORSO FOUND IN CENTRAL PARK

On this June 10, he got bored with the Classifieds and went to the big titles. And this immediately caught his attention.

WOMAN'S TORSO FOUND IN CENTRAL PARK, he read again. His heart was racing, going boom-boom-BOOM against his chest. He took a deep breath. Then another. So they found it. He wrung his lips, then stretched them into a one-sided grimace.

> The woman's torso found in The Lake in Central Park is believed to belong to a Mrs. Dorothea Sishy, owner of Open Page bookstore-cafe on East Side Sixty-Sixth Street. Dorothea Sishy had disappeared since May 4, and despite the state of decomposition of the body part, forensic specialists have been able to identify the DNA.
>
> Medical examiner Faye Gambetta stated that "a prolonged immersion produces wrinkling, maceration, and blanching of the skin, but will not prevent body identification." Loose hair found on the victim's body helped confirm the victim's

ID. When asked if hair that did not belong to Sishy was also found, Gambetta did not respond. She said instead, "Looking at these factors, it is reasonable to assume that Dorothea Sishy died shortly after she disappeared." The examiner added that the precise time of death cannot under these circumstances be established. But something can be asserted more definitely, according to Dr. Gambetta: "The torso has been found without the rest of its body parts, and with clean cuts at neck, arm, and leg points. This indicates foul play. The instrument used to separate the torso from its extremities is most likely a chainsaw."

The criminal psychologist analyzing this case is looking over two possibilities. One of them profiles a serial murderer with ritualistic tendencies. The fact that Dorothea Sishy's head, arms, and legs were not found with her torso could classify the crime as bizarre and even indicate some form of cannibalism. The other possibility suggests that the murderer could know his victim, even be a member of her family. The use of the chainsaw would then reveal two things: extreme anger and violence and a defying need to mystify authorities. Dorothea Sishy's torso was immersed in a trash bag with two heavy rocks, perhaps an indication that the murderer might not want the body found. This explains why it took three days of searching the bottom of The Lake to find the torso. In typical cases of drowning, the bodies eventually refloat.

But why drop the body part in the middle of Central Park and not at the bottom of some more isolated body of water in some rural, unfrequented place? Or even the Hudson River, where its disappearance could almost be guaranteed? Could it be that the murderer is playing with the police?

NYPD crime psychologist suggested that the cutting of the body into several parts could signal a morbid sense of game-playing but that more needs to be known. Additional clues and facts will help to definitely categorize the crime. "We have been investigating the disappearance of Dorothea Sishy for a month now. But the latest discovery changes everything. The disappearance investigation is now closed, and the murder investigation is just beginning. Detective Leek and I are working closely with our medical examiner as well as with the two possible murderer profiles drawn by our crime psychologist," said Detective Hoffman during last night's press conference. When Leek and Hoffman were asked which profile was in their opinion more plausible, they suggested either possibility leads to the conclusion that the murderer is psychologically unbalanced and certainly very dangerous.

When asked what led them to search The Lake in Central Park, the detectives claimed that they had reliable sources but refused to give the names of such sources. "My partner and I feel it would obstruct the progress of our investigation," said Detective Leek.

When Leek and Hoffman were asked if they were working with other forces, such as the FBI or even paranormal personnel, such as mediums—as is sometimes the case when police faces challenging investigations—they remained aloof, only alluding to the fact that the FBI is often active in cases of disappearance and so are mediums, but that the Sishy case is now officially a murder case.

The FBI knew where to find Dorothea's bust? Could that be? He had been very careful and was almost certain that the cops' fucking reliable sources came from elsewhere.

Like from that Russian old witch. People around here knew she was a psychic of sorts, but they didn't take it seriously. Thought it was a Russian thing, like borsch and vodka. Well, he knew better. His damn mother had been a psychic and had predicted no good would come out of her own son. Her own son! Imagine that! Now she was six feet under, had been there for years. Only a few bones remained there, probably, a shadow of what she was in any case. A heart attack had brought her to her grave. The woman ate too much. Ice cream, fries, sausage, all that shit. He didn't cry at her funeral, thought he was rid of her at last. Then why did he feel she was still here, watching him, invading him?

And then there was the NYPD, with Leek and that dyke. Invasive as well. When they were at the Russian bitch's house again, he knew what he had to do. Burn the damn house.

But he had failed. Fire only destroyed her car and part of the garage. He had waited till three a.m. or so, making sure all lights were out in the neighborhood. Chainsaw Jane went to bed late, after two a.m. But even Russian bitches need their rest.

It hadn't worked as planned. Nobody was killed. It just dawned on him that the Zimmerman girl had been at the Russian's house. A black guy was there too. Was the Zimmerman girl fucking the black guy? Weren't white dicks good enough for her anymore?

One thing was sure, he had fucking miscalculated. When he had seen that Crown Vic go, he had thought that Jane would be alone in her house and that he could set his fire in peace, at last. What he hadn't realized was that Jane had left with them. The big bag the black guy had carried on his back from the house to the car was no luggage. Looked like a bag; wasn't a bag. It was Chainsaw Jane.

The man swallowed his last drops of coffee and punched the desk with his cup. The handle got detached in the process, and the rest of the cup flew in the air until it crashed on the floor and broke into pieces. Shit!

He bent down to pick them up. One, two, three, four, five. Six. Six pieces. It went into six pieces. Just like Dorothea after he was done with her.

He had to smile.

But now he heard a bang on the door that led to his basement. Boom-boom-boom! She would end up breaking his door. He couldn't believe the strength of that woman. Maybe it was all this bowling every Tuesday. She didn't go there just to show her array of miniskirts and her still pretty hot legs.

She was starting to get on his nerves, though.

He threw the broken cup in the waste basket by his desk and started to walk out. He then thought of something and returned to grab one piece of the broken cup. "This should help," he said.

Walking down the stairs was painful. His leg was acting up again. The banging on the basement door got louder as he descended. So did the screaming. "Let me out! Let me out, you bastard!"

"Boy, she got lungs too! Must be those big boobs helping!" he thought.

He went to his dining room, got his gun out of the top left drawer of a battered dresser, placed it between his pants and his butt, and slowly progressed toward the basement.

"LET ME OUT! LET ME OUT! LET ME OUT NOW, YOU CREEP!"

To think he had fucked her once. Or twice. No regret, though. She was good. Matter of fact, there was nothing that equaled the hot temper of a Latina.

But he couldn't afford this one anymore.

He approached the door very slowly, silently, forcing his bad leg into regular motion and tightening his teeth in the process.

"LET ME OUT, DAMMIT!"

Considering the yelling and screaming, she didn't suspect he was that close. Good. But he had to be cautious. He had to make sure his bad leg wouldn't pound on the floor the way it did when the pain hit him. And today the pain was near unbearable. That bitch would have to pay.

"I WANT OUT! WHAT DO YOU WANT FROM ME? YOU THINK YOU CAN HURT ME? YOU THINK YOU CAN HURT ME, YOU S.O.B.?"

He was there now. He silently unlocked the door, then opened it with such speed that she was left speechless and immobile for a moment. He pushed her down the stairs.

She was now lying on the basement cement floor. As he descended he noticed she was not moving anymore. Well, if she was dead, that would simplify things. He now leaned over her. As he extended his hand to check her pulse, she suddenly grabbed him by the collar. Her face was bleeding.

He tried to take her hand away from him and regain control. He twisted her fingers, but she didn't feel it. All he saw on that face was blood and rage. She was not the woman he knew. A woman couldn't be that strong. He couldn't bear the humiliation. He let go of her fingers and picked up the broken cup piece he had placed in the right front pocket of his baggy work pants, noting in the process that dirty kleenex had been keeping it company. He thought for a second and wondered if he should get the gun instead. No! He had a plan. And he would make this one suffer before she died.

Her hands were still on his collar, lead tentacles flattening his neck. He wanted to swallow saliva, but couldn't. Oh, the bitch would pay! Very slowly, almost imperceptibly, he moved his shoulder, then raised his arm, and in a swift gesture he sliced her cheek.

Next target was her neck. As soon as he could reach it, he would slash it and then let her bleed, slowly, like they used to do with pigs.

But first, she would have to let go. It would happen any time now. He was sure of it. She was just a woman. How strong could she be?

A loud roar burst out of his mouth. She had plunged her teeth into his fingers. Now *he* was bleeding and in pain. It felt as if he had been bitten by a wolf. He went for his gun. Was it the brusque movement, the pressure on his neck, the insufficient breathing that suddenly stopped him in the middle of his action? He felt dizzy all of a sudden, as if he were there but not there. How stupid was that! He tried to twist his body one way and the other, but her hands were still on him. He had to recover his strength; he had to get his gun.

He was on top of her. Then how come she was the one controlling the situation? Beneath him, and in charge? Her arms would end up being tired. Actually, they already were. Her hold was loosening. She would get it! She would get it soon! He heard her take a deep breath.

He took a deep breath. He reached for his gun.

"AAAAHHHH!"

"What did you think, *hijo de puta*? That I couldn't kick you in the *cojones*? How does it feel, eh? How does my knee feel on your stupid balls?"

He wanted to get up, but his body wouldn't follow. The pain between his legs had only made his bad leg worse. He instinctively took a fetal position, oblivious of the gun in his hand.

She crawled out from under him, wiped the blood from her face, but more got out from where it came from. She tightened her teeth. It suddenly dawned on her that she was wearing stilettos. Stiletto heels were named after stiletto daggers. Her feet were weapons. She saw the gun, extended her right leg, and hammered his hand with her daggered heel. Fucking crucifixion for someone who truly deserved it. His scream came strong and strident, soon to be followed by the cold metallic sound of the gun hitting the cement floor. She got on her hands and knees, grabbed the weapon, and got up.

"Sit up!" she ordered, pointing the gun at him.

"I can't," he said. "My leg."

"Sit up, or you'll see what happens to your third leg, if you know what I mean!"

"Can't. S...sorry!"

"Okay, you crazy bastard. Then tear a piece of your shirt."

"What!"

"You heard me. Tear a piece of your shirt. Yeah, like that, bigger, bigger. Now give it to me!"

He handed her the torn piece of cotton. With her free hand, she snapped it and applied it to her bleeding cheek.

Clack!

"Oh, no!" he cried.

"Oh no what? So you're just a wuss without a gun? You never heard the wind shut a door before? Are you afraid of the fucking wind, huh, is that it?"

He got out of his fetal position.

"Don't move or I'll shoot!"

"Okay. It's just that—"

"Just that, what?"

"The door. You can't open it from—from here. When it shuts, it locks up automatically."

She pressed the dirty piece of shirt on her cheek, produced a small circular motion with her gunned hand as if she were drawing a special target on his chest, and gave him a predatory smile.

"So, hijo de puta, it's just you and me having a little rendez-vous. Actually, during my stay in these deluxe quarters, I saw a rat hanging by a beam on the ceiling somewhere. So it's gonna be ménage à trois."

He looked frightened. Frightened and surprised, she thought. She hoped he wouldn't realize that's exactly how she felt. She had never held a gun before, and the thing was heavy. It looked much lighter when she was watching cop shows on TV. Fatigue was taking over and she didn't know how much longer she could hang on. And help was not coming. She had spent what seemed like an eternity in this filthy basement. And no one came.

Surely Jane was worried.

Surely she wouldn't die here. Surely. She kept applying pressure on her cheek with the dirty piece of shirt and a few tears came in to join the blood. At this point she didn't know what was comfort, what was pain.

He looked to see if the gun, by any chance, had forgotten its aim. No such luck. It was there, an extension of her arm, watching him like the eye of a Cyclops. He lowered his gaze toward the floor. The broken piece of cup lay there, unseen by her.

ETECTIVES LEEK, HOFFMAN, AND Rippon were at the precinct, each facing their mug on Julie's stormy desk. "So I am not the only one undercover, your laptop is?" Aimé enjoyed repeating each time he saw the detective's computer buried under her reports. "Not missing Chief Dumasky's coffee, Rippon?" Julie said, ignoring her colleague's sarcasm.

"FYI," Aimé responded.

"FYI what?" Julie narrowed her glance.

"Fuck your ID."

"Sure, but not in public, sweetheart."

"Hm," Leek commented. The two younger cops sent a side glance to the older, mustached one.

"What now?" Aimé asked. "I suppose I go back to routine."

"Undercover is pretty interesting routine. And you now have liaison duties, Rippon," said Leek. "It seems Chief Dumasky is keeping his word about informing you about the state of affairs in Noliar."

Julie poured herself some additional brain juice. "That fire at Jane's place. Disturbing."

Leek frowned but said nothing.

Aimé finished his cup and rose. "Well, I guess it's back to the yellow cab. See you when I see you!"

"Wait!" said Julie as she ran after him. "Take this!" She handed him a thermos. "Dumasky juice!"

"Ugh! Sounds like disgusting porn."

"Okay, socks' juice, then."

"Even worse. You're out to torture me, 'that it?"

"This cop just wants to have fun. Oh, this cop just wants to have fun." After a beat, Julie added, "Are all French guys that sensitive?"

"Only when it comes to coffee."

"It's Star-fucking-bucks in there, dense enough for a couple of massive heart attacks. Enjoy!"

Aimé emitted a luminous, broad smile, then went to apply a big smack on Julie's lips.

"Nice try, but you know I don't do guys," she said.

"No chance, uh?"

"No fucking chance. Not even with Parisians."

"I knew that. Hope your girlfriend is at least as good-looking as moi."

Julie rolled her eyes.

"Thanks for the coffee all the same." And with these words Aimé was gone.

When Julie returned to her desk, Leek was waiting, face and mustache impassible. "What did you think of our press release?" she asked her partner. "A bit surreal, I suppose."

"Leek, what—"

"I mean, Julie, the finding of a torso. No head, no limb. I know Mrs. Dzhugashvili warned us. Still, it doesn't happen every day, even in New York. And being there on the field yesterday while they dug it out, all the more surreal. Someone is playing us."

"Well, yeah, but—"

"I don't like it."

"Does that mean you *like* other murders?"

Leek's mustache twittered. "I mean, Julie, that this murderer is not the ordinary type of murderer. The intent of a murderer is to get rid of a person or persons for a definite motive—money, passion, revenge. But most murderers are not defiant. And I feel this one is."

Murderers, not defiant? Julie frowned. Leek was not making sense. She planted her gaze into her partner's. "Explain."

"It seems he —"

"Could be a she—"

"Could be. But I don't think so. I don't want to offend your feminist sensitivities, Julie. Not even with a chainsaw murder. But humor me for a second, and let's assume the murderer is a man."

Whatever. Julie sighed as she tapped on her desk. "So defiant, you were saying."

"Yes. This murderer got rid of Dorothea Sishy for a reason we are not aware of yet. While at the same time, this crime was some sort of provocation."

"You're not saying that the murderer killed Sishy to provoke the police, are you?"

Silence.

"Well, are you?"

More silence.

"Because it doesn't appear that the murderer wanted the body to be found, for one. I mean the torso was bagged with stones in it. It wasn't supposed to resurface on the lake. How could that be provocation?"

Leek closed his eyes. "With stones, no, but right in Central Park, yes. There is a contradiction here. You saw our profiler's report. And I concur."

Julie observed her partner, the tension in his facial muscles, the long wrinkles curving inward around his mouth, the mouth itself slipping down toward the chin, as in discouragement. He had been in the force for thirty years and was close to retirement. He never spoke of it. But was it time? He seemed to have lost that special glow in his green eyes, something that made him move with a blend of smoothness and enthusiasm when he was on the trail of a prey.

For ultimately, that's how Leek saw the murderers, as his prey. Which was fine with Julie. He was a true feline, with hardly a useless movement, everything calculated, precise, both sides of the brain balanced until the right moment, when Leek's claws would make their gradual incisions, and the murderer would be too numb to realize what was happening. But what she saw now was a tired cat, ready to nest by the fireplace and sleep, body all rolled up. Cocooned. Worse, locked to the world. A safe with mighty doors. She swallowed. And in that swallow there was the emerging taste of salt. Tears were not far. She used the quick movement of her lids to wipe them out.

"You say you have a list of suspects?" Leek produced a half-grin, a wink.

Sigh of relief from Julie. Damn old cat.

"Yeah. I have a few names. The lovers Sishy saw recently. And you had officers check her store and apartment?"

"Nothing of interest there. Open Page is a nice place. One of the best bookstores in the city, if you ask me. Friendly, efficient. And good coffee for our friend Aimé." Leek smiled. "But nothing suspicious. Nothing. And her apartment is nice and clean. Strong interest in contemporary art. A couple of interesting paintings. Books, of course. But not as many as you'd think."

"Well, there's plenty at her store. And she probably owned a Kindle or Nook."

"Correct."

"Disappointed?" Julie made a face.

"By what?

"By the aridity of Sishy's place, I suppose."

"It's not arid. It's a lovely place."

"Come on, Leek. You know what I mean. The place is clueless, is what I mean. Too clueless?"

Leek shrugged. "Let's look at these names."

She handed him a piece of spotted, wrinkled paper. "Here are names with photos and profiles. I'll make you a copy in a minute."

"I see that you have been studying these for a while."

"You could say that." Julie failed to tell her partner that she had taken the liberty to e-mail some of these photos to Marc. She had done so on a whim, on a "crazy idea," as Marc had put it. She could hardly call it a theory. It was the germ of an idea. Only a guy like Marc, whom she had known since she was a kid, could have humored her. Lucky for her.

Maybe.

"Indeed a clean copy would be nice."

Fucking cat, thought Julie, who nevertheless rushed to the copy machine, and got back with several sheets. "Here's a couple, in case one of them gets dirty."

"Steve Knight," Leek read, then looked at his partner. "*The* Steve Knight too."

"Read on."

"Famous photo-reporter...Mm...I knew that. Am a fan of his work, actually...Yes... okay...Works for *Newsweek*, *Paris Match*, *Vanity Fair*. Books on Calcutta. On Iraq and Afghanistan Wars. On Brazilian ghettos. Shows all over the world. Fearless. They say a picture is worth a thousand words. With this man, it's really true, Julie."

"Can't judge a book by its cover, can you? The guy goes to the most dangerous places in the world and looks like Larry King. Go figure."

"The glasses and the myopia, but that's about it, Julie. So Steve Knight was Dorothea Sishy's lover?"

Julie nodded. "At least they were close. We'll find out."

"Well, it says here he read and had book signings at Open Page."

"Perhaps they met there, then."

"They could have known each other before that. But it makes sense, doesn't it?" Leek sat perplexed for stretchy seconds.

"Leek, are you all right?"

No response.

"Leek, hello?"

The old detective seemed to wake up from a bad dream. "Quite, dear. Quite. It's just this case. It reminds me of something else."

"Well, Leek, tell!"

"That's where the problem lies, Julie. It reminds me of some thing. And I just don't know what. Or, to be more accurate, I have a hint, but it just doesn't click the way it should." Leek bent his head once more toward the document. "Says here that Mr. Knight has a mentally challenged son. That's something that doesn't come often in his bios. At least I haven't seen it."

Julie finished her coffee and rose. "Have to go pee. Will be right back." That was her excuse. But she couldn't take it. Something was wrong with Leek. She could feel it right down to her bones.

While Julie was away, Leek took a peek at the second profile. Walter Gother. Artist living in Queens. Not successful, but young. Mm, quite a change from Steve Knight, fame-wise, wealth-wise, and age-wise. Julie had put in a bit of physical profile as well. Six foot two, one hundred and eighty-six pounds. He went back to Knight's physical info: six foot two, one hundred and ninety pounds. That face. He had seen that face before. But this Walter Gother wasn't old enough for Leek to know him. The face that he vaguely remembered came from the past and, Leek sensed it, a past he didn't want to revisit. But would he have to? Would that past hold some clue?

He went on to the third profile. Jack Teddy. Deputy Mayor for Legal Affairs. Yes, of course. Six foot three...Six foot three? He knew Teddy. He was more like six foot two, perhaps two and a half. Ah, politicians. Think themselves taller than what they really are. One hundred and eighty-eight pounds. Oh, but that was interesting. He went on looking at the profiles of the other suspects and noted the similarity of height and weight. With the exception of Walter Gother, there was a similarity of age as well. Most of the men were in their fifties, with five or six years' difference, give or take.

He returned to the beginning of the list, this time looking only at the photos. There were two for each suspect, face and profile. Each one of these men had a strong convex nose, dark eyes. Mouths were middle-sized, except for Gother, whose lower lip appeared to be thicker than the upper one. He knew that age reduced the fullness of lips, so he examined the pictures once more. The mouths of these men were not that different from Gother's. To be sure, if Dorothea Sishy had many lovers, she stuck to the same type of men. She stuck to a rather exacting criteria, in fact.

And then it dawned on him. In a most uncharacteristic fashion, he pushed papers and reports away from Julie's laptop and clicked a few times on the keyboard. "But of course!" he whispered. "She never got over him. So this explains that."

He thought of that man who was living with Zoe Zimmerman, a doctor. Dr. Marc Trenton. He was a plastic surgeon, wasn't he? Julie had mentioned him; she was friends with him as well. And he had actually met him, once. The man seemed solid, reliable. On the stern side, even. Quite a contrast to his companion, Leek reflected with a smile and a mustache thrill. He went through Julie's e-mail to see if there was an address. Ah, there it was. He moved to his own account and forwarded a brief message with a couple of references and website addresses. "Just a hint," he added at the end of his message. "But I would be grateful if you could take a look and give me your professional opinion."

When Julie returned, Leek had, against his better instincts, returned his partner's desk to its original and cluttered state. That his colleague could have such a clear mind and function in such a disarray was a mystery that even *he* could never solve.

"Let's go," Julie said.

"Where to?"

"Why, to pick up Jane."

"Of course, of course."

Jane Dzhugashvili. Another mystery Leek might never solve. And a mystery with a temper at that.

■ 12 ■

"**M**R. KNIGHT, ARE YOU the one who placed the ad on...on...let's see." Detective Leek turned back a few pages of his memo pad. "On May 10. It read: 'HAVE YOU SEEN MY FRIEND? Urgent. Dorothea Sishy, owner of Open Page bookstore-cafe on East Side 66VANCE\u3ʳᵈ St. Has disappeared since May 4.' You admit being the author of this ad?"

"Well, yeah, Detective. I was...uh...I was worried."

Hercules Leek, Julie Hoffman, and Jane sat in Steve Knight's living room. The only clue indicating that Knight was a rich man was his address on the Upper East Side—once known as Silk Stockings District—at the corner of 5ᵗʰ Avenue and 82ⁿᵈ, a few steps away from the Met. The luxurious entrance of the building with its sleepy guard and tea-for-two concierge reinforced the notion. So did the fresh smelling and smooth elevator with its polite jazzy-bluesy music. So did the humongous rubber and snake plants with their fancy porcelain pots. Rugs thick as mattresses were there to kill the sounds of heavy steps, if these happened to be too unpleasant. Each floor, with the useless hugeness that luxury demanded, unused armchairs and end tables, could have hosted useless international conferences.

In fact, nothing prepared the visitor for what would happen after Knight's door would be pushed open. Eyes were immediately assailed by chaos. Lamp shades bent this way and that like miniature Pisa Towers. Fallen objects and bibelots, papers scattered on the parquet floor. This was a war zone, a scene not unlike what could be found time and again in his photographs. Walk at your own risk.

Even athletic Julie Hoffman tumbled a bit. Hercules Leek approached the lieu like a feline, stepping in slowly and carefully. And when Chainsaw Jane fell on her ass, she uttered a series of words in Russian. Although the people present were no experts in Slavic languages, they suspected that the expressions used by Jane wouldn't be acceptable during, say, a baptism or some presidential inauguration. When she looked at Knight and finally switched to English, it went like this, "What kind of shitty place is this? Can't filthy rich man like you get fooking cleaning lady?"

Suspicions confirmed. The Russian used previously was not excerpted from Pushkin.

Steve Knight squinted toward the woman on the floor. "Who is she?" he said with a voice that had known tobacco for decades. He wore his thick glasses, impeccable hairdo, silk shirt, designer pants, and half-century (with a few bonus years) on this earth with an air of resignation. The contrast between a groomed appearance and unattended quarters always had the power to vex Detective Leek. And today was no exception, despite—because of ?—his forty years of experience in the police force. But there was something else about this place that troubled him, and he couldn't put a finger on it. The place was in disarray, but it seemed to him that it was fresh disarray, that it had just happened. Violence, that was it. There was a great deal of violence in the disarray. He pressed on his mustache with his thumb and forefinger and reflected for a moment before moving on.

Going to one of the living room sofas was an expedition, and not only because of the general bedlam. Unnerving were the proportions of the room. Obviously, the decorator had taken coziness out of her lexicon and dreamed of Grand Central Station the night before she got to work on the place. Instead of the intended grace, the curves of a spiraling staircase added a disturbing quality to the decor. Even its owner seemed to be out of his element there. Leek had tried to straighten a picture on the wall, pushed aside a cigarette butt with the end of his foot, and unfortunately met the stare of his partner who was shaking her head. And why was he so surprised to see pieces of gum sticking to Oriental rugs in the midst of such chaos?

"Who is she?" Knight repeated.

"None of your business," Jane retorted while Julie was helping her up.

Because he couldn't straighten anything else, Leek went at his mustache again, adjusting it, despite the fact that it was perfectly in place and trimmed to perfection. "Mr. Knight. I want you to meet Mrs. Jane Dzhugashvili."

"You're kidding me, right?"

Jane slowly walked toward the nearest sofa and chairs.

"Right?" Knight repeated, turning now toward Jane, who was installed in a leather armchair. Loose pages of newspapers, half-torn magazines, and pieces of paper covered with what looked more like mad scribbling than colored drawings, were suffocating under her butt with a whistling-crackling sound. "Is that your last name, really? Are you related to Stalin?"

"I have interesting family tree," Jane said. "But relax, they call me Chainsaw Jane now."

Knight's tan complexion suddenly turned as white as his silk draperies were supposed to be. He opened his mouth like a carp and froze for a few seconds.

Julie fixed her gaze on Knight. "Are you ready for some questions now?"

■ ■

"SO YOU PLACED AN ad because you were worried." Leek scribbled briefly on his memo pad.

"That's correct, Detective," Knight answered.

Leek tapped his mouth with his pen. "I see. Don't you think that worrying about a friend so shortly after her disappearance is somewhat strange?"

"What are you getting at?"

"Well, you wrote in the ad that Ms. Sishy disappeared on May 4. But we checked: she was at her store on that day. She even closed at seven p.m. So why did you assume she disappeared then?"

"We were to meet that night at Studio 54. It was her birthday. She never showed up."

Julie opened her eyes wide. "Wow! Studio 54! Could she afford it?"

"Dora was a good businesswoman. Her bookstore did well. In any case, I can afford it. And it was her birthday. So it was my treat."

"Yeah, I suppose so. Still, with famous people and all that, she might have found Studio 54 kinda intimidating."

"You've got to be kidding me! Famous people amused her. She enjoyed observing them, imitating them even. Many people don't realize that Dora was a fun, witty person." Knight swallowed and repressed a tear.

Leek index-tapped his temple. "So you took Ms. Sishy to Studio 54 often?"

"Often enough, yes. She got a kick out of it every time. Well–"

"Well, what, Mr. Knight?"

"There was that one time. Dora had had one too many. She loved champagne. She was not exactly drunk, but quite tipsy. Alfred DeCallo was there."

"Quite an actor."

"Yes, a connected actor, Detective Leek."

"What you're saying is that he's from *the* DeCallo family, am I right?"

"You got it."

Leek nodded. Julie frowned.

A beat.

"Italian man. Bad temper," Jane mumbled.

Julie heard. "As opposed to Russians."

Jane discreetly raised her middle finger.

"Nice nail polish," Julie whispered.

Leek briefly directed an austere gaze toward the two women, scratched his throat, then resumed his questioning. "Why was that, Mr. Knight? Why was Mr. DeCallo unhappy?"

"Dora started doing an impression of him. She was quite good. Many people laughed. But not DeCallo. He came to our table and confronted Dora. 'What duya think you're doin', eh! What duya think you're doin'!' I stared at him for a while, hoping he would move on and leave us alone. But that didn't deter him. He said to me, 'Whatcha lookin' at!'"

"Was he inebriated?"

"Hard to tell with DeCallo. I suspect he's a functioning alcoholic. An intimidating man in any case. And his voice that night was close to threatening."

"I see. How did Ms. Sishy react?"

"She just said, 'Let's get out of here.' So we did."

Julie frowned. "Well, that might have been a deterrent. Maybe she didn't want to return to Studio 54 after that."

"I don't think so, Detective. We went several times after that. DeCallo actually bought her a drink. That was his way of apologizing."

Leek underlined a few words on his notepad after jotting down the date, June 11. "So you're telling us Ms. Sishy loved Studio 54."

"Absolutely. She never missed an opportunity to go there. That's why I was so worried when I didn't see her that night."

"Well, she could have been sick."

"She would have called."

Julie nodded. "Perhaps. But she could have dozed off as well. Why place an ad so early after that?"

"What are you implying?"

"Sometimes placing an ad is a way to hide in plain sight."

Knight's lower lip trembled. "Oh, I see. What you're saying is that I pretended to be worried and wanted the whole world to know that when in fact I killed Dora, is that it?"

"Why not?" Leek asked.

"Why not? Why not! I'll tell you why not! I called her, left several messages on her machine, and got no answer. It's not like her not to answer. I went to her place, rang her bell, and still got no answer. I was worried sick.

"And I—I loved Dora."

Silence.

Jane seemed lost in thought. Her eyes were slits, Julie noticed.

Leek looked intently at Knight, then said, "And you didn't mind that she had affairs on the side?"

Julie looked at her notes. "Boy, the lady was busy! Was she ever! There were not one, not two, but *several* other men."

"Several other men? Mm. Didn't you mind, Mr. Knight?" Leek's eyes spread on Knight like green laser beams, while his voice maintained its caressing tone.

Ah, my cat is back, thought Julie.

While Leek went on his interrogation, Jane picked up a sweater on the floor, a sweater far too large to fit Knight's body. Her hands immediately shook and her face tensed up. She and Julie exchanged glances.

"Later," Jane whispered.

Julie nodded.

Knight's face trembled, but he remained silent.

"You're sure you didn't know?" Leek bent his head sideways. "You didn't know, Mr. Knight, that Ms. Sishy had several beaus?"

"What are you doing with that sweater? Please leave it alone!" Knight told Jane.

"Please answer my question, Mr. Knight."

"No."

"No, you won't answer my question? Or no, you didn't know?"

"No, I didn't know."

"Are you sure?"

"You think I am lying?"

Leek smiled. "You're not only a photographer, Mr. Knight, but a photo-reporter, am I right?"

"What has that got to do with anything?"

"Isn't a photo-reporter somewhat like a journalist?"

"And?"

"And isn't a journalist somewhat like a detective?"

"What are you getting at?"

"What I am getting at, Mr. Knight, is that someone like you, especially someone like you, having seen what you have seen around the world, someone like you is not naive. Someone like you develops instincts of suspicion like us in the police force. I know the public is told otherwise, but in our world everyone is guilty until proven innocent. That's how we do our work. So I assume that when Ms. Sishy told you she was going to dinner with a lady friend, or to the theater, when she told you her little lies—for she had to lie to you, didn't she? She was a busy lady. I assume that you didn't necessarily believe her. You might even have followed her. Or have her followed. And then, when you found out she cheated on you, you got mad. I do believe you loved her. But you couldn't handle it, could you? It was too much! So you killed her."

Knight opened his mouth and his eyes wide. If the horror of a silent scream could have been emitted, there it was.

"So you're ready to admit it, Knight," said Julie. "Jealousy makes us do things we wouldn't do otherwise. This is a crime of passion."

Knight's whole body shook like the *Titanic*; his complexion was the one of an iceberg. And then he breathed again and words burst out, "When was the last time you saw a crime of passion involving a chainsaw? Decapitation? Just the notion that Dora was...God!... slaughtered like that. Killing was not enough. He had to...Who would do something like that? What type of monster? You think I could do that kind of massacre! You think because I witnessed massacres I am capable of making one of my own? What kind of sick people are you? Do you know how many times I have had to throw up after taking my shots in India, Haiti, even in the Bronx? Hey, do you? Well, I don't give a damn if you are cops but I'll say this, fuck you! Fuck you! Get me busted if you like. But fuck you! Just fuck you!"

Jane discreetly applauded. "That was good performance," she mumbled to herself.

Knight held his stomach.

"Try vodka. Helps stomach," Jane said.

Knight turned toward the Russian woman, "I've got Potocki."

Jane made a face. "That's Polish vodka."

Silence. The two detectives went bipolar on their expression. One second it went scowling, the other, reflective. They were, however, both insisting on the importance of being earnest.

"But if that's all you got, I'll drink it. Just this once," Jane told Knight resignedly. "Sometimes one's got to compromise."

What was Jane doing? The cops exchanged glances.

Julie looked down the floor. "So much mess here, yet no broken glass."

"I keep my liquor cabinet locked," Knight said.

"Good idea," said Jane. "Can't mess with vodka. Even Polish vodka."

"Jane!" Julie said. "We're investigating. This is no drinking party."

"Fooking cops," Jane whispered. Knight smiled.

Julie rolled her eyes.

Leek slid his fingers on his eyelids and let silence set for a while. Seconds would feel like minutes. Jane would settle, although he was not sure if she needed to. Her little interruption might have been a strategy. One never knew with Jane Dzhugashvili. Possibly, Knight would talk. Really talk.

But nothing happened. It looked as if everyone was comfortable with the impromptu quietness.

Until a huge scream exploded out of nowhere. Followed by a howl. That went on and on. Then it died down, and laughter began, hitting like percussion, ha-ha-ha, ha-ha, ha-ha-ha, ha-ha. A demented staccato.

"What's that?" Julie asked.

Jane kept quiet. Attentive. She looked at the sweater she had touched a moment earlier and then thrown on the arm of her chair, and waited.

Leek looked up toward the spiraling staircase which, at this moment, seemed under the transforming influence of kinetic energy. It moved somewhat like a Calder mobile. A muted, drumming noise added a rhythm to the approaching laughter. Heavy legs appeared then disappeared behind the curves of the stairway.

And then he was there, straight, huge and suddenly as immobile as a tower, facing them with immense gray eyes and an empty stare. And a smile. A smile that went nowhere, addressed no one. Some streaks of gray seemed out of place among the abundant dark mane. How old was he? Twenty-eight? Thirty, maybe?

And how tall? A little under seven feet, Julie assessed.

"Hello," Leek said. "And who are you?" The young man stared, grinned, chuckled, but said nothing.

"Who's he?" Julie asked Knight.

"Who's-he—who's-he—who's-he." A little boy's voice came out of the giant's body. "Woos-he, woos-he, woos-he. Woos-he—woos-he—woos-he—wooshe." And then, the repetitions grew quicker and sounded like, "Wussy-wussywussy."

Jane evaluated the newcomer for a second, then closed her eyes. "His name is Lance. Lance for Lancelot. He's Mr. Knight's son," she said after a few moments of silent concentration.

Julie raised her brows. "Lancelot? The son of Knight?"

Knight turned toward Lance, then toward Jane, his face gray and hollow. "How—how did you know?"

Jane shrugged.

"Wussy-wussy-wussy," Lance repeated, his mouth the only moving part of his body.

"Cut it out!" Knight told his son.

"Wussy–wussy–wussy–wussy–woo–woo–si–sissy–sissy–wussy!"

"CUT IT OUT!"

Julie got up. Lance threw an empty stare at her, then started running around the room, gliding among the scattered paper on the parquet floor, never falling, as if he knew precisely the geography of such bedlam. He occasionally picked up a loose sheet, tore it apart, and threw it around like confetti while engaged now in a new litany: "cut-it-out, cut-it-out, cutitout, cutit, cutit, cut, cut, cut-cut-cut-cut-cut-cut."

Knight ran after his son. Julie went on the other side in an attempt to stop Lance. But athletic as she was, she was no match for the furious giant who brushed her aside like a feather. Julie fell on her side.

Leek grabbed his gun.

"No!" Jane said. "Wait!"

"But he's dangerous, Jane!" Leek said, for a moment forgetting the formality he had used, up to now, with the Russian psychic.

Jane grabbed the sweater on the armchair and observed the young man running around the room. A colossus with feet of clay was the image that kept coming to her.

Julie massaged her hip as she got up. She touched her holster, Jane noticed, but decided against pulling her Glock out of it.

"Let Julie handle it, Detective Leek."

"She needs my help."

"Not right now. You're no good to her right now."

Jane's remark provoked some hair rising on Leek's mustache. He nevertheless held his pistol while the psychic held the giant's sweater. "Lots of hurt here. Lots of hurt," Jane mumbled.

"I don't know how you can feel that from a piece of clothing. But that's why you're here." Leek, attentive to the circular chase around the room, kept tensing up on his chair, his index finger dangerously flexed on his pistol trigger.

"I feel vibration in hands. Like electricity. Sometimes it's fluid. But here it comes with intense, acute pain. This kid suffered a lot."

Leek didn't relax his index finger. Lance was in a frenzy, screaming his lungs out, running in one direction, then in another, extending his arms toward the ceiling, then curling up, as if in a tribal dance, and always able to glide away from his father or Julie.

Gang fights were unsettling, dangerous, unnerving. But this— this! This could shatter the nervous system of the Great Master of Zen.

And Leek was tired. Jane could tell. At this point, she was not afraid of Lance. She was afraid of what used to be the calmest cop in the city.

"Detective," Jane said, "Put that fooking thing away."

Leek stared at Jane, then at his Glock.

"It's no use here," Jane insisted. "It will make things worse. You've got to trust me here."

"We've got to stop him!"

"Not with stupid gun."

"We've got to stop him." Leek stared into space.

Jane grabbed the detective's arm. "Yes, we've got to stop *him*."

Without letting go of Leek's arm, and while the chase and mock-voodoo dance continued, Jane said, "I had more pain in hands just now, but that came from you. There are things you know and that you don't want to tell. But you have to talk to Julie. Soon. You hear? Now, let go of fooking gun. You're freaking me out. You're not yourself right now. And that's because you're keeping secrets."

"I am not sure those are secrets. It just doesn't make any sense and it's driving me crazy, Ja...Mrs. Dzhu..."

"Call me Jane. What's with you and fooking formality anyway?"

Leek laughed softly. Jane grabbed Leek's Glock and planted it in its holster. "Now, how is that for metaphoric porn?"

Would that make Leek a convert to familiarity? Right. He would probably go back to fooking formality as soon as he got enough sleep and went back to his old self.

She observed the man sideways. And her hands were at it again. There were vibrations, painful vibrations. She was worried.

And she knew Julie was too.

■ ■

AFTER THE RONDE MARATHON had gone for a while in Knight's living room, Jane placed herself in the middle of the room, followed each and every one of Lance's movements, displayed his sweater like a banner, and kept repeating, "Lance, stop, you're going to catch cold! Lance, stop, you're going to catch cold!" She never changed her tone of voice, was relentlessly steady with her mantra, and after a minute or two, Lance slowed down, then stopped like an unwound toy. He was as sweaty as a colony of Danes in an oversteamed sauna, but he put the sweater on nevertheless, and this appeared to soothe him.

Knight, not as out of breath as one might have expected, disappeared for an instant, only to return with a syringe and needle. He rushed to his son, grabbed his arm, and swiftly gave him a shot. Lance did not react. Obviously the needle was as familiar to him as his father's face.

The glances of two cops and one psychic convened in one impromptu conference, during which surprise was manifest, but typical of any conference, no conclusions were made.

They all convened however that, had Knight not been such a brilliant photographer, he might have been a hell of a nurse. How long had he been giving shots like that? This obviously was not the first time.

Could he have killed Dorothea Sishy this quick, efficient way, and later cut her body to disguise the nature of the murder itself? He certainly had the brains for it. And physically, well, looks could be deceiving. Appearances, appearances. One thinks of silk as this delicate, fragile fabric. And yet they used to make parachutes out of silk. Knight was like that. He gave the impression of breakability, of confusion, but the face of a creative mind—and Knight the photographer was certainly one— assumes expressions that confound the casual observer. For a weakling he wasn't. Otherwise, how could he handle a son named Lancelot and shaped like Gargantua?

And he drove a Mercedes-Benz M Class, a one hundred thousand dollar SUV. When Julie had read the report, the first lines sounded like a love affair between the cop in charge and the vehicle: automatic transmission, up to 11 cty/15 hwy mpg, all-wheel drive, navigation system, Bluetooth, iPod input, satellite radio, and a few more details that made her wonder if the guy had not gone orgasmic before starting the real search. But the cop had noted the SUV was loaded with cameras, various sizes of tripods, and computers. It was certainly big enough to transport a body and even hide it under all the equipment. There were spots on the vehicle's carpet that looked like blood spots and were now examined at the lab.

"Can someone give me a hand?" Knight said.

Lance was now fast asleep on the floor.

"Sure," Julie said. "You want me to help you carry him on one of the sofas?" The nearest couch was made of black leather and big enough for Lance's body. Luckily it was only ten feet away. While the female cop went to help Knight, she asked Leek and Jane to clear the piece of furniture from its papery mess.

"No!" said Knight. "That won't be necessary."

"Don't you think he will be more comfortable that way?"

"What I mean to say is that I need help to get him back to his bedroom."

Julie looked at the spiraling staircase. "You've got to be kidding me! You want me to help you transport the Himalaya through that?"

"He needs his sleep."

"Can't he sleep on the couch?"

"You see what he does in here!" said Knight. "It's not always like that but...he's safer in his room."

"In that case," Julie said, "Let me call for some backup."

"No, no, no!"

"Can't your colleague help?" Knight looked at Leek.

Leek rose.

Jane pushed him back down on his seat. "Detective Leek broke his leg not long ago while arresting a gang," she lied. "He can't help you."

To the detective she whispered. "You're old man, are you crazy? This monster would break your bones. Even asleep he would break your bones."

"Thanks for preserving my pride, Mrs. Dzhugashvili."

"Don't fooking mention it, Detective."

"Let's go back to plan one. Backup." Julie picked up her cell.

"No, please no!"

Julie scratched her blond mane, frowned.

"Lance is afraid of strangers," Leek continued.

"And what are we?" Jane mumbled. "His aunts and uncles from fooking Utah?"

Julie sent a not-so-amicable glance at Jane. "He's asleep," she told Knight. "He's not going to know who carries him upstairs. Looks to me you gave him of good dose of sedatives. Were you a nurse in a past life, or do you shoot yourself with drugs? When we're done with Lance, you'll have some explaining to do." She started dialing.

Knight grabbed her arm. "Please. I don't want to take that risk. Are you ready to have a scene just like the one we had just now? I am so, so tired."

Julie evaluated the situation. Knight weighed one hundred and ninety pounds, and, late fifties or not, he was as strong as a thirty-year-old man. She, with her lean and muscular one-twenty-eight, could use what she had more efficiently now that she knew what she was facing. She put her cell away. For a minute the two discussed a strategy, and then Lance's heavy but now limp body was suddenly lifted like a colossal bag of potatoes. Both breathed rhythmically, with the inspire equaling the expire. As painful as the effort was, giving balance to the breathing was an enormous help.

During the slow progression of a tall man, a fairly svelte woman, and a huge hobble mass dragged across the floor, Knight's glasses had slid partially away from his eyes and formed a diagonal line across his face. They were about to fall off when agile hands placed them in perfect symmetry on Knight's nose. Leek had rushed to fix the problem. Of course, Julie thought.

They were getting out of breath. Julie squinted at Knight. "Say, when you had the place decorated, who decided on this binding staircase? Someone as nuts as your son?"

Deep breath. Again. They both resumed their inhale and exhale counts.

"Excuse me, Detective, but—"

"Carrying that huge thing through twists and turns is gonna be a real trip. Couldn't you at least have his bedroom on this floor?"

Silence. More breathing.

"Okay," Julie resumed. "Let's go. Ready? One, two, three!"

The ascension began. Jane and Leek got up to watch, then resumed their sitting in Grand Central revisited. If the staircase had trembled when Lance descended, now it was a magnitude three.

"Is that staircase going to hold?" Leek had gone back to sitting next to Jane, but he was about to rise again when the Russian psychic spoke.

"Well, I suspect staircase is not as dangerous as it looks. They use flexible material now for these annoying pieces of shit. Material similar to the stuff they use in California and other places that have earthquakes. So even if spins and turns give you fooking headache, it's stable. I know because there is architect in my family. Or maybe it was Stalin's daughter, Svetlana Alliluyeva. Or maybe Svetlana was married to architect. Something like that."

"William Wesley Peters. Frank Lloyd Wright's protégé."

"What?"

"Stalin's daughter married Wesley Peters," said Leek.

Jane frowned. "Whoop-de-fooking-do. And why would you know that?"

"Why wouldn't I, Mrs. Dzhugashvili?"

Silence.

Leek scratched his mustache.

Huffing and puffing was heard amidst the localized earthquake, to be followed by the irregular thrumming of heavy steps on the top floor. The staircase, a moment ago alive like a weeping willow under the wind, gradually stopped its motion like a yoga master.

■ ■

THERE WERE NO BOOKS, no bibelots, no pictures on the walls of Lance's room. It was beyond monastic. Slightly above prison decor. A hospital room. Childish scribbles on the walls didn't manage to break the cold monotony. As they were placing Lance on his bed, Julie noted that there were straps hanging from the bedspring.

"You're gonna attach him?" Julie wiped her sweaty forehead with the back of her hand, ran forked fingers across her hair, breathed, breathed again.

"Well, you saw what he did downstairs," Knight said. "But no. Not now. Sometimes I have to, though."

"Mr. Knight, do you think this is the right place for someone like your son?"

"What do you mean?"

Julie bit her lips, then said, "Perhaps your son needs more professional attention."

"A mental institution, is that what you are alluding to, Detective?" Knight straightened his glasses, which had once again traced a perpendicular path on his face. "What on earth gives you the right to say that?" Knight stroked his son's hair.

Now in his bed, with lids colored like late autumn leaves, Lance looked surreal, like an overgrown baby. On such colossal visage the rosy cheeks looked like soft little hills. Had Hercules mated with the mother of the Little Prince, their sibling would have ended like this: a head like a planet, inhabited with delicate features. And had Julie not witnessed the disturbing scene downstairs, she would have,

like that Swedish group from the seventies—the ABBA, wasn't it—
believed in angels. Actually, all devoted atheist that she was, she liked
that song, perhaps out of hearing it time and again at Jane's house
when she was a kid and went to play there with Zoe. The two even
did a mocking dance to the refrain. But the result was that it never
left her brain.

*I believe in angels. Something good in everything I see. I believe in angels.
When I know the time is right for me. I'll cross the stream. I have a dream.*

Sitting on Lance's bed, his face relaxed and loving, Knight was a
man who had renewed his faith. Once more, he renewed his faith, for
he believed in angels. His unconscious son was now an angel.

It was as if what happened a floor below had never happened. For
the contrast was absolutely astounding. This was another floor; this
was another planet. As sweet and as dreamy as the upper floor world
seemed, Julie didn't like it. The contrast between upstairs and downstairs gave her the creeps.

But here was a man who has photographed men and women at
war, limbless, disfigured, or about to go mad. He had shot hate in the
eyes of ghetto and gang members, and in the photos of women who
had just been raped, he had captured a peculiar type of imploration,
a special prayer to Death. Leek had brought a book of Knight's photography to the precinct. First, Julie had leafed nervously through the
volume, then her pace had slowed. It was as if the people portrayed
were actually examining her. These were accusatory eyes.

Then she had closed the book and taken some distance. Knight
was good—a tough cookie. As tough as they come. He had unflinch-
ingly faced horrors. His camera eye was lucid and merciless. But when
it came to his son, Knight seemed in a state of total delusion. Still,
the needle he had planted in his son's arm was not. This was a soldier's
reflex. A cop's reflex.

Or a criminal reflex.

Knight's nearsighted coup d'oeil was directed toward Julie, to whom he muttered, almost imploringly, "Look at him, Detective. Does he look like he belongs to a mental institution?"

"He's heavily sedated," said a gentle voice behind him.

Knight jumped. "Detective Leek. I didn't hear you come up."

Neither did Julie. But *she* didn't jump. Old cats remain agile.

"So you don't think Lance should go in a mental institution?" Leek asked Knight.

"Of course not."

"Then what are these straps for?"

Silence.

"And who taught you to give shots like this?"

Noise was approaching—heavy puffing, the resounding born from steps hitting every stair with the rhythm of a duck, the resolution of an elephant, and the unmistakable punctuation of "fooking architect."

Mouths had shut. All was quiet in Lance's room as the woman born in the former USSR stood panting before two NYPD detectives plus one renown photo-reporter. She took a few deep breaths, then went at it. "Get out of here, all of you!" she said, her voice as steady as the Cheka. "Jesoos-fooking-Christ! Can't you let child sleep!"

The trio looked at the giant in his bed, at Jane, at each other, unable to utter a response.

"I fooking repeat, can't you let child sleep!" And then in unison, tongues still paralyzed, they left Lance's room.

■ 13 ■

"**H**OW YOU DOIN', SHAWN?" Dumasky put on the brakes of his patrolling car.

"Hey, Chief, what's cookin'? Did you catch a thief today?" Shawn Doogy was smoking a cigarette in front of his house on Drumerer Alley, a cul-de-sac that dropped on one side into Heritage Lane and was barraged on the other by about 10,000 square feet of woods that were part of Doogy's property. Only natives belonging to Noliar Historical Society knew that Drumerer Alley had been baptized as such by mistake. It was supposed to be called Drummer Alley, in homage to a local musician who had passed away in the 1800s. (This musician had a name, but in the nineteenth century Noliar was but a village, and surnames were then less relevant than occupations, so this glorious villager went by "The Drummer.") But the man in charge of the sign was a drunk, a misspeller, and a stutterer. Time being an effective memory eraser, Noliarites ended up forgetting who or what the name was about, and Drumerer Alley stood. "Nope. Not a good fishin' day, buddy. Just same old, same old."

"Drunk driving. A couple of accidents, I saw in *The Noliar News*." Doogy walked toward the police car in a relaxed, neighborly way.

Dumasky smiled at him. Friendly chap. Funny walk, though. It always seemed to him that one of Doogy's legs was slightly shorter than the other. Hey, he wasn't a great walker, either. Arthritis was starting to play its tricks, and spending hours in cars or writing police reports didn't help any. To each his own, he supposed.

"Yup! These kids, you know. Go to a party. Booze, drugs. More and more drugs these days. And then they drive."

"I hear ya. Can't control them anymore, can you?"

"You got it. Looks like this drug thing is getting organized, I mean *real* organized. Just like in the city."

"You don't say!"

"Oh, we caught a few sellers. But they ain't the ones in charge, Shawn. I say there's a guy in the area, or maybe 'couple of guys who are arranging things and gettin' rich out of the kids' backs. My guess is they're members of a network. Some kind of mafia or somethin'."

"Mafia? In Noliar?"

"Well, Pittsburgh ain't far. And there's Philly and New York pretty close by."

"New York is pretty far. Six hours by car, ain't it? Maybe you're pushing it a little, Chief."

"Yeah. Maybe. It's just frustratin'. Wish I could catch these guys and teach 'em a lesson, 'know what I mean?" Dumasky tapped his holster.

Doogy threw his cigarette butt in the grass. Dumasky stepped out of his car. "Gotta stretch a little. Have been patrolling all day." He lit a cigarette. "Say, you wouldn't have some coffee in the house, would ya?"

"Can't go in the house right now."

"No? Why not?"

"Cleaning lady. She makes a scene every time I take a smoke. Imagine with two guys smoking!"

"Hey, it's your house!"

"I know. But last time I tried smoking inside, she opened every window in the house, plus the front door, said she couldn't stand the smell and all that."

"She's a little dictator, ain't she?" Dumasky took a drag. "Is that why you got all red all of a sudden? Or is she an attractive girl?"

"No! It's hot, is all."

"It's hot, or she's hot?"

"Don't know about that."

"Personally, I wouldn't want a girl who wouldn't let me smoke in my own house."

"Why, does your wife let your smoke inside?"

It was Dumasky's turn to get red. "Well, the missus, uh...You ain't married, is all I'm sayin'." He scratched his throat.

Doogy grinned. "I think she's a Jehovah's Witness."

"Your cleaning lady."

"Yeah. And they're kinda funny about smoking. They think it comes from the Devil. Read somewhere on the net about a case where one of them got expelled from the sect because he liked his snouts."

"Huh! But you never had problems with girls and ciggies before, eh, Shawn?"

"Nope. Why?"

Dumasky noticed that the lower part of Doogy's right hand and his wrist were bandaged. "What happened there?" He asked.

Doogy squinted. "That? You know my job, Chief. Comes with the territory."

"Really? I thought you didn't cut trees yourself. You have men to do that, don't ya?"

"Had to let one of them go."

"You mean Monkey?"

A.k.a. Ed Reed, but no one in Noliar called the most agile tree climber and cutter in town that way. Doogy nodded. "Couldn't hold his liquor anymore." He looked at his hand. So that what happens when you haven't practiced yourself for a while."

"Looks to me that, booze or no booze, he could handle a chainsaw better than you did."

Doogy shrugged.

"Gotta be careful with those," Dumasky went on. "Could have cut your whole arm, just like that."

Dumasky squinted toward the sun as he took another drag. "Have you heard of that crazy murderer? The chainsaw murderer? It's all over the news. Man! There's some real sickos in New York! Boy! And you know one of the cops in charge used to be a Noliar cop? Julie Hoffman? Remember her? Let's see, she left six-seven years ago?"

"I don't think I know her."

"That's right, that's right. You were not a Noliar resident by then."

"I came here about three years ago."

"Jeez, that long already? You're from New Hampshire, aren't ya?"

"Jersey. New Jersey."

"That's right, that's right. Boy, it's hot out here! Only June. What day are we? June 11. Not even official summer yet, and it's hot as hell. I wouldn't mind going inside. I can drink coffee without a smoke for once."

"Why don't we go have one at the AM EYE Café?"

"Your cleaning lady really scares ya, eh?"

Dumasky looked straight into the eyes of Doogy. "Tell you what. There's a bit a shade on your porch. Let's sit there for a while. There's something I have been meaning to ask you, and now is as good a time as any."

Doogy looked at his watch.

"Don't worry, pal," Dumasky said. "Won't take long. I thought you had a bit of time anyway, since you were ready to go to AM EYE."

"Sure," Doogy said. "It's just that I forgot I had an appointment."

"With a girl?" Dumasky asked.

Doogy smiled.

"Bah, the girl can wait 'couple of minutes. The thing I wanted to talk to you about was about girls, anyway. Two girls: Cruz and Chainsaw Jane.

■ ■

"YOU SURE YOU DIDN'T see Cruz after you two had that fight on Heritage? Sorry to insist, but my guys and I have been looking for her and asked around, and there's no trace of her. And from what everyone's telling me, you're the last one to have seen her." Hands on his beer belly, eyes squinting toward Heritage Lane, Dumasky's large frame fit tight on Doogy's patio chair. Although unable to spread his legs, the man seemed oblivious of his discomfort.

"I already told you, I haven't seen Cruz since. Nor do I want to see her again." Doogy, albeit stocky, could move on his chair. And so he did, as he seemed to have trouble finding a comfortable position.

His visitor, as much by choice as by furniture imposition, remained like a statue, except for the head, which on occasion, tilted lightly this way and that.

"That must have been some fight, eh!" He pointed toward Heritage Lane with his chin. "It happened over there, in front of Jane's house, right?"

"I don't quite remember. But I guess. We broke up that night, somewhere on that street, is all I remember."

"That was what, a week ago, right?"

"Something like that."

"No, no. June 6." The Chief frowned and nodded. "Yeah, that's right. I remember because there was that black guy who came to see me the day after it happened, on June 7, from the NYPD of all places."

"Someone from the NYPD came to see you about Cruz?"

"Yeah. Black NYPD cop with a French accent. All stuck up."

"What was he doing here?"

"Oh, I guess he's a friend of Zoe Zimmerman. You know Zoe, right? Pretty redhead. Is a writer now. Lives in New York, like Julie. Well, I guess he decided to come with her or something. And then, when they arrived, Jane told them about your fight with Cruz."

"Jane was the one who saw me break up with Cruz?"

"Didn't I tell ya?"

Silence.

"So I guess he came to see me as a favor to Jane. Because, you know, Cruz is Jane's best friend. And Jane at this point was worried sick. Going into hysterics. So this guy promised her he would talk to me. That's why I am here."

Doogy massaged his bandaged hand.

"Hurt, hm?" Dumasky said.

"I don't know how I can help you."

"She was cheating, is that it? Cruz likes men, we all know that."

"Let's just say it didn't work out."

"Yeah, it happens. There was a neighbor who overheard something. Something like." Dumasky scratched his head. "Let's see if I can remember. Ah, memory ain't what is used to be. But this neighbor said that Cruz told you, 'They'll find out, it's over.' Yeah, I think that's right. What does that mean?"

After a beat, Doogy emitted a satisfied smile. "I think that's pretty obvious, Chief. Cruz was alluding to the other women."

"Ah, you were the one cheatin'."

"Guilty, Chief." Doogy took a pick at his watch. "Which reminds me..."

Dumasky ignored him, looked straight across him at the burnt house on Heritage Lane.

"Say, it's a good thing Jane was not there when that fire started."

"She went to New York, didn't she?"

"Oh, you knew?"

"I assumed. With Zoe's visit and all."

"She left in the nick of time. As if she knew."

"She's a psychic, isn't she?"

"You believe in that stuff?"

Doogy shrugged. "Police do."

"Not me."

"They use mediums and psychics in the city. The LAPD, the FBI. That's what I hear."

"Yeah, they do. I hear it works sometimes. Go figure."

Doogy wiggled his stocky legs in his chair, wiped his forehead. "It's hot, even in here." A beat. "There are rumors that Jane is working for the NYPD."

"Yeah? Where did you hear that?"

"Gossip, I guess."

"Uh, don't listen to all the gossip. Me, I rely on tangible stuff. Facts. Who did what, when, why. And you know what, Shawn, that fire at Jane's house, that tickles me. During the night of June 7, Cruz disappears. On June 7, that NYPD detective pays me a visit. On June 8, Jane's house burns down. You're a pretty smart guy, Shawn, how would ya connect the dots?"

"Maybe there are no dots to be connected."

"Think so?"

"Well, Cruz may have gone to a friend's house."

"We checked."

"I mean, out of state."

"Mm. She's from Jersey. Hey, like you, in fact. Maybe you knew her there, eh?"

"Jersey's a state, not a village."

"Mm, I see what you mean. You must be a small town man yourself, though, since you ended up in Noliar."

Doogy made a face. "Newark."

"Say what?"

"That's where I come from."

"Oh, yeah, really? That place got a monster airport. The missus and I almost got lost there once with the gran'kids. On our way to Disney World, we were. That thing gotta be bigger than Noliar County. It's a huge, ugly thing, ain't it?"

Doogy shrugged, lit another cigarette. Smoke stretched away into a thin ribbon, then lazily expanded into a grayish veil, muting the two men's view of the blue sky. With the cigarette slowly dying on Doogy's mouth, so did words. Hush settled in at this end of the cul-de-sac on Drumerer Alley.

One of these men was comfortable with hush.

The other was not.

Dumasky sent a relaxed grin to the sun.

Doogy squinted and discreetly threw a sideways glance at the cop.

Dumasky let hush hush away.

"As for the black guy, who knew he was a detective?" Doogy suddenly spurted out.

"Eh?"

"Well, Chief, you asked, didn't you? You asked me to connect the dots. I mean, you say Cruz disappears, then an NYPD cop comes here, then someone sets fire to Jane's house. And, frankly, I don't see connections there. Who in town would know that black guy was a detective?"

"That's what I'm wonderin'," Dumasky said.

"Probably no one around here. No one saw him here before."

"Mm."

"As for Jane's house burning, you know her electric system is from Neanderthal. It was bound to happen."

"Eh, you're probably right." Dumasky let his thumb rest on his cheek while the rest of his hand curled into a fist, covering his mouth. After a while he let the hand glide sideways on his face and added, "Say, there's no love lost between Chainsaw Jane and you, is there?"

"What do you mean?"

"Taking her to court."

"Jeez, Chief. That's a long time ago. She didn't want to pay her bill after we did a job for her. What was I supposed to do?"

"Yeah, I know that. But that's not how we do things 'round here. Well, it's your business. In any case, Shawn, it was good talkin' to you. I let you go to your mm...appointment. Or rendezvous, right?" Dumasky winked, then got up, and the garden chair followed him. He calmly detached the piece of furniture from his body and settled it on Doogy's porch. After shaking hands with his host, he said, "Say, have Jehovah's Witnesses got somethin' 'gainst electricity?"

"Why do you say that?"

"Well, looks like your cleaning lady don't like vacuum cleaners very much. I didn't hear a lot of electrical sweepin' noise while we were talkin'."

■ 14 ■

As soon as they left Knight's apartment, Julie called a cab for Jane. "Why can't you take me home?" Jane argued.

"Leek and I have to discuss the case, write reports. You know how it is."

"I don't like cabs," said Jane.

"The NYPD will pay for it, don't worry, Mrs. Dzhugashvili," Leek offered.

"I can pay cabs, I just don't like cabs. Specially yellow cabs."

Ah, yes, the color yellow. Julie had forgotten about that. And Zoe's place was full of it as well. Ouch! Why Jane was allergic to that shade, no one knew. "Just close your eyes, Jane. I'll call someone you already know." She pressed a key on her cell.

"That you, Aimé? Bored, no one to spy on this very second?" She explained the situation. "Will be right there to pick up Catherine III of Russia!" was the answer.

Five minutes later, the brakes of the undercover cop's yellow cab screeched on 82nd Street, causing other brakes behind him to react, honks to blow their annoyance, middle fingers or lower arms to raise, and swearwords to do their acrobatic routine into the New York polluted air. To this Jane added her very own, and Aimé, stepping out of his now double-parked cab, added his irresistible Parisian smile. Julie rolled her eyes. Women and a number of men who didn't suffer from myopia or a poor sense of aesthetics, smiled back. Suffering from the aforementioned diseases, or from envy, or impatience, or the simple modern-day addiction to rush and self-importance, the macho population multiplied the obscene gestures. New York at the corner of 5th and 82nd had become a cacophony of sounds and expressions, among which a USSR and a Guadeloupe native appeared very comfortable. After all, they had sounds and expressions of their own—continuous grin on the Guadeloupe-Parisian side and a series of drumming "What fook!" on the Soviet side. No rush. One of them walked gallantly toward the other, kissed her hand, and slowly directed her toward his vehicle. New York drivers were about to explode.

Meanwhile, Leek remained impassive.

"That was interesting circus number you did just now," Jane told Aimé as soon as they were on their way. "Did you do that to distract me?"

"From what?"

"From fooking yellow, what else?"

Aimé lifted one eyebrow and drove in silence.

"Or is it because you were seeking forgiveness?" Jane continued.

"Forgiveness?"

"You fooking kidnaped me!"

"Oh, that!"

The Russian woman held her handbag tight on her lap. "Yeah, that. Just kidnaping. Matter of little importance. Who gives shit about that?"

"Ma'am, there was a fire at your house. There is the possibility that we saved your life."

"And what am I now, a Russian woman without a house! Like turtle without shell!"

Catherine III of Russia without a house, that was kind of funny, Aimé thought.

"Sorry. But I am sure you can stay at Zoe's for as long as you like."

As soon as Aimé had said that, he felt a little sorry for Zoe.

But that Jane's imperial presence would torture Marc somewhat gave him satisfaction.

When they reached 72nd Street, Aimé went to open Jane's door and was about to take her to Zoe's building entrance, but she refused. She took money from her purse and handed the bills to the cop.

"I can't accept that." Aimé chuckled.

"Why not?"

"I am a faux taxi driver, you know that."

"What fook do I know! If you're undercover, you should be undercover all the way!"

"You're playing with me, aren't you?"

Jane shrugged. "Go, go, go! You and your ugly taxi, go!"

Aimé left at all speed, and the commotion that occurred minutes earlier on 82nd was duplicated here to a degree. Jane gave a nod of approval and mumbled to herself, "Kidnaping aside, he's pretty nice man. If he were not undercover cop, he could get good tips at Chippendale's."

■ ■

JANE STOOD ON THE sidewalk, oblivious of the passers-by, her gaze distractedly fixed on Mr. Liu's flower shop, where Marc bought flowers for Zoe. Her thoughts went to Cruz. Immediately after that she had the vision of a cave. Cruz and a cave. All of a sudden New York

City felt wrong. But did it feel wrong because she shouldn't be here?

Or because she should?

She still had the tip money Aimé had not accepted. Enough to buy a couple packs of cigarettes, she thought. So she walked toward the drugstore half a block away, dragging her steps.

■ ■

"SO, HOW DID IT GO?"

"I am not talking to you."

"How long are you gonna stay mad at me, Aunt Jane?" Zoe looked at her watch. "Let's see. It has been two days now. Two days, two hours, and twenty-two minutes, to be precise."

"Precise, my ass! You wear watch, only God knows why. You have no notion of fooking time. Never had, never will."

The hell with Russian psychics, Zoe thought. Even if Jane was telling the truth. But, hey, she was a writer, creating her own schedule and ignoring artificial measurements like minutes and hours. When she was invited for a reading at a city bookstore, café, college, and even a strip-joint once, she tried to be punctual. Really she did. She set up a loud-ringing clock an hour ahead. She even remembered to look at her watch. But hours were never as long as they should be. They only stretched for the bored. For the busy, they behaved like inflation. You could never put in as much as you thought you could. It got more complicated if you operated in a threesome: you, the laptop, and the rat.

Zieg II liked to travel from her shoulder to her desk and had even tried his own version of creative writing. Like the time she went for a cup of coffee and a cigarette and when she returned to her desk she read on her laptop:

"&W#@

*jaU+" ;xxxxewwaww μ¾ ."

Good thing she backed up her files. The time this happened, she had arrived at a reading fifteen minutes late. It was at a cool place too, a bookstore/café with plenty of room to read and relax. She remembered the owner, a petite middle-aged woman with short dark hair and the face of a mouse. "Miss Zimmerman," she had said, "we were starting to worry about you. You were supposed to start thirty minutes ago."

"Fifteen," Zoe had replied.

"No, I am pretty sure it was close to thirty minutes. Maybe twenty-eight."

"Twenty. Tops."

"Maybe twenty-two?" The owner had said.

"Twenty-two it is. Sold!"

The little woman had emitted a soft laugh. "That's expensive, my dear. Say you give this nice audience a nice apology and maybe a few extra minutes for questions and book signing."

Zoe didn't tell the little woman that she actually never failed to give extra time at every reading. This, out of guilt for coming late, of course. "Okay, but just this once," she told the bookstore owner. "And as a special favor to you."

The memory made her smile, chuckle a bit. And then, all of a sudden, her face narrowed. Oh-God-oh-God-oh-God-oh-God. Oh, shit! That reading! That was at the *Open Page* bookstore-café on 66th. Dorothea Sishy had been the mouse-faced woman. And now, not only was she dead, but she was transformed into some macabre jigsaw puzzle. A deconstruction game made of flesh. Jacques Derrida meets Dexter. How would she go about it if she wrote Dorothea's story? Once upon a time, there was a woman who owned many books and then, one day, she didn't even own her head?

She felt dizzy, went to sit on the living room sofa.

Jane followed her. "What's matter? Okay, don't take it like this. I'll talk to you now. Okay, you drugged me, and then you kidnaped me. But that's okay, I guess. I'm ready to forget that! Transportation in yellow cab, I can forget—"

"You can forget because you have no remembrance of it in the first place. You were snoring like a regiment of asthmatic sailors then."

"Then I woke up in strange yellow room. What fook were you thinking! Yellow, yellow everywhere. You know I don't like yellow."

"Why is that, Jane? You never said."

"Yellow is color of pee."

"What about the sun?"

"What about it?"

"Well, it's yellow, too, and kinda beautiful, don't you think?"

"Who gives shit about sun?"

"So when I am wearing a yellow top, you think I have urine on my back, is that it?"

"Not like yellow pillows. Imagine sleeping on piss!"

Zoe wondered if maybe one day Jane would tell her the real reason of her aversion to yellow. How much time had she spent with good old Aunt Jane? And yet, what did she really know about her? Chainsaw Jane, eccentric Jane, temperamental Russian Jane. She was just like the Noliar natives, finding comfort in clichés. She mentally slapped her face. What the hell, Zoe! But Jane! She was guilty too, who liked to talk about everything except herself.

Jane picked up a cigarette and suddenly her hand shook. "And look! You have yellow in living room, too!"

"Jane, what the fuck! I switched cushions, okay? I removed all the yellow from your bedroom. I put colored lightbulbs and Marc bought blue drapes, so the mimosa walls look more like green now. Just don't allow daylight in. Leave the curtains as they are. I even changed the sheets. And I certainly hope you like red. So you've got red and green. Early Christmas, what do you say to that? If you don't like it, tough! Because I'm done!"

Jane managed to control her shaking. "What's wrong? PMS? If so, take it out on Marc. That's what men are for. But don't throw bad mood on poor kidnaped, not to mention homeless, Russian woman."

Silence.

Followed by more silence.

"You're worried about something." Jane sat on Marc's chair and lit a cigarette.

"You're the medium. You figure it out."

"Oh, stop shit, Zoe. I am on psychic break."

"Rough day, hey?"

Jane nodded.

"Perhaps you should get some rest, then," Zoe said.

Jane examined Zoe's face as if it were a map. "I see."

"See what?"

"Dorothea Sishy."

"I thought you were on psychic break."

"I fookin' wish! But sometimes I can't control visions. They come and I can't stop them. So it looks like you knew her."

"Yeah. I did. Why didn't I realize that before?"

"Subconscious. Bastard likes to play tricks on mind. Sometimes gives mind vacation, though."

"I didn't want to remember, is that it, Jane?"

"Correct. Because you were involved in criminal case before."

Zoe nodded.

"And you are afraid you are going to be suspect again," Jane added.

"Damn right," Zoe mumbled.

"You have conflicting emotions. You liked victim. So you're sad. But you're a bit mad at her for being dead too, because it's criminal case, and it's a little too close to home. So you're scared of going through same kind of shit again. But you shouldn't be."

"Really? So Julie and Leek found Dorothea's murderer?"

Jane crushed her cigarette in the red porcelain ashtray on the coffee table. "Not as simple as that."

"Great!"

"Besides? Who do you think you are?"

"What?"

"No one in right mind would think you capable of this crime."

From the tone of Jane's voice, Zoe didn't know if she should feel relieved or just plain insulted. "Why the hell not?"

"You can't handle chainsaw for life of you!"

That, Zoe was sure, was insulting. Her mind went to Jane's yard, her limbless trees. "And you think you can?"

"Damn right I can! Have you seen my yard? How nice it looks?"

Zoe's silence was punctuated by a mental "oh boy!"

"Well, have you seen it, have you seen it?" Jane started yelling and shaking at the same time.

"Jane, Jane! What's the matter?" The Russian woman let her face fall between her hands then burst into tears. Zoe wrapped her arm around her. "'T's okay, Jane. 'T's okay."

"No, no! I don't think so, Zoe! Cruz! I am so worried about Cruz! But I can't see. I can't see clearly. Do you know what kind of torture it is for medium not to see clearly? Specially when best friend is in danger?"

"Are you certain Cruz is in danger?" Zoe handed Jane a tissue.

"Certain? I am not even sure she's alive!"

■ ■

JULIE BOUGHT A HOTDOG from a street vendor. "Add more mustard, would you?"

She paid the vendor and turned to Leek. "Not hungry?"

Leek looked at Julie's dog. "Not just yet. Let's walk."

Whereas Julie liked to swallow junk food while in action, Leek preferred to sit down and eat mostly balanced meals, although his well-rounded belly indicated that he seldom missed dessert. Their individual tastes differed not only in food, but in basically everything else, with few, but significant, exceptions. For instance, cops to the bone, they both had a passion for truth. Both enjoyed the city streets, rain or shine. That afternoon on June 11 was warm and gray, with a little breeze, increasing humidity, and a threat of storm. In other words, a pretty satisfying atmosphere for the two cops. Passers-by giving the tempo on the sidewalks with their staccato steps served as percussion, hurried conversations on cells and Blackberries became wind instruments, the continuous roar of cars and trucks were electric violins and cellos; city noises were more symphony than cacophony— music to their urban ears. It helped them think clearly. Not to mention they were anonymous amidst the crowd and could discuss their case freely.

"So do you think he did it?" Julie asked with her mouth full.

Hercules Leek's figure was round, but his step was brisk. "Steven Knight? Jane says he's innocent."

"You? What do *you* think?"

"It could be a crime of passion," Leek said.

Julie wiped mustard from her mouth with a paper napkin. "Yeah. Jane did say in her reading that Dorothea *fooked* a lot."

"He's certainly very adroit with a needle."

"The explanation he gave made sense, though. With the places he goes to, he has to be able to give himself anti-venom injections."

"Right. He probably met a few scorpions and snakes during his expeditions," Leek said.

"He could just as easily inject some poison into someone else." Julie took another bite into her hotdog.

"That could make for a rather sophisticated crime. A bit complicated, perhaps. How does he distract Dorothea Sishy's attention so he can plant a needle into her thigh?"

"Or neck. Or anywhere else. He can kiss her and shoot her. Make love to her and shoot her. He can be as fast as lightning, Leek. You saw him with his son. Thing is, could he handle a chainsaw afterward? I mean, butcher her? He said he loved her. And, Leek, that part, I believe."

"You're still young, Julie. Me, I have seen crimes of passion involving cannibalism, body parts kept in the freezer. I never get used to it, thank God. But Steve Knight probably met and photographed cannibals. In many cases, these photo-reporters are as tough as the most hardened criminals. At least their eyes are."

"You mean—" Julie let her dog hang in the air. Some mustard fell on the sidewalk.

"What I mean is when ordinary people would close their eyes at unbearable sights, professionals like Steve Knight have theirs wide open and keep shooting from every angle."

Julie looked at her hotdog, swallowed hard. There was a trash can a few feet away. Coming closer as they walked briskly. Julie took a deep breath. The trash can was within arm's reach now. She directed a tender, almost nostalgic, gaze toward her hotdog. But her stomach was telling her to get rid of that thing, like now. The detectives passed the trash container. Too late, Julie thought with a certain amount of relief as the dog stubbornly remained in her hand.

Leek squinted.

"What?" Julie said

"It's just that you're handling your hotdog as if it were a newborn."

"Yeah, Leek. I am now figuring out the right lullaby for it."

"It's a great risk, though."

"What? Holding my dog like a newborn?"

"Not to mention eating that kind of crap," Leek said. "What I meant was that Knight is in the league of Annie Leibovitz. Not style-wise, but income-wise. Why would he murder someone? Especially now? At the peak of his fame?"

"Passion makes us all crazy. Haven't you ever been in love?" Julie held her half-consumed dog as if she were on a rescue mission. "Like Leibovitz, eh? Do you know she was Susan Sontag's lover?"

Leek half-smiled then frowned. Julie, who was not the literary type, had once loved a writer. Patricia Something. Patricia Whingham. No, Goodwin. That was it. Julie was usually very discreet about her love life, but that affair had ended badly and she needed to cry on someone else's shoulders. And he had been the only pair of shoulders available that day. Reluctant shoulders as well, he remembered. Most of his life, he had tried to avoid dealing with raw emotions, his or others'. And Julie was that way too. Except for that one time. He had never seen her that way, so lost. It was not like her to be so openly vulnerable. So his shoulders had become an emergency device. He had held her in his arms—he, the man who had hugged no one. No one after his niece had died. Their relationship was never the same after that. Against his better judgment, he saw Julie as the daughter he never had.

He would never tell her, of course.

The cops walked for a few moments without uttering a word, letting the rhythm of their steps accompany their reflection on the case. If Knight looked like a strong suspect, he appeared under scrutiny more possible than probable. But possible was still plenty for a case like this.

Julie looked at what was left of her hotdog. It felt cold in her hand. Among the traffic that had stopped at a red light, there was a garbage truck maybe ten feet away. Julie's eyes went from dog to truck, and back, once, twice. After a swift but precise evaluation, she propelled the remnants of paper, bun, and sausage toward the truck. The hotdog flew like a small missile then plunged into the trash. Either blasé or pretending to be, the New York citizen does not react to unusual behavior. But now a multiracial group of teenagers who, judging from the ball one of them was carrying, were going to or coming out of basketball practice, rushed to give a five to Julie. Julie fived them back with a grin. Leek quietly watched and waited.

"Is that your dad?" one black boy asked Julie.

"He don't look like you," a Latino kid added.

Julie and the basketball gang exchanged jokes for a minute or two. She then consulted her watch. "Look at the time. Must go, kids. How come Alberto isn't with you?"

"Got a girlfriend, is why," a blond, skinny kid said.

Julie smiled and waved them good-bye. "Don't get into trouble, okay?"

"We don't get into no trouble. Alberto's the one in trouble with his girl," said the ball carrier.

"You jealous," Leek heard one of them say as they faded into the crowd.

"Obviously you know these boys," he told Julie.

"Neighbors," Julie replied vaguely.

"Looks like you're popular with teenagers."

"I do a bit of work in the community, teaching them about gangs and such," Julie mumbled. Leek could hardly understand Julie's half-eaten words right now. But he could decipher in an instant that indelible cop reserve.

And then, Julie uttered, "I would kill for brain juice."

Understood.

■ ■

DINO'S LITTLE ITALY BETWEEN 77th and Amsterdam, not far from the Planetarium and Museum of Natural History, was one of the detectives' favorite joints. The coffee there was strong and thick enough to cut with a knife; the steaks juicy; the prices as sensible as Miss Marple's shoes; and the atmosphere, warm, jovial, and relaxed—all good reasons for cops to patronize the place. They sat and peered through the window, contemplative of the city turmoil they had left just moments ago.

"What about the son?" Leek asked as he rearranged the salt and pepper shakers on the red and white tablecloth.

"Lance? Motive?"

"Jealousy. Dad is not often home."

"And he is being taken care of by a couple of private psychiatric nurses when he is away, right?"

"That's Knight's story. Easily verifiable, but totally plausible. So when Dad comes back, Lance, who is like a child—"

"We certainly heard Jane about that!" Julie chuckled.

"He probably wanted Dad all for himself. And here comes this woman, whom Dad is apparently very much taken with. And Dorothea was petite. A giant like Lance could have crushed her in a fit. Knight could have gone to the kitchen to get a drink, and Lance could have been done with her in seconds, maybe even without realizing it."

"And Dad would have covered the murder."

"He's got the brains." Leek ran his index fingers on the edge of the table.

A smoothing out gesture Julie was familiar with. Her partner was perplexed.

"There's just one problem with that theory."

"Yes, I know. Jane Dzhugashvili doesn't think any one of them is responsible for Dorothea Sishy's death."

"Yes, Leek. And what makes the problem more complex is that Jane is not herself these days. What with Cruz' disappearance, the fire at her place."

"So she could be wrong."

■ ■

THE DETECTIVES WERE BACK on the street, their steps brisk, their heads stooped under the slaps of the rain. Lightning had cracked the sky open minutes ago. And now it seemed that invisible hands were furiously emptying gigantic buckets, transforming the city into a messed-up watercolor, with no precise line, no center of attraction to direct the eye.

"There's something I have been meaning to tell you," Leek said.

"What?" Julie was pushed away by a passer-by afraid of wetness. "Hey! Watch where you're walkin'!"

"It's about Dorothea Sishy's husband," Leek continued.

No response from Julie.

"I think he might still be alive." The rain caught Leek's words. And, after a moment of puzzlement, so did Julie.

■ 15 ■

THIS HIJO DE PUTA managed to get out. She thought she had a handle on the situation, but he managed to trick her. And now, she was back to square one.

Square one minus some. For she was tired. Tired and angry. But soon, she knew she would be too tired to be angry.

A burning sensation traveled down her cheek. And that piece of shirt she had used to stop the bleeding was soaked with blood. Blood and his filthy germs. She touched her face, brought the finger to her mouth. Tears. Tears, and blood.

He had cut her neck too, with some broken glass. Probably the same piece he had used to slice her face. But he had gone deeper there, stabbed her with it.

At this point she was pretty sure she wouldn't make it. She had been dizzy. That was the bleeding. She needed some rag. Anything. She tore a piece of her silk blouse, wrapped it around her neck, tight. Her breathing was uneven. She sounded like an asthmatic.

Or like a woman about to deliver a child.

What a joke! A sinister joke! Deliver a child. What she would deliver was death. *La muerte. Sólo la muerte.*

Her neck was not a neck anymore, but a thousand electric needles attacking every nerve. Of course she wouldn't make it. *Claro que no.* How could she? She had been careless, confronting him like this. Instead of going right to the police. Although it had happened outside. Surely there were witnesses. With all the gossips in town, *Madre de Dios!*

And there she was, in this filthy basement, her beautiful fuchsia skirt no longer beautiful but spotted, her pantyhose torn, her underarms acid with perspiration under her silk blouse, her panties . . .

When she had begged him to go to the bathroom, he had refused. Instead, he had brought a bucket. That was it, a bucket. No paper, nothing.

Her mouth was dry. No food, no drink for hours. Hours?

Days?

There was no light, no window in this basement.

She tried to find a switch, but soon realized that it was on the other side of the door. So the light came on only when *el hijo de puta* came to pay her a visit. She lived in a dungeon and he played the fucking lord.

He had always liked to play the lord. How come she hadn't recognized him?

True, he had some work done on his face. But the voice. The voice was the same.

He was supposed to be dead, six feet under. In a place not unlike this one.

That's where she was, wasn't it?

At the center of the earth.

In a cave.

In a grave.

Maybe she was already dead.

Dead, or delirious. What was the difference?

Her throat was dry. So, so dry.

She let her lids grow heavy and dozed off. Until she heard the unnerving sound of drops falling on metal. A leak. There was a leak somewhere. She crawled to a wall and started feeling its surface inch by inch while at the same time listening to the regular beat of the drops. After ten minutes, she found the leaking pipe, felt the drops on her head. She repositioned herself, formed a cup with her hands and started collecting the drops. When a dozen or so dropped, she drank them. She repeated the operation for an indefinite amount of time.

Drip, drip, drip, drip, drip. Drink.

Drip, drip, drip, drip, drip. Drink.

She had a smile on her face.

This felt like victory.

Drip.

Drip.

Drip.

Drip.

Drip.

Drink.

Hip-hip-hip-fucking-hurrah. Drip.

Drop.

■ ■

SHE HEARD VOICES.

Besides *el maricón*, she had not heard other voices until now. Sounds, yes. Especially when it was dark—darker than now. When all light died off, when sight became useless, when the smallest of noises conquered space. She heard it all. The wind. Steps. Light ones. Rabbits, Foxes. Foxes running after rabbits? Heavy ones among leaves. Bear steps, maybe. Men's?

Swift ones, blending with the breeze. Deer?

Was she somewhere in the woods?

But then darkness would thin out, and the birds would announce a new day and sing their *libertad. Libertad de mierda.* And she wanted to scream her rage. Damn birds with wings.

AAAHHHH!

And now, voices.

Real voices.

That's what she heard.

Right?

Voices.

Muted voices. But voices. Human voices. Listen, listen. Yes.

Male voices. The *hijo de puta* and at least another guy.

And she screamed her lungs out. Some blood gushed out of her throat. For a second it felt good. She was out of it, in another world. "HELP! HELP! *AYUDA! POR FAVOR! POR FAVOR! Por favor, por favor, por favor...El hijo de puta ese me va a matar.* This son of a bitch gonna kill me. HELP!"

Because I know. He's gonna kill me because I know. That's why he killed Dorothea too. Because she knew. And she knew because I told her.

She felt something hustling on a beam above her. The rat. The rat that shared the abodes with her.

HELP!

It's no use. *Voy a morir con una rata.*

Imagine that.

I am not gonna die alone. She pressed her hand against her throat.

Not alone, imagine that.

But in the company of a fucking rat.

■ 16 ■

THE PLACE WAS DARK and in want of a decorator. There were some pictures plastered on dirty walls, a carpet that had not interacted with a shampooer for a decade or two, tables that, if able to talk, would have reminisced about the good old days when computers and cell phones, not to mention Wal-Mart, didn't exist. The shocking part in such decor was the shiny new bar, which would have stood proud in a fully remodeled place. Here, it looked like an insult. It told the rest of the furniture just how shitty it looked.

Nevertheless, the Moisol Bar was a popular place.

Local business people, workers, and the occasional farmer who had done some shopping in town went there at the end of the day.

Nat, a petite no-nonsense brunette in her fifties, was in charge of the bar tonight.

"What's gonna be for you, Chief? The usual?" she asked Dumasky as he let his massive body drop on a bar stool.

"Yep." Seconds later she placed beer from the tap before him.

"Thanks, Nat. Big crowd tonight."

Not that the Moisol population would drop dramatically at this time of the night, but Dumasky, somewhat preoccupied, was just making conversation.

"Always on Tuesdays, right? When drinks are half price and snacks are free, the whole town is here." Nat wiped the counter with a wet cloth.

The voices of FOX News commentators were buzzing out—and the stingers would soon follow. Dumasky knit his brows.

Nat shrugged in a what-can-I-say fashion. "The FARTS are here."

Short for Foreigners Allergy & Rash Tension Sufferers, FARTS was an appellation given years ago by a Noliarite to a group of local racists and xenophobes. This name had stayed to the point that even the FARTS called themselves the FARTS.

And here there were, on their assigned stools, Dumasky observed, among them a few with distinct signs. One with the same unkempt goatee, one with a Doberman tattooed on the side of his bold head, one with cowboy boots that had seen better days—and emitted better scents—and one with his unnerving finger tapping.

All of them with eyes riveted to the TV monitor.

"Do you want me to change the channel?" Nat asked.

"Why change the channel?" Shawn Doogy yelled from the door. He walked unevenly toward the bar, grabbed a stool next to the tattooed head, and made a sign to Nat. A J&B soon appeared and Doogy took a sip. "Keep a tab, Nat."

The barwoman nodded.

"Fox is good TV," Doogy told Dumasky. "How's your hand?" the cop asked the tree guy.

Doogy looked at his bandaged hand. "Ah, shitty, but better."

The FARTS chuckled.

"I say you shouldn't use a chainsaw for a while." Dumasky swallowed some beer.

"'Probably right," Doogy answered. "What are you doing here tonight, Chief? You're not usually here on Tuesdays."

"I've got the night off this week. Guess it's my lucky night."

"Why do you say that?"

"Because for once I don't have to pay full price for drinks."

Nat smiled. The Chief winked. Doogy mumbled something inaudible.

The FARTS frowned.

"Who's that?" one of them, looking at a black man seated across from him, asked Nat as she refilled his drink.

Nat took a pick. The man wore a Pittsburgh Steelers cap, designer jeans, and a shirt that showed off his beautiful biceps. Not the talkative type, he had been nursing his drink for quite a while, raising his head to the TV from time to time, but basically keeping to himself.

"Why don't you ask him?" Nat retorted. "If I were a bit younger, I sure would ask him myself. He's pretty good lookin'."

The FART made a face. "Never saw him here before."

"And?"

"I was just sayin'."

"Hey, I know that girl!" The tattooed guy exclaimed as he watched the TV monitor.

"She's from 'round here! She used to work for you, Chief." The boot guy cried out.

It was past ten and *On the Plate* was on. Gilda Snider's two guests appeared somewhat tense.

"The dyke's on TV," mumbled another FART while unknotting his goatee.

"Looks pretty good, too. I mean for one of them lesbian women," commented the finger tapper, slowing his pace all of a sudden.

The black man at the bar looked up. So did Dumasky a few stools away.

Doogy massaged his hand.

Ed "Monkey" Reed chose that moment to burst into the Moisol, his walk not so steady, the cornea of his eyes not so white. When he saw Doogy at the bar, he staggered his way to the other side of the bar next to the black man.

Noticing that all eyes were zoomed in on the TV, he did the same. "It's Ju–Jul, it's JU-LIE," he finally managed out. "It's our Julie. What's she doing there? Eh? What's she doin'? Did you see? It's Julie—Julie with that mustache guy."

Nat looked Monkey straight into the eyes. "Will you shut up?!"

Here they were: Julie and Leek on FOX NEWS, sitting around a table on Gilda Snider's set.

"Sometimes she comes with that guy to see—to see Jane. But now Jane's gone. Her house is—well—"

Nat grabbed Monkey's lips. "Will you shut the hell up, Monkey?!"

"Our guests tonight are the two detectives in charge of a mystery that is grabbing the interest of the whole country," Gilda Snider said from the box. "Dorothea Sishy, the owner of the New York City Open Page bookstore, disappeared weeks ago. The drama turned not only into a tragedy but into a bloody horror story. Here is a widow who was murdered in the most gruesome way, cut into pieces by an obviously demented, dangerous killer."

Julie glowered. Leek stood impassive.

"Detectives Hercules Leek and Julie Hoffman have accepted to come to our studio tonight, hopefully to shed light onto the matter," Snider continued. "Let me start with you, Detective Leek. Sources tell us that famous photographer Steve Knight is a prime suspect in the Dorothea Sishy murder."

"He's one suspect," answered Leek.

"But he *is* a prime suspect, do we agree on that?"

"We can agree on that. But there are other possibilities." Leek's voice flowed smoothly.

"This would mean that a brilliant artist like Steve Knight is also an insane man."

"As I said before, there are other possibilities."

"I see, yes. There's the possibility that this could be a random killer. Someone mentally deranged?"

"Whoever the murderer is, there is something dysfunctional or, as you put it, 'deranged' in his or her mind. At least during the time of the crime. As for the theory of a random killer, to answer your question, no, we haven't rejected it at this point." Leek pressed his hands on the table.

Snider turned to Julie. "And how far along, may I ask, are you in your investigation?"

"It's progressing nicely." After a beat during which Julie's lips contracted, she added, "This said, there are still a few blurry zones left. And we have not interviewed all of Ms. Sishy's friends and acquaintances."

"So in your view the murderer would be someone who knew Dorothea Sishy."

"It's the most probable hypothesis. Most murderers have a motive. Chances are that as soon as we find the real motive, we find the murderer as well." Julie started to relax under the studio lights.

Snider addressed her two guests. "Tell me, Detectives, are all of Ms. Sishy's friends right here in New York City?"

CHAINSAW JANE 163

"Well, there may be a link in western Pennsylvania. But we're not sure yet," Leek said.

"Ugh?" the FARTS stated in unison.

People who were not at the bar, but busy socializing at the Moisol tables, or moving to and fro helping themselves with snacks and appetizers, creating buzzing and laughing noises typical of drinking places, were now making signs to each other, showing the TV screen. Voices progressively died down, and the whole bar fell into an eerie silence.

"May I ask you where in western Pennsylvania? Pittsburgh, perhaps?" Snider continued.

"We shall inform you on the matter, if and when the connection is confirmed," Julie produced a professional smile.

"Fair enough. Let's revisit the profile of the murderer."

"Haven't we drawn it a moment ago?" Leek noted.

"Sure, we have," Julie said dryly. "On top of that, the NYPD established a profile as well, which first appeared in *The New York Times* and has been discussed time and again in the media. If I remember correctly, I have seen experts discuss the matter on this very show."

Leek scratched his throat.

"Well, Detective Hoffman, perhaps we could remind our viewers. Isn't that why you're here? The experts on my show were intriguing but, shall we say, somewhat argumentative." Snider paused and faced Julie for a second.

Julie returned the intense gaze.

"As for the profiles I have read in the press," Snider went on, "they were a bit confusing. They suggested someone obviously violent, with ritualistic tendencies, the possibility of cannibalism included. They also portrayed some sort of agent provocateur. Someone in want of attention—Ms. Sishy's torso having been found in the middle of

Central Park. I think the NYPD profiler added to that the possibility that the murderer might be playing with the police, trying to mystify it. Well, which one is it? A cannibal, a sick egocentric, or a morbid teaser?"

Leek showed a tense smile. "All the factors you are mentioning, Ms. Snider, could be included."

"Really? Nothing more precise?"

"Detection can be a precise science, Ms. Snider, but it is not a sprint competition." Leek tapped the edge of his mustache with his forefinger.

"You say detection can be a precise science, Detective."

Leek pressed the tips of his fingers against each other. "Can be."

"Is that why you are using a psychic for this investigation?"

"Where did you get that information?" Julie sat straight in her chair.

"Well, are our sources correct? Are you using a psychic?"

Leek bent his head as in a half-bow, then rose it again and said nothing for a while.

"Well, Mr. Leek?"

"You're a journalist, Ms. Snider, are you not? You know police occasionally use mediums. It is no secret." A side grin came with Leek's observation.

"That mustache guy gives me the creeps," said one of the FARTS.

"Me too!" said another. "He's like an old tiger, ready to pounce at any moment."

Doogy frowned. "A bit too old to pounce. A bit too weak, I'd think."

"He don't scare ya, Shawn?" said the goatee guy.

"The guy's fucking good TV, if you ask me," said someone from a table.

Several "Ssshhh, ssshhh!" came from various spots and, but for the TV, the bar fell silent once more.

"But this is no 'scientific' method, is it—the use of psychics," said Snider from the box.

"Neither is this a philosophical discussion. I can say we work with them, but I am not really familiar with their methods."

"You are not trying to tell me that the method of psychics is based on science, are you, Detective?"

"We prefer to call them mediums."

"Can you give us the names of some of the mediums you're working with?"

"J...J-J-Jane!" Monkey burped out as he nearly fell from his stool. Dumasky, Doogy and the black guy simultaneously sent the drunk man a dirty look. "What's with Jane? You mean, Chainsaw Jane?" one of the FARTS questioned. "Sshh!" The assistance reiterated. "Will you shut the fuck up!" was added to this as a bonus by a raspy male voice from the back of the room. Once more, the TV took dominion.

"So you don't wish to give names," Snider noted.

"Surely you can understand that, Ms. Snider." Leek smiled at the camera.

"Do you give the names of all your sources?" Julie sternly faced Snider.

"Then why exactly are you here, Detectives?"

"To explore another possibility, if we may." Leek looked at the camera. "This case may be geographically more extended than expected. We thought it was contained in New York City and vicinity at first."

A pause. "But, as mentioned before, there may be links with western Pennsylvania." Turning to Snider. "We would like to address members of your audience." Back to the camera. "And ask them if they knew anything about Dorothea Sishy." Another pause, longer than the first one. "Or Cruz Mojada."

Snider looked at her notes. "I don't see that name mentioned here. Is there a link between Dorothea Sishy and this...uh...Cruz Montoya?"

"Mojada," Julie corrected.

At this point, Detectives Leek and Hoffman had the forum, and no one in the Moisol population dared interrupt.

■ ■

MANY MOISOL HABITUÉS STAYED longer than usual that night to discuss what they had just seen on *On the Plate*. They put tables together and, after briefly evaluating the TV performances of former Noliarite Julie Hoffman and her mustached colleague, they discussed the Sishy case. What intrigued them most was the mention of another fellow Noliarite, Cruz Mojada. Some of them believed the Cuban librarian to be on vacation. The few who didn't visit the town library to admire her flamboyant and length-challenged outfits were not aware she was absent. One at the table who asked who Cruz Mojada was, was looked at as if he came from another planet. They revisited what Detective Leek had suggested, that there might be a connection between the savage murder of Dorothea Sishy and Cruz. What could be that connection? No one had ever heard of Dorothea Sishy before the murder. Faces grew long and worried.

For, FARTS excluded, everyone loved Cruz.

Actually, some of the FARTS were Cruz' fans in the closet.

Shawn Doogy had not joined the discussion. Looking somewhat pale and haggard, he had left the Moisol immediately after *On the Plate*.

"Should have that hand looked at," Dumasky told him before he walked away.

"I need sleep is all," Doogy answered.

"Too many women, eh?"

"Could be." Doogy winked a tired wink and disappeared.

Nat was cleaning the bar while observing the black guy who was still sitting there, still silent. The FARTS had gone shortly after Doogy. Monkey had gone to the discussion table, contributing inebriated comments about Jane and how she would solve the case.

But no one listened to Monkey.

"What did you think of the show?" Dumasky asked Nat.

Nat finished drying a glass. "I hate to repeat what one of the FARTS said earlier. But here it is: gives me the creeps. I mean, Cruz! I had no idea she was in danger. Did you?"

Before he could answer, someone from the improvised panel called, "Hey, Chief! Care to join us? We need a cop in this discussion."

Dumasky scratched his head. "Sure, why not?" He looked at the black guy. "Why don't I ask this gentleman here to join us as well?"

"I am not from here," the man mumbled.

"All the more reason," Dumasky uttered. "Plus that will give Nat the chance to clean her bar in peace."

The barwoman showed a grateful smile to the Chief. She'd had a long day.

As she rested for a moment, her eyes followed the movements of the two men. She had worked in bars all her life, served all sorts, and was able to classify customers. She could tell from their expressions, the way they held their glass or bottle, and the tips they gave what type of life they were having. When it came to guessing about their job, she was right 95 percent of the time. The stranger and the Chief walked together to the discussion group, and Nat noticed they both walked with a similar type of walk.

Cop walk.

◼ 17 ◼

"**T**HAT WAS AIMÉ," JULIE told her partner as she put back her cell in her blazer pocket.

"Back on the road, I presume?" Leek replied.

The detectives were at Leek's neat desk, examining dossiers. The air conditioning was down again; and mixed odors of stale and fresh coffee, doughnuts, and abandoned fast foods were polluting the air, already too humid this June 15. The buzzing of voices, with pitches rising now and then, was part of the daily cadence. Visitors tears and screams were not unusual, and the detectives would have been far more disturbed with a silent precinct. Silence, they associated with the finding of bodies at murder scenes, and they much preferred noise, even while expressing despair, than its nihilistic counterpart.

What Julie had trouble with today was the tenacious heat. She removed her jacket and opened the window behind Leek. But the New York air seemed more charged outdoor than indoor.

She went back to her seat. "Looks like Noliarites were impressed by your performance on that bitch's show last night."

"Is that what he said?"

By golly, vanity made Leek's mustache bristle, nearly levitate. Julie shook her head.

"Some also said that you gave them the creeps."

Leek grinned. "Good."

"You like giving the creeps to people, don't you?"

"I like giving the creeps to the right people, Julie, that's all."

"Do you think we reached someone yesterday?"

"We had to shake things a bit. At least try, Julie. Perhaps tongues loosened a little bit in Noliar. What did Aimé say?"

"Nothing definitive, he and Dumasky agree. There was that big discussion at the Moisol. With a skinny guy called Monkey who claims he knows who the murderer is. But he's the town drunk. Not exactly a reliable source. In any case, Dumasky will talk to him when he sobers up. Otherwise, most of the conversation was about Cruz. Some knew she was from Jersey, others didn't. But no one was able to tell whether or not she knew Dorothea Sishy. If you ask me, the theory is a bit far-fetched. New Jersey's population is about, what, nine million or so? So two women from the same state would be like, what? Two needles in two haystacks?"

"Two women from the same town. It narrows things a bit, don't you think?"

"Say what?" Julie opened her eyes wide.

"Newark. Dorothea Sishy was from Newark. And Cruz was born there as well. Newark is no small place, granted. Less than three hundred thousand, but still. It's starting to look less and less like a coincidence."

Silence.

"Remember what you said when we came back from talking to Steve Knight?" Julie grabbed a small notebook from the blazer she had hung around her chair.

"We talked about the case," Leek responded tensely.

"Yes, that was at Dino's. But afterward, when we left, you added something."

Leek kept quiet.

"First I thought I misheard you. But I decided to write it down nevertheless."

Leek crossed his hands under his chin and listened to his partner.

"'There's something I have been meaning to tell you,' you said." Julie looked at Leek straight into the eyes. "Of course you chose to say this right under a merciless rain." She went back to her notebook. "'It's about Dorothea Sishy's husband. I think he might still be alive.'"

Leek nodded.

"Are you going to elaborate on that, or what? I looked into it. The guy was also from Newark." Julie addressed her colleague sternly. "I know you can be pretty Byzantine, Leek. But I am your partner, damn it! Shouldn't you be straight at least with your partner?"

"Yes, I should. And I meant to. But we had to appear on TV and—"

"Oh, p-le-ease, Leek! That's bullshit, and you know it."

"Yes, you're right. I don't know what to tell you, Julie."

"How about telling me why you made that remark under the rain?"

"I suppose I had to vent it out. It was driving me crazy. But the whole case is making me crazy."

"You, crazy?"

"Thinking that Doug Sishy is still alive? Don't you think it's a crazy idea?"

"Coming from any other cop, I might dismiss it."

"I am getting old, and memories—"

"Come on! What's going on here?!"

"When you reach a certain age, Julie, the past becomes alive again. It basically coexists with the present. And when we were assigned the Sishy case, part of that past slapped me in the face. And I didn't want it. See, I knew Doug Sishy once. And, Julie, he was, as they say, bad news."

"What did he do?"

"He was connected to the mafia. To the DeCallo family."

"Wow! The same family Knight mentioned before we had to carry the Colossus of Rhodes."

Leek nodded. "They were all there at Sishy's funeral. It was a beautiful, opulent ceremony. Excessive, like only the mafia can do it."

"So Doug Sishy's dead!"

"Do you know Dorothea Sishy never saw the body of her dead husband?"

"What's that gotta do with our case?"

"He was cremated without her consent. Although cremation was mentioned in his will. This happened at the time her German Shepherd disappeared."

"Leek, you're not suggesting—"

"That they cremated the dog in lieu of the man? I've seen the mafia do worse things."

"When did you start suspecting Doug Sishy might not be dead?" Julie asked.

"Only recently. And by association. At the time I thought he was dead, and good riddance! I had been after him for so long."

"By association? How?"

"When you showed me the list of suspects a few days ago. I looked at their pictures and saw that they had the same type of features. I then noted that they also had a similar physique—height and weight not so far apart. One of them, Walter Gother, is notably younger than the rest of them. But the others are about the same age."

"Give or take a few years."

"So you noticed."

"I did, Leek. And I asked myself why would Dorothea Sishy go out with the same type of man? I mean, she had several lovers, but they all looked alike. And I thought, who would do that?"

Leek closed his eyes. "Well, there are people who only date a certain type. But, you're right, at Ms. Sishy's age, criteria—at least physical ones—tend to relax. It's more about companionship, compatibility, comfort, and good times at this point. Whether the person is short or tall, skinny or fat, is really secondary. But not with Dorothea."

"Exactly. Something was wrong with this picture."

"With *these pictures*. Absolutely." Leek took a deep breath. "Mrs. Dzhugashvili implied someone disoriented in her portrayal of Ms. Sishy."

"You mean Jane thought Dorothea was kinda nuts."

"You could put it like that. I think 'imbalanced' would be a better word."

Julie rose her eyes to the ceiling. Precise mustache and precise words for Leek as well. "How about 'obsessed'?"

"Yes, I came up with that word afterward." Leek clicked on his laptop and turned the screen toward Julie. "See?"

"I came up with the same picture when I did my research."

A look of surprise from Leek that his partner ignored.

"It's not the same face, exactly," she continued. "But there is a definite resemblance. Let's see, how old was Doug Sishy then? Forty-two, I see here. If he were alive today, he would be—"

"Fifty-four."

"So features can be affected by a few more wrinkles. Even height could be affected. Bones, posture."

Leek let his gaze wander, as if he were not at the police precinct, facing his all-too-neat desk and his all-too-energetic partner, but living through a messier scene in his life, not liking it, but assuming the obligation of going through it. "Absolutely."

Julie opened a folder and extracted four enlarged photos. "This is Jack Teddy, deputy mayor, to whom we will talk soon. This is Steve Knight. Here is Walter Gother, the young one. And here is a printout of the photo on your screen. Doug Sishy."

The two cops sat close to each other and dissected every detail of what was before them, pointing in silence to a chin, or a lid, a hairline. All in all, it was a frustrating examination.

"You know, if I saw these men walk from afar in the street, and if I were nearsighted, I might assume they were from the same family," Julie finally concluded.

"They're just the same *type* of men. Features are different. Except for Walter Gother. He does resemble Sishy." Leek made a face. "But he's quite young. Maybe we should start talking to him and see the deputy mayor afterward."

"Disappointed?"

"What on earth do you mean, Julie?"

"That none of these men could be Sishy? That he's probably dead?" Julie smiled a cop smile.

"You're playing games with me."

"I learned from the master."

"Have you got something up your sleeve?"

"Probably something similar to what's up yours!"

"Julie!"

"Oh, my dear old cat!"

Leek chuckled. "It's just a crazy theory."

"Me too. Let's have it."

Leek's mustache shivered with excitement. "Let's still assume that Doug is not dead."

"Let's."

"As we said before, with age, his features could have changed."

"And with his connections, his name could have changed."

"And with his money, his face could have changed."

"You're thinking plastic surgery?"

"I have to tell you something, Julie. I e-mailed your friend Dr. Trenton."

"Oh, Leek. We have been partners for too long. We think the same, act the same. I e-mailed photos to Marc as well."

"Any response?"

"He's busy. But he took a glimpse. He's noncommittal for now because he needs more time. Says there are 'possibilities,' though. That's his word."

"Possibilities?"

"Possibilities is pretty good coming from a doctor like Marc."

"Well, we should call the Chainsaw woman," she added after a brief silence.

Leek nodded, then pressed keys on his cell. "Mrs. Dzhugashvili?. . .Yes, I see. . .Well, thank you! . . .Well, what do you say we pick you up in about twenty-two minutes? Looks like we need your expertise again. . .Till soon, then."

"Twenty-two minutes?" Julie rolled her eyes.

"You know, Mrs. Dzhugashvili was perfectly charming on the phone."

"Yeah, right! How can anyone named Dzhugashvili be charming? And why don't you call her Jane like everybody else?"

"Would that make her more charming?"

"Hell, no! Are you sure you talked to Jane—not her angelic twin?"

"She watched Fox News last night and—"

"Oh, I get it! And she saw your little torture number with Snider. She might not even feel the nails just yet. But Jane saw what you did. She probably approved, for she can't stand Snider. In her mind, you're probably Saint Hercules right now."

Silence.

"Surely you don't mean what you just said." Leek's mustache glistened with pride.

"Surely I fucking do, Leek. And am I glad you're on this side of the law. Otherwise, you would make the most dangerous criminal of all time."

■ 18 ■

THE HUMID HEAT HELPING, every shape and form had lost its definition. Blurred out like this, cars and trucks in constant motion were nearly indistinguishable. Thick air and kinetic energy turned traffic into a giant, sinuous, colorful reptile. And with the honking as a leitmotiv, the monster was definitively a grouch.

Ah, the New York spirit.

"Where are we going?" Jane asked as she climbed into the back of the Crown Vic.

"Queens. To see our next suspect," Julie answered.

Jane lit a cigarette.

"Can't smoke in here. You know that, Jane."

Jane took a drag then threw her cigarette out the window. "Fooking cops."

Julie adjusted the car mirror and turned to Leek. "Charming, huh?"

"Let's go!" Jane yelled. The monster roared non-stop.

"Have you seen the traffic, Jane?" Julie yelled back.

"So what are sirens for?"

"Emergencies, Mrs. Dzhugashvili."

"Well, this is fooking emergency. I need cigarette as soon as possible. And if we wait here, we won't reach Queens till next century and I'll be dead by then." Jane tapped on Leek's shoulder. "You realize, Detective Leek, that Julie is behind wheel."

"I do, Madame."

"Then you don't know."

Leek stretched his head back. "Know what?"

"Julie drives like Zoe. Who needs criminals when there are drivers like these two?"

Julie clenched her teeth, thought of a few swearwords to yell out but decided to save them for better occasions, grabbed the siren, stuck it on the Crown Vic roof, and plunged into traffic.

"Works every the time," Jane whispered in Leek's ear.

"I know," Leek whispered back.

■ ■

IF THERE WERE ONE region that could symbolize the diversity of the US, Queens could be it—America at its most culturally dynamic. Criminally speaking, it wasn't undynamic, either. There were Irish, Hispanics, Greek, Italians, Croatians, Chinese, Indians, Koreans, Filipinos, and a growing population of Arabs. And there was a bit of Russian occupation as well—something Jane definitely approved of. That is, until she discovered that the Polish presence was numerically superior—just slightly superior, but big enough for Jane to burst out a ritual but resonant, "WHAT FOOK!"

Her consolation came when she was told that 63 percent of Queens was Democrat against 15 percent Republican; and, as far as the 22 percent with no affiliation or classified as "other," she decided they could only be extra-legionnaires on their way to crush the 15 percent *de trop*.

An Independent herself, she didn't care for either major party. One party with two faces, she would claim. The arch-conservative and the conservative. The one that chose the elephant as its symbol couldn't be trusted. Its members were out of touch with reality, not to mention geography—with the exception of zoos, where could you find elephants in this country. On the other hand, you could still find plenty of asses, which made Democrats slightly more in touch.

The fact that US natives made up only a little over half of Queen's population brought some comfort to an immigrant like Jane as well. Among the natives, African-Americans, Latinos, American Indians, Alaskans, Hawaiians, and others made up a solid 70 percent of these demographics. The 30 percent that was left was white. But there were Jews, Catholics, artists, gays, and atheists among them too! Ha! Jane thought. The WASP was really a small minority. The male WASP *half* that small, desperately hanging onto power, but hanging by a *fooking* thread. So one day it would happen: all that would be left for the WASP would be accounting and S&M.

Jane loved to read about demographics. There was an old computer in Zoe's apartment guest room with an Internet connection, and that was plenty good for her. When she declared that she had never learned to type properly, she really meant it. She would attack a keyboard with her middle fingers and nothing else. She had to do something while Zoe was locked up in her study and writing away most of the day and Marc was medically busy with reinventing bodies and faces. Queens was an interesting case. She had lived there once, few people knew that. But that was in another life.

The red brick buildings had not changed much. The atmosphere was more neighborly than Manhattan. Elegance had been traded for character, and that was a-okay with the Russian psychic.

Julie hit the brake in front of an old warehouse.

"So we've reached destination. Thank God, I can actually breathe freely now," Jane said as she stepped out of the car and lit a cigarette.

Julie frowned, looked at her watch. "Listen, Jane. After you're done, go to the second floor. That's where we will be, interrogating Walter Gother."

■ ■

THE PLACE REEKED OF turpentine, linseed oil, and, oddly enough, bleach. The detectives had anticipated a messy decor and were rather surprised to find fairly neat surroundings. Shelves built into the walls ran up to the ceiling. Everything seemed in its proper place. Leek couldn't refrain from smiling. Paintings of all sizes were plastered against the red brick walls, forming an uneven dark fence of sorts, a dented shadow. Large pots of paint laid on an old butcher stand that had also been roughly fenced in with boards nailed on each side. Thick brushes burst out of plastic flowerpots like clown hair. Here and there, homemade easels supported works in progress, all with a black background. Natural light filtered through large windows from the north side. Julie noticed a couple of skylights as well. Close to ideal conditions for an artist, if she remembered what her artist friend Marcel Pavie had told her once. "Better to have windows facing north. Or skylights. That way you don't have to fuss with drapes or shades. The sun won't come and trick you and your colors."

In one corner, odd objects were agglutinated: old typewriters, three-legged tables, broken lamps, discolored pots, pans and lids, cabinet doors, window frames, rusty bird cages. Next to this mountain of rubble stood an installation, with a stove, a pan, and inside the pan, a Barbie doll. A teddy bear was sitting near the pan, holding a lighter as if ready to cook Barbie. The sculpture was surrounded by a wire fence holding stabbed posters of female Hollywood stars.

An old sofa splashed with paint rested against the north wall. In front of it, an old kitchen table with a huge spherical ashtray pushed on one side and legs amputated halfway reminded Leek of a basset hound. A little further, there was a Japanese folding screen, which seemed incongruous in such a rugged place. He wondered what was behind it. A bed would be his guess. And, as it happened, a good guess.

Leek's eyes traveled now to the center of the room.

A sizable canvas laid flat on the floor and on all fours over it, Walter Gother was splashing black paint, à la Jackson Pollock. The artist's nervous sweeping gestures made the detectives protect their faces with their hands. Julie caught dark paint on her new pair of jeans. Leek miraculously avoided damage.

"Mr. Gother," Julie yelled out.

No response.

"Mr. Gother!"

No response. Gother kept splashing. Julie ran toward the action like a soldier on a battlefield, caught additional black stains on the way, and pulled the iPod earphones out of the artist's ears. Gother stopped all movement like a character in a DVD put on pause, then slowly straightened up his body and saw Julie.

"Hey, man, why did you do that?" He got up, examined Julie's spotted jeans and top. "Cool clothes! Where did you get these?"

Gother's red hair and clear blue eyes reminded Julie of something—someone. Doug Sishy, sure, but someone else as well. She knew this intense glance, she was sure of it. "Not far from where I got this badge. Is that cool too?" She told the artist as she flashed her professional ID.

Gother's face dropped. "You a cop?"

Seeing that the ground was relatively safe, Leek carefully approached, but not without asking Gother to put his brush down first.

"Say we are, Mr. Gother." Leek showed his badge as well.

The artist dried his hands on a rag. "It's about Dorothea, isn't it?"

"What fook!" Puffing and panting, Jane dragged her steps and her smell of cigarettes across the room. She first walked toward the stove installation and paced around it, nodding now and then. She then went toward Gother with careful steps, as if she were seeing a ghost, and started examining his left ear. "Mm...intact. So you're not him! Good. I am not seeing ghost."

That's it! Julie thought. The guy looked like Van Gogh! He fucking looked like Van Gogh. His palette didn't, though, thought Leek. Where did the yellow go?

"That thing starting to get old, man!" Gother said. "Do you know how many people examine my ears when they see me for the first time?"

Jane gave Gother's painted oeuvre a quick, circular gaze. It was dark as hell. Looked like hell as well. She definitely preferred the satiric touch in the installation. She needed to ask him when he planned to have Teddy Bear use that lighter on Barbie. She wanted to be there when it happened.

■ ■

"How long have you known Ms. Sishy?" Julie asked.

"Two years, I think. Yeah, I've known Dorothea two years." Gother seemed nervous.

"And you two had an affair?" Julie was looking around, taking notes.

"Yeah, if you wanna call that an affair, fine with me, man!"

"Well, Mr. Gother, what would you call your relationship with Ms. Sishy?" Leek's half-closed lids and velvety, gentle voice invited confession.

"*Good old fooking*," answered Jane to herself. She was relaxing on Gother's paint-splattered sofa.

"Good old fucking, man!" said Gother.

"I see." Leek twitched his mustache as he looked through his note-pad. "But you could have that with someone...uh...a bit younger."

"Don't mind if I do," said Gother.

"How old are you, Mr. Gother?"

"Twenty-eight."

"And Ms. Sishy was fifty-four, is that right?"

"What's it to you?"

Leek gave Gother a one sided-smile. "Just double-checking facts, Mr. Gother. Nothing more." The detective touched the tip of his mustache with his notepad while examining his prey. "Nothing less."

Julie paced a few steps, handling a painting here, a sketch there.

"Hey, be careful with those, man!" Gother's face was anxious.

"Just being a cop, *man*!" retorted Julie.

"Cool. But I worked hard on those."

"Could have fooled me," Julie mumbled.

Jane saw the monumental ashtray facing her, nodded in approval, and lit a cigarette.

"Could I have one?" Gother asked. "I'm out."

Jane handed him her pack and her lighter. She didn't know yet what to make out of the faux Van Gogh. But the large and butt-filled ashtray ruled in his favor so far.

Leek scratched his throat. "What you are trying to tell us, Mr. Gother, is that your relationship with Ms. Sishy was without constraint. You were both free to see other people."

Gother took a drag. "Yeah."

"And you apparently like older women."

"I like women, period, man."

Julie walked toward the artist. "You don't think Dorothea would have been jealous of your other relationships?"

"Why? She had other men in her life. And I wasn't jealous."

"You weren't?" Leek insisted.

"If he says he wasn't jealous, he wasn't." Julie sent a glance toward Leek, who gave her a discreet nod. "So let's talk about something else. Finances, for instance. How do you make a living?"

"Uh...I sell my work."

"No, you don't," Jane said.

Gother turned to Jane. "I sell my art, man!"

"You sold total of two paintings to one person."

"How...do you know?" Gother raised his head toward Julie. "Who? Who is she?"

"Special task force for lying artists." Leek adjusted his mustache and grinned.

"Paintings cost pretty penny to Dorothea, didn't they? Fifty thousand dollars, that's expensive for unknown artist," Jane said.

Leek looked at his notes and saw that indeed on May 3 Dorothea Sishy had written a $50,000 check to William Gother. And when he and Julie had checked her apartment, they had seen two very dark abstract paintings on her walls. Aha! They thought.

"So what if she bought paintings. Dorothea liked to support artists."

"With preference for young handsome artists she fooked, maybe." Gother shrugged.

"She also gave you cash on regular basis."

Gother's complexion turned as red as his hair. The only colorful thing in the decor, so far, Leek reflected. The detectives looked at each other and decided to let Jane do the talking for a while.

"So you didn't have to work for living, did you?"

"Can I see a badge?" Gother asked Jane.

"Special task force don't carry badges," Julie deadpanned. "Answer the lady, please."

"Okay, so what if she gave me money? Is that a crime?"

Jane's glance seemed unfocused, floating.

Silence.

"Is your task force on drugs?" Gother finally asked.

The detectives didn't reply and waited.

"She told you she was about to leave you, right?" Jane's eyes were focused again.

"She wasn't gonna leave me!"

"Yes, she was." Jane plunged her cigarette butt into the ashtray.

Gother took a last drag. "You've got no proof."

"Special task forces need no proof," Jane said with conviction.

The detectives looked at each other, made faces.

"Just who the fuck is she?"

"Just answer her, Mr. Gother!" Leek's face was stern.

"Why would she leave me, eh?"

"You mean, why would a middle-aged woman decide to break up with a hot thing like you, is that what you are implying, Gother?" Julie was making careful steps, her eyes on every element, her hands handling an object here and there, her feet sensing the floor under her.

"She left you because you kept asking her for more money. That's why she left you, young man." Jane lit up another cigarette.

"Can I..." Jane handed Gother her pack before he could finish his sentence.

Gother took a shaky drag. "Okay, so I did accept a little bit of her money."

"Little bit of money?" Julie lifted one painting, looked through the back.

Gother's body stiffened.

Julie glided one finger to the back of the canvas supporting frame, and pulled a few bills out of it. "Guess that's a little bit more...All in hundreds."

"That's stupid hiding place," Jane said.

Gother's body shrank. "It's not what you think; it's not what you think."

"American fooking gigolo."

Gother's body curved downward. "No...it's not that."

"Mr. Gother, would you care to tell us what exactly happened between you and Ms. Sishy?" Leek's eyes were squinting.

Fooking pouncing cat, Jane thought.

"Nothing happened. We...broke up, is all." Gother slowly rose his head.

"SHE broke up with you," Jane corrected. "You didn't want break up. Dorothea was like ATM machine with infinite supply. And ATM machine you could fook."

"Again, Mr. Gother, would you care to tell us what happened?"

"Or I will," said Jane.

Gother folded again, a fatigued Thinker, he put his head between his hands. "All right, man."

"If he adds another 'man' to the conversation, I'm *really* gonna make him look like Van Gogh," grumbled Julie who was now examining a painting knife.

"I guess we had a fight." Gother scratched his head. "I mean a big fight, not like the other ones."

"So you fought often?" asked Leek.

With some couples it makes fooking better. Although. Although, what? Something didn't click there. Jane took a last drag and let the thought go with the smoke.

"It got better afterward." Gother's voice was dead.

"What was particular about this fight?"

"I got mad when Dorothea told me she didn't want to see me anymore, that it was too painful. I mean, at first I thought it was just one of our regular fights..."

Julie put the painting knife down. "So she threatened to leave you several times before?"

"Yeah, but I never took it seriously."

"What made you take it seriously this time?"

Gother remained silent.

"What changed?" Leek repeated.

Silence stretched on.

"Paul...no, Paulo. Pablo, that's it, Pablo," Jane said, her eyes lost in space.

Gother froze.

"You know someone called Pablo, Mr. Gother?"

"No."

"Pablo Barreta... no, Ibañeta. Yes, Ibañeta. Crazy Basque name. Young, young man." Jane closed her eyes. "Hot young man. Also artist."

Julie pulled out a chair and sat across from Gother. "Looks like Dorothea found a new...uh...how shall I put it?"

"A new interest," Leek completed.

"A new gigolo," Jane punctuated.

Leek remained silent, his stare dead.

Gother's face reddened. "Pablo is bad news, man."

Julie cringed. "Judging from your viewpoint, he might be. He could become the new special funds deviator. No more money flowing your way. So let me tell you what I think happened, Gother. You had a big fight, just like you said. And maybe you had a few drinks as well. I saw a nice collection of bottles behind the folding screen, right beside the bed."

Jane rose, eyes lit up.

"But no vodka," Julie continued and Jane sat back down. "Dorothea Sishy was not a fool, I hope you realize that, Gother."

"Fool for sex, maybe." Jane commented. She was about to add a few more remarks when she met Julie's Napoleonic stare. Jane thought she owned the copyright for such a stare. She then turned to Leek, who remained still, eyes half-shut.

"She told you that she was done with you," Julie continued. "But you didn't take it well, did you? It felt like an insult, a kick in the butt. It was the end of easy street, a kuhl-dee-sak."

"Cul-de-sac," Leek corrected.

"French for ass of bag," Jane completed.

"Well, that about says it," Julie continued. "You found yourself in a bag ass. So first you begged her to stay. But when someone like Dorothea Sishy has made a decision, she doesn't go back, does she? It may have taken her a while to reach it." Julie paused for a second, gave Leek a side glance, then continued. "Hell, considering all the dough she poured on you, I'm quite sure it did take her long. Fifty grand for your paintings and, let's say, fifty more for various expenses. I mean, she couldn't have poured all that dough on you in three days, could she?" Julie suddenly stopped, turned, squinted, and went toward a can of paint on the butcher stand. She opened the can, dug into it. "Well, what duya know? Here's another special savings account. Let's see, one...two...aha...mm. Four more grand here, and a few small bills for dessert. What the hell, Gother! See, I knew something didn't fit, and I couldn't nail it. And then it suddenly dawned on me. One can of paint looked clean. Light and clean. How can a used can of paint look so clean? Well, you wash it, duh! But why would you wash it? Usually, we wash cans to use them for other purposes. But shit, don't you believe in banks, Gother? I know they're definitely thieves. Legal, though. They give ya low interests if you invest and ask for high ones if you borrow, but they keep money pretty good. I mean, it ain't that easy to rob a bank."

Julie placed the money back in the can, handed it to Leek, who put it aside as evidence with the rest of the cash.

Jane wondered if now was a good time to ask for an increase.

"So where were we?" Julie bent over Gother, touched his arms. "You're a pretty strong guy. So when you realized that Dorothea would no longer be your own personal bank, you decided no one else should, either. You were drunk and flew into a rage. You strangled Dorothea, waited until she got cold maybe, and then cut her into pieces. Got to admit, found no blood here. But this floor has been bleached."

"I bleach my floors regularly."

"Why?"

"To kill odors."

"Say what?"

"I like to paint with oil, but the smell of turpentine makes me sick sometimes."

"How about blood? How about cut limbs, guts sliced with a chainsaw?" Julie walked toward the pile near the installation. Behind cabinet doors she unraveled pieces of a tree trunk. "I mean, look at this. How did you cut this, Gother? If you can slice this, you can slice a body, can't you?" Julie made another round around the room, stretching, bending, touching shelves and walls. The atmosphere had grown dense in the large studio, as if air and the sudden silence had coagulated into lead. Julie fixated on a point close to the ground, squatted, and grabbed a heavy object from a bottom shelf. "Mm. An Echo C-S 400. Not bad. Heavy-duty. About three hundred dollars. A very respectable chainsaw, actually."

Gother, who had turned white, ran to the bathroom.

"I don't know if you two are able detectives. But you're certainly good at making people throw up." Jane got up, went behind the folding screen, and returned with a bottle of scotch. There were no glasses in sight. So when Gother returned from the bathroom, she started handing him the bottle. She then reassessed her decision and said, "Wait." She opened the bottle, took a swallow, then gave it to the artist. "Cheap shit. But will help digestion."

■ ■

BACK IN THE CROWN Vic, this time with Leek behind the wheel, the detectives and Jane let silence settle for a few minutes. When Julie broke it, she said, "This might be our guy."

Leek shook his head ever so slightly.

"Throwing up doesn't mean he's innocent. He might have realized the horror of what he did. And he had plenty of motive."

"The chainsaw doesn't mean he is guilty, either. Artists work with heavy-duty tools these days," Leek retorted.

"The thing was abnormally clean."

Leek wrinkled his brows. "Things that are too clean are not normal to you, dear."

Julie emitted a silent "Fuck you, old cat."

Jane remained silent.

"So Jane, what do you think?" Julie asked.

"That he's fooking liar, but no murderer."

"I know he's a liar. Murderers usually are."

"Suspects, even when innocent, can lie out of fear as well," Leek added.

"Gother is major liar. He never slept with Dorothea Sishy."

"What do you mean, Jane?"

"And he loved Dorothea Sishy. He truly loved her."

"You care to elaborate on that, Mrs. Dzhugashvili?"

"She was there," said Jane.

"She, who?"

"Do you mean Dorothea Sishy?" Leek took a left turn while ignoring a red light. "But you called him a gigolo, Mrs. Dzhugashvili."

"Girl's got to have fun."

Julie lifted her eyebrows and sighed. "And she told you something?"

"Yes, the bitch did. She said, 'Leave my son alone'!"

19

"**W**AS MS. SISHY REALLY a...a —"

"Say it, Leek. A bitch." A beat. "By the way," Julie added. "In Jane's mouth that's a compliment."

"Compliment? Sishy's ghost was major pain in ass. She kept repeating: 'Leave my son alone, leave him alone!'" Jane rubbed the sides of her head.

"Fooking ears hurt."

"Why would she say that? Do ghosts lie?"

"Sometimes. But I don't think so with Dorothea. She told truth."

"So she had a son?" Leek was perplexed. Jane nodded. "How come we didn't know that?" Julie turned to Jane. "Maybe because she didn't have him with her husband—that it?"

Jane grimaced. "Very good. Maybe someday you can become detective."

"Did she have him before her marriage? Gave him for adoption?"

"No."

"Can we be a little more loquacious, Jane?"

"No."

"No?"

"No."

"Why?"

"Because."

"Because?"

"Because!"

"Because, what?!"

"Just because."

Leek listened to the two women, counting the beats and wondering. He finally said, "You don't know?"

"Not everything."

"But you think she had him with someone else while being married." Leek scratched his mustache.

"No. What I am thinking is that son didn't go with marriage."

Julie tightened her jaw, then took a deep breath. "I don't get it, Jane."

"I need more time. Vision is not clear yet."

A beat.

"It's kind of sick for a guy to say he slept with his mother," Julie said.

Leek smiled. "Oh, dear, you're so retro. Gother is an artist. Part of his job is shocking the mainstream."

"Shocking mainstream replaces talent in his case," Julie said and, after a beat, added. "Did you just call me 'retro'?"

"How fooking shocking. Calling a lesbian that, imagine! I have you know girls sleeping together is not new invention. It's pretty retro thing. Hell, there are lesbians among seagulls."

Leek laughed. "Really, Mrs. Dzhugashvili, seagulls?"

"Really! And all those assholes with constipated religion telling it's not natural thing. What fook do they know?"

Julie shook her head. "Can we go back to our main topic here?"

"Maybe Walter Gother didn't know Dorothea was his mother," Jane mumbled to herself.

"Ugh?" said Julie.

"Nothing."

"Nothing?"

"Nothing!"

Not again, thought Leek. "How about Ibañeta?"

"Yeah, we could do a checkup," Julie said.

Jane shrugged.

They had arrived at the precinct. Two male police officers were talking at the entrance. When they saw Julie's tight body glide by, one of them muttered, almost inaudibly, "Such a hot thing and she only does girls. What a waste!"

Julie turned and walked back toward the commentator.

Echeverria had been his name once. Some years ago, a cousin living in the Basque Country, told him that the "ch" sound was originally written with an "x" in Basque. So, for authenticity's sake, he had changed the "Echeverria" into "Exeverria."

Bad idea when you are a NYC cop.

From then on, everyone called him "X."

"I wouldn't fuck an X. Don't ask me why," Julie told him.

The other officer chuckled.

"But since you're in a garrulous mood, why don't you put it to good use? I need you to check on a Pablo Ibañeta. A Basque, like you, apparently. Written report tonight, tomorrow morning at the latest."

"Okay."

"It's *yes, Detective*, for you, X."

The other officer chuckled again.

"Why don't you go with X, Vee? She grinned. "Looks like there might be something between you two."

No more chuckle.

■ ■

LEEK AND JANE WERE having coffee at the detective's desk when Julie joined them. "What now?"

Leek looked at his watch. "It's after two. We could have a late lunch."

"You want me to get you a couple of hotdogs?"

"You still like that fake sausage shit, Julie?"

"Perhaps we could take Jane to Dino's."

Julie made a face. "Fine!"

■ ■

A LITTLE BEFORE FOUR o'clock, the threesome were out of Dino's and on their way to 51 Chambers Street. If New York City Hall was listed in the National Register of Historical Places, it was for a reason. Built in 1811, it was an imposing yet elegant combo of French Renaissance and Georgian architecture. Surrounded by the magnificent gardens of City Hall Park, it made Jane exclaim, "New York Mayor works in fooking palace. Who says Louis XIV is dead?"

■ ■

A MIDDLE-AGED ASSISTANT WITH oversprayed hair, a double chin, thick glasses, and an air of self-convinced competence sat behind the desk of the Deputy Mayor for Legal Affairs antechamber.

"Mr. Jack Teddy, please," Julie asked.

"Mr. Teddy is in a meeting right now."

Leek and Julie flashed their badges.

"I'll see if he can get out of conference. Won't you please sit down?"

The cops and Jane sat and waited.

Five minutes.

Ten minutes.

Fifteen.

Jane went for her cigarettes.

"Ma'am, you can't smoke in here," the assistant said.

"What kind of city hall is this?"

"You can't smoke in here," the assistant repeated, glasses gliding down her nose.

"Is that how you welcome taxpayers?"

"You can't smoke in here." The assistant's binoculars were about to downslope all the way when she slid them back up her aquiline ridge.

"What are you? Secretary or scratched vinyl record?"

"Put your smokes away, Jane," Julie said, then thought about it. "Hey, what the hell! Gimme a cigarette, Jane!"

"You can't smoke in here."

Leek went to pick a cigarette from Jane's pack and grabbed her lighter. He walked to the assistant. "We can't smoke in here? Is that what you are saying, Ms.?" He looked at the sign on her desk. "Ms. Konsteepatud? Is that a German name?"

"You can't smoke in here."

"Then let's make a deal, shall we? If Mr. Teddy appears in, let's say, one minute, we won't light our cigarettes. Otherwise, we shall be on a polluting mission."

The secretary pressed nervously on phone keys, and fifty seconds later, a handsome man looking ten years younger than his officially declared fifty-five appeared.

Impeccable haircut, smile as broad as the Grand Canyon.

"Ah, Detectives, sorry to keep you waiting. Won't you please come into my office?"

The voice was warm, caressing, perfect for a *politique*. "To what do I owe the pleasure of your visit?"

After introducing himself, his partner, and Jane, Leek gave a brief synopsis of Dorothea Sishy's disappearance and ensuing murder.

Jack Teddy's grin could have won him a contract with Colgate. "Ladies and gentleman, I am just a deputy mayor. I don't see how—"

"Our records show that you were well acquainted with Ms. Sishy," Leek said.

Mr. Colgate's smile was plastered on his face. "I assure you I don't...didn't...know this Ms. Sash..."

"Sishy," Julie said crisply.

"Yes, well. I certainly read about her tragic ending. But I can assure you—"

"There are people ready to testify that they saw you with Dorothea Sishy." A bluff couldn't hurt, thought Julie.

"Well, perhaps at Open Page."

"So you knew her bookstore," Leek said.

"I do read, Detective."

"But the witnesses I just mentioned saw you elsewhere with Dorothea Sishy." Julie liked to play poker.

"Well, Dora was—"

"Aha! So it's Dora now. So you did know her well."

The Colgate grin tightened.

"Okay, we did have an affair. Very brief, though. Very brief. But can we please keep it, uh, under the rug, uh, at least for the time being? I'm a married man and Mayor Blushborg will be retiring after this term and—"

"And you are thinking about replacing him, Mr. Teddy?" Leek adjusted his mustache.

"If the people of New York will have me. And you know very well how the press would exploit my relationship with Ms. Sishy."

Jane tapped her foot in restive fashion and all eyes turned on her. Hers went to the politician.

"Why don't you go to France?"

"Excuse me?" said Teddy.

"You think you invented fooking on side? It has been happening since beginning of time. Kings did fooking on side. Czars did fooking on side—Nicolas II, Ivan Terrible. And Catherine? Catherine II did serious fooking on side. And then she killed fooked up guys. American news creates scandals out of fooking on side. Italians, Russians, they don't give shit about fooking on side. They just practice it and then shut up. Well, Italians like to flaunt fooking on side. So do some Russians. But truth is, American news makes scandal out of old, old fooking story."

"Ahem, you mentioned France."

"Yeah, Mr. Teddy, I did. You know what happened at President Mitterrand's funeral? Wife was there, sons were there. Mistress and daughter she had with Mitterrand were there. They all shook hands. And Mazarine—that's mistress' daughter, named after famous Cardinal on top of things— became the one in charge of President's cultural heritage. Not legitimate sons, but daughter that came from fooking on side. And what did French press do? Nothing. Nobody knew about Mazarine until funeral. And when French people heard, they just shrugged. Another president that fooked like mad rabbit, so what else is new?"

Leek observed.

Julie frowned.

Teddy sat open-mouthed and scarlet-complexioned, and after a moment, asked, "Your point?"

Jane was about to speak up but Leek interrupted. "I think Mrs. Dzhugashvili's point is that this is murder. We're investigating a murder. Serious matter."

"Her name is Dzhugashvili?"

His gaze parked on Teddy, Leek slant his head slightly. "Is that a problem, Mr. Teddy?"

"Am I a suspect?"

"Yes, Mr. Teddy."

"But you just said that it was about murder, not sex."

"Not exactly," Julie said. "This murder could be connected to sex."

"I don't understand."

Jane resumed her foot tom-toming. "Here goes. American media and politicians inflate what's silly, so important stuff looks less important. They fill American brains with games and gossip and sex scandals. Some don't like to think, so they swallow junk food for brain. If politicians and press want monopoly of analysis, so be it, they say. But other Americans say: 'Analyze this!'" She tapped the side of her ass to illustrate her comment.

"I certainly don't agree with that, Ms. Dzhugashvili." Teddy's breathing became audible. "Is that really your name?" A pause. "And I really don't see the point of this diatribe." Teddy turned to Julie with appraising eyes. "Do you?"

"I do."

"You do?" Teddy let his eyes linger on Julie's figure.

Wrong fooking target, thought Jane.

"I do." Julie smiled at the deputy mayor.

"What is it?" Teddy seemed puzzled.

"Can't you tell?"

"I can't."

"You can't?"

"No, I can't."

"I can."

Oh boy! Leek rubbed his hands. "It seems you have a serious motive for killing Ms. Sishy. She might have wanted more out of the affair. She might have threatened to make it public."

"That's silly."

"Is it?" Leek's eyes had become slits.

"It is."

"Really?"

"What is this?"

"Murder is not silly, Mr. Teddy."

"But you just said it. Murder is important; sex is silly."

"Except in America. Remember Chappaquiddick?" Leek said.

"That was a long time ago, Detective."

"And yet we didn't get it."

Jane was about to open her mouth. Julie discreetly shushed her, but the Russian was on a roll.

"If this country had grown up, nobody would have given importance to fooking on side. No death would have occurred. But puritanical system encourages politicians like you to be criminals."

Teddy grew very tense. "But I didn't kill Dora, I swear."

Julie raised her hands. "Okay, so let's all go. Mr. Teddy says he didn't kill Dorothea Sishy, so we should believe him. After all, he's just a politician. As innocent as they come. I say, let's leave the poor man alone!"

"You don't have to be sarcastic, Detective." Teddy pressed his hands in front of his mouth and closed his eyes, as in prayer. "Listen, I am willing to cooperate. There may be things about Dorothea that can help your investigation."

A beat.

An exchange of glances.

Another beat.

Teddy stared at Julie for a long time.

Leek took advantage of the moment to bend toward Jane and whisper. "Good job."

Julie gave a broad grin to the deputy mayor, as if she were about to give him her phone number.

"She's pretty good too," Jane whispered back.

They had Teddy where they wanted him.

20

"**Y**OU KNEW Ms. SISHY had a son? At least she suspected he was her son. His name is, let me think. Gotham. No, Gother. William Gother."

Julie nodded. "Not Sishy? Gother. So she had an affair with a man named Gother who apparently acknowledged his paternity. Is that it?"

Jane, the detectives, and Teddy were having coffee in the deputy mayor's office, trying to fight fatigue. Teddy had called earlier his robot-assistant Ms. Konsteepatud to have her cancel all of today's appointments and engagements, as he was spending the afternoon with two NYPD detectives and one Mrs. Dzhugashvili.

Occasionally, one of them would get up to stretch, peer through the window, and watch the day slowly dye over City Hall Park.

"Not exactly."

"What do you mean?" Leek asked.

"Dora told me that she had a very good marriage. Except for one thing. He—?

"You mean the *late* Doug Sishy?" Leek's eyes were slits.

"Yes. He didn't want children. But she got pregnant, apparently at his request."

"I don't understand," said Leek.

"Neither do I," said Teddy. "She could never finish her story. She would burst into tears. All she would tell me was that after many years she had found her son, that his name was Walter Gother."

"Looks like she had to give up her son early on," said Julie.

"That's what I figured," Teddy replied.

"Did she tell you how she recognized him? From child to man, features change, obviously."

"Mother's instinct, that's what she claimed."

"This is New York City. Can mother's instinct find a guppy in a school of sardines?"

"Okay, this is what I remember her telling me. One day a young man came to Open Page, looking for an art book. *Black Paintings*. I remember the title because I was at the opening of an art show once where the paintings of Rauschenberg, Reinhardt, Rothko, Stella, all the artists who were exploring the color black in the 1940s were..."

"Well, this explains that," Julie interrupted. "Have you seen Gother's paintings?"

Silence. The politician didn't like to be cut in.

"In any case," he resumed, "Dora had a shock when she saw him. He looked exactly like 'Doug as a young man,' as she put it. Up to the dark, wavy, auburn hair, which Sishy lost in part in his early forties. But 'handsome no matter what,' she added. She was still in love with her dead husband."

"Could that have been wishful thinking? Apparently, she did not accept her husband's death."

Leek insisted on the word "death." Jane made a funny face.

"I thought so at first, Detective. I mean, seeing Gother with such a strong resemblance to Sishy. And finding the son she had not been able to keep. It probably felt like a miracle—a resurrection, if you'll pardon the religious expression."

"She could have asked for DNA," Julie said.

"She wanted to, so she said."

"You don't sound convinced, Mr. Teddy."

"I believe Dora was afraid to find out the truth. If Gother happened not to be her son, this would have crushed her. She was very emotional and, uh, hormonal."

"Hormonal?"

"Fooking menopause, Mr. Leek!"

"That's correct," said Teddy.

Tired of sitting, Julie had gotten up and paced around the plush office. She scratched her head. "When you talked about Dorothea's husband a bit earlier, you referred to him as simply 'Sishy.' Did you know Mr. Sishy, Mr. Teddy?"

Teddy swallowed and his Adam's apple stuck out. "I did."

"Well, why didn't you say so before, Mr. Teddy?"

This was the first time Julie heard anger in Leek's voice. Refrained anger. But a real, raw feeling.

There was astonishment on Teddy's face.

Leek rebuilt his mask. "Well, Mr. Teddy? Were you friends once with Doug Sishy?"

Teddy shook his head. "Sishy is not a memory I care to revive. I know he's dead. We should not speak ill of the dead."

"Bullshit," said Jane. "Do you really think the dead are so thoughtful about the living?"

"Who are you?" said Teddy.

"Why didn't you like Doug Sishy?" Julie asked.

Leek was all ears.

"The most aggravating part is that I don't know exactly why. But first of all, you should know that I met Dora when she was a widow. I learned she was married to Sishy only later, when our liaison was well under way."

Silence—during which Julie compared notes. First the deputy mayor talked about a brief affair with Dorothea. Now, it was a liaison that was "well under way."

"I came into contact with Sishy about twenty years ago. I was a prosecuting attorney then. We prosecuted members of the DeCallo family."

Here they come again, thought Julie as she scribbled on her pad. "The family of the actor?" She made sure her attitude was nonchalant as she asked.

Leek's whole body tensed. "Among other things."

Julie sent a side glance to her colleague.

"Yes, exactly, among other things," Teddy said. "Linked to a drug and prostitution ring. Pleaded not guilty and won."

Leek observed Teddy intently. *Of course! That was thirty years ago, or pretty close. But of course!*

"And Sishy was connected to this?"

"We could never put a finger on it. But I was convinced he was part of it."

"And Dorothea never knew?"

"Dora idealized him. She told me he showered her with jewelry, expensive furniture, clothes. She thought he was the most attentive husband in the world. The only time the idyllic image broke somewhat was when she mentioned her son. Oh... oh, my!"

"What?"

"I just remembered. The name of one of the DeCallo family law-
yers was Gother. Walter Gother."

■ ■

THEY WERE ON THEIR way out. Jane was dragging her steps behind
Julie.

But where was Leek?

Julie turned back and saw that her partner was having a private
conversation with Teddy.

■ ■

"WHAT WAS THAT ALL about?"

"I don't know what you are talking about."

"Don't play coy with me, Leek. This tea-for-two talk with the
deputy mayor. Why wasn't I invited?"

"You said it. Tea for two."

"Very funny."

They were back at the precinct, which at that time of night was, if
not deserted, certainly quieter than during the daytime. Many patrol cars
were on duty, for one. Julie looked around. A few officers were writing
reports at their desk—X was there; was he writing his report on Pablo
Ibañeta? None of them was talking. Relentless, the humid heat did not
encourage loquaciousness. Neither did overextended working hours.

Leek had made a fresh pot of coffee. Thick and dark. It wouldn't
kill their exhaustion, but it would keep their gray cells active a little
longer.

Jane was snoring in a corner. Actually, she was sitting on a chair
with her head resting on an empty desk.

Leek took a deep breath. "It's the past rushing back and hitting me in the face, Julie."

"Explain."

"Where shall I start?"

"In the beginning."

"No so simple. Let me just say that I knew Teddy when he was a young prosecuting attorney. Still in his twenties. An assistant, actually. And I didn't remember the name. Just the face."

"Really? Didn't look that way. Not till you two started a private conference, at least."

"I knew the face was familiar, albeit changed." A pause. "But familiar, why? Because we had just looked at photos and compared his features with Doug Sishy's? Or was it something else? That's when he mentioned DeCallo. And Doug Sishy. That specific connection. I was young myself—even younger than you are today, dear. And while in court, I tended to confuse them, you know."

"Confuse them?"

"Yes, they were wearing similar suits. One was in the courtroom and one at the witness stand; one was that young attorney."

"You mean, Sishy and Teddy. Sishy, I assume, was at the witness stand for the DeCallos. And Teddy was the assistant prosecuting attorney. And you had trouble telling them apart."

"Yes, let me explain. I...uh...I *inverted* things. I expected Sishy to be sitting at the prosecution table and Teddy to sit with the public in the courtroom. I thought Sishy was Teddy, and vice versa. Like the way sometimes people confuse their left and right. It was sort of people dyslexia. Does that make sense?"

"They looked that much alike?"

"No! That's my point. It's as if there was one man they were making a movie about, and one actor playing the part. Well, the actor doesn't really look like the real character. But, he knows how to make believe just by imitating the original's expressions. Roughly, it was something like that. To make things worse, one man had a slight limp, and the other didn't. And back then, I could never remember which one of the two had it. The limp was hardly noticeable, that's one excuse; Sishy and Teddy were not the main actors in the unrolling drama back then, that's another. Compared to the overwhelming presence of the DeCallos, well, these two looked insignificant, to tell you the truth. The main excuse was my youth and inexperience. Little did I know back then that Sishy would be a name that would be so significant in my professional life."

A beat.

"But Doug Sishy would come back to my life later."

"Was he the guy with the limp?"

"Yes, he was."

"Did you notice something weird about Teddy's walk? Is that the real reason why you stayed and talked to him?"

"There was no limp. As I said, Sishy's limp was hardly noticeable at that time."

"Sishy worked for the DeCallo clan, you said earlier. What did he do exactly?" Julie finally asked.

"He was an intermediary. He supplied them with narcotics and young women—many from US ghettos, but also from Asia, the Philippines, Santo Domingo—who thought they were being hired by a modeling agency."

"White slavery."

"Yes." Leek swallowed hard. "Yes. At the beginning, they give these women luxury items, beautiful lodgings, things they have never known in their lives. Then they drug them. And soon, it's over ..."

Leek didn't finish his sentence. But Julie guessed what her part-ner could not express. For she had heard rumors, then verified those rumors. Something similar had happened to Leek's niece. She had been one of them. When she could not afford to buy drugs, his niece had sold her body. And received coke as a recompense. And was deprived of it until she sold herself again. And so the vicious circle never ended.

But it had for Leek's niece—for she had overdosed. Whether vol-untarily or involuntarily had never been established.

Of course, Leek never talked about his niece. And Julie never asked. Did he know that she knew?

He knew that she was a cop to the bones, so he had a pretty good idea.

But Leek was a man of secrets. Not only an old cat, but a sphinx of sorts. It dawned on Julie that he was not unlike Jane. While the Russian woman was flamboyant, he was reserved. While she was loud, he was soft-spoken. While she went into expansive gestures, he adjusted his mustache. But they were two sides of the same mir-ror. They hardly spoke about themselves. They both carried baggage where pain was packed tightly at the bottom, for no one to see.

A while earlier, Leek had declared Jane "charming." This com-ment appeared no longer odd to Julie. These two, as different as they appeared on the outside, recognized themselves.

"In any case," Leek continued. "I kept a file on Sishy. But although I was sure he was involved, I couldn't knock him down with solid proof. I watched him, I followed him, and he played me."

"You were never able to lock him up."

"I got him arrested for traffic violations, hoping this would lead to more revelations. But the man was as sly as an eel. As I said, he played me."

"Playing you, Leek? I thought that was not possible."

"He had a good cover. He owned several businesses in Jersey."

"Good spots to sell narcs as well and make shady deals."

"Of course."

A beat.

"Dorothea never knew? You never talked to her while investigating on her husband?"

"God, that was such a long time ago!"

"You must have talked to her."

"Of course I did. She was self-effacing then, though, easy to forget."

"And when she was murdered, didn't you make any association?" Leek suddenly turned very pale.

"What's wrong?" asked his partner.

"Me. Me. That's what's wrong, Julie. I failed. I failed miserably."

"What are you talking about?"

"When Dorothea Sishy disappeared—that is, before we even knew she had been murdered—I just saw it as another case. I didn't even associate her with Doug Sishy."

"In your mind you had buried Doug Sishy. Case closed. How many cases did you go through since then during your—what—forty year career as a cop?"

"Thirty-eight. Still. That's a name I should never have forgotten. I need never forget this name. But I did."

"For Chrissake! What you need is a good night's sleep."

Leek ignored Julie. "And I didn't pay close attention to Ms. Sishy back then, either. As I said, she was self-effacing. Or I wanted her to be. She was the good wife. The good wife, you understand. Convinced that her husband was an honest businessman. Or at least played the part very well. It was hard to tell, and I had little time for her well-intentioned smiles, obsessed that I was by her husband's chicanery." Leek shut his eyes for a second. "And indeed he was a businessman, the owner of several successful gardening stores. Not only did that sound legitimate to her, but she seemed proud of her husband's commercial savvy." After a moment's hesitation he added, "And then my niece died. Did I talk to you about my niece?"

No answer.

"You found out, didn't you? Of course, you did! I wouldn't expect any less of you, dear. You look a bit like her, you know." Julie smiled. Swallowed. Nodded.

"I held Sishy responsible," Leek continued. "That's why Sishy is a name I should never have forgotten. Because it feels as if I had betrayed my niece." A beat. "Back then, I was set on revenge. I would get him. "

Silence.

"And I almost did."

"What happened?"

"I went undercover, changed my appearance."

"No more mustache, eh?"

Leek drew a sad smile. "I played a drug dealer, made contact with Tony DeCallo—"

"The Godfather, I presume?"

"Yes. I assured him that I could provide quality cocaine for a good price. DeCallo was reluctant at first. But I managed to convince him. I could provide a few ounces for free, so he could judge for himself. He accepted. A week later he called me and placed an order. He would send one of his men to pick up the merchandise."

"Let me guess. That man was Sishy."

"Correct. I had backup that night. I was to meet him in a club in Jersey. But before I could have him arrested, he recognized me and managed to escape. But I was determined. I would get him."

"He recognized you. I thought you had a disguise."

Leek shrugged. "Shortly after that, he called me. 'You'll never get me,' he said. And I never did. He died a week later."

A beat.

"But now, I don't know anymore," he continued. "Or rather, the nagging thought that this devil has resurrected somehow won't leave me alone."

The two cops swallowed brain juice in unison.

Jane's snoring flew across the semi-deserted precincts.

Julie put her coffee down on Leek's desk and rubbed her eyes.

Leek went to the coffee machine, poured himself another cup, and went back to his seat. "Remember when I mentioned him being cremated?"

"Vaguely. I remember you talking about his dog."

"His German Shepherd. Who disappeared at about the same time he died."

"So he would kill his dog and have it cremated in his stead? What kind of funeral parlor would accept doing that?"

"DeCallo Funeral, my dear."

"So they're in the prostitution, drug, and death business."

"These are all variants of the death business, don't you think, Julie?"

Julie yawned. "True. But you need sleep. And I need sleep."

"You think I am going crazy?"

"You're the least crazy person I know. But fatigue—"

"Here's the scenario I have worked out in my head," Leek said, ignoring his partner's hint. "First, there is a hurried cremation. The

DeCallo funeral branch might have informed Dorothea that by cremating him, they did her a favor. Sishy's accident happened in one of his Jersey stores and he was so disfigured that they decided to cremate him as soon as possible. That way, Dorothea would remember her husband as a good looking man."

"And you think she accepted that explanation?"

"I think that when one's heart is broken, other parts of the self malfunction as well. The fact that her beloved German Shepherd had disappeared as well didn't help. So she accepted whatever the DeCallos were telling her. And why not? They organized a fancy funeral service, sent her beautiful flowers, took her to dinner or sent restaurant food to her place, and minimized the burial costs. Come to think of it, they might have paid for the whole thing. They also helped her sell the gardening tool stores that Sishy hadn't had time to liquidate. They might have taught her a thing or two about finance and management, especially if they liked her or took pity on her. They can be as easy with sentiment as they are with bullets. But business is never out of the question. I bet they retained some fees after the sale. Still, it helped Dorothea see the future without too much financial concern."

"At least she had that," Julie said. "It probably helped her start her Open Page bookstore."

"Indeed."

"As for him, he probably had plenty of assets besides his stores."

"With his extracurricular occupations, absolutely. Plus loads of cash. If he is alive like I think he is, he's probably doing what he did before under another name. Or at least selling drugs while keeping a completely legit business."

"In that case, Dorothea might have recognized her dead husband somewhere. And she let him know she found out he actually had not died."

"And he killed her." Leek swallowed some coffee. "The irony is that Dorothea was so traumatized by the loss of her husband that she only dated men who looked like him. A form of denial. A way to bring him back to life. But when she found the real thing, that was the end of her."

He placed his cup on his desk, and Julie saw that his hands were shaking. "How many cups, Leek?"

■ ■

"I DON'T KNOW HOW many. But there are a few more things we need to discuss." Leek joined his hands, as in prayer.

Julie looked at her empty cup. "It's gonna be one of your all-nighters, ain't it?"

Leek massaged the bridge of his nose. "Jack Teddy mentioned the DeCallos' lawyer. Walter Gother."

Julie ruffled through her notepad. "Yeah, I know. And we visited the son this morning, didn't we? The artist." After a pause, she added. "Weird, isn't it? Maybe all the money we found in his place didn't come from Dorothea. Apparently, he had a rich daddy. So he can afford being an unsuccessful artist. Plus, Dorothea—"

"Who doted on the one she thought was her long-lost son." Leek finished his partner's sentence.

"Was, too, her son," mumbled a sleepy voice.

The detectives turned toward waking Jane with questioning eyes.

"Do you know what happened, Mrs. Dzhugashvili?"

"It's clearer now. I had dream."

After convincing Jane that, no, the New York police did not have vodka, or even whisky, at their station, Detective Leek brought her a cup of coffee. She began narrating her dream.

"Once the Sishys were poor, or at least in debt. He was developing his gardening tool business, but was in trouble with banks because he did not meet deadlines. At that time, Dorothea got pregnant. They couldn't afford baby, so they thought about abortion.

"One day a man came into gardening store. Sishy was upset and hardly paid attention to him. The man was displeased. He said something like, 'Come on, man! Don't you want my business?' Sishy apologized. They started talking and, for some reason, Sishy mentioned his financial problems and then baby situation. Man's face lit up. 'You don't have to abort baby,' he said. 'Let me adopt him.' He gave him business card. 'Think about it. Talk to your wife and call me.' Those were his last words before he left tool store.

"On his way home, Sishy thought of idea. The man had said there would be no adoption paper, no agency, just a handshake. Sishy could sell baby directly to him, no question asked. Sishy was tempted. After all, man was lawyer and, judging from clothes and hair, successful lawyer.

"Before he talked to his wife, he called lawyer."

"What was the name of the lawyer?" asked Julie.

Jane pressed one index finger on her forehead. "William...no... Walter. Walter Gother."

The two cops stared at each other.

Jane swallowed some coffee, made a face. "Could be a little stronger, but will do."

"Maybe you're thinking about Irish coffee, Jane," said Julie.

"I'm thinking about feeding your fooking tongue to New York pigeons right now," retorted Jane.

"Go on, Mrs. Dzhugashvili."

"Sishy made deal with Gother. Sold baby for million dollars."

"How did Dorothea take it?"

"Not good at first. She refused to sell baby. But Sishy managed to convince her. She met Walter Gother and wife Sandra. She liked Sandra. Sandra couldn't have children, see. And she couldn't go to adoption agency because of her husband. He was lawyer with lawless connections. Mafia connections. So business between Sishys and Gothers happened. No one knew Sishys sold baby because no one besides them and Gothers knew Dorothea was pregnant. And she hid at Gothers' house when pregnancy started showing. She and Sishy were Gothers' guests until doctor made house call to deliver baby. And there was shenanigan with Sandra wearing pregnancy clothes. Apparently, charade worked.

"Sishy became rich. One million dollar is lots of money. And. . .how old is son now?"

"Walter Gother is twenty-eight now," said Leek.

"So twenty-eight years ago, a million was even more money. Sishy could pay banks, develop business. And he got even richer."

"His gardening business picked up fast, eh?" said Julie.

"That took time. But he got other jobs, thanks to Gother's connections."

A beat.

"During sale of baby, Gother had detected ruthless businessman in Sishy. Sly man too. He knew godfather needed intermediary man for prostitution and drug business."

"Do you mean the DeCallo Godfather?" asked Leek.

"Yes. Gother thought that Sishy could work for him. After having him run small errands, Godfather gave Sishy more and more responsibility. Some in Atlantic City. And Sishy's gardening tool business became good cover."

"Didn't Dorothea realize that her husband ended up working for the mafia?"

"Dorothea was smart woman, but she had stupid adoration for husband. It was not totally her fault. Sishy had double personality. Or was good actor. And great manipulator. After he had her give up baby, he gave her many, many presents. He took her to trips. In his way, fookhead loved her. The way he knew how and with part of him that was not completely evil."

"Perhaps we should talk to Walter Gother Sr. tomorrow," Julie suggested.

"Don't waste time. Gother is dead," said Jane.

"Natural causes?"

"Man ate like pig. Yes, natural causes, Julie."

"And Sishy, is he dead?" asked Leek.

Jane kept silent for long minutes, her eyes seemingly unfocused.

"What?" Julie said finally.

"It's Dorothea. She's here now. And very agitated."

"And Sishy, is he dead?" Leek repeated.

"No, he's not dead," Jane finally said.

"Then where is he?"

"I wish I could tell you."

"Would Dorothea know? Can you ask her?"

"Did he kill Dorothea? Did Sishy kill Dorothea?" Julie suddenly asked.

Jane closed her eyes. "Yes, he killed her."

"Then where is he?"

■ ■

LEEK HAD GONE AND taken Jane home. Julie was still at the precinct, reading the report on Ibañeta that X had thrown on her desk a while earlier. Pablo Ibañeta was not as shady as Walter Gother Jr. had implied. Unless he meant by that a talented artist. Ibañeta had a major show in the city at the moment. And, she saw, another one in Los Angeles. She happened to know the guy who made that one happen—Marcel Pavie, who was friends with her and Zoe. He was a brilliant artist with integrity. So things looked beyond reproach on Ibañeta's side.

What was his relationship with Dorothea? Well, X had the answer right there: "I doubt there was anything intimate between him and Dorothea Sishy," the report read. "A year ago, she showed some of his work at her bookstore. He also mentioned they became good friends and that when he learned of her death, he cried. He is presently living with another man whom he calls his 'partner.' He displays very few masculine attributes. I suspect he's not the killing type. Plus, he has no motive for murdering a woman who seemed to give him emotional and professional support."

That X was not the king of objectivity was no surprise. That he was a macho fuckhead was no surprise, either. But his report was clear. He didn't smell any form of criminality, and despite her reservations, she knew that X was a pretty good nose.

She looked at her watch. 3:15 a.m. Pavie would be up. It was only fifteen after midnight in LA, and Pavie was a night owl, anyway. She dialed his number. But she already knew that Ibañeta was not connected and would not lead her to the author of Dorothea Sishy's murder.

Pavie confirmed with fervor and a French accent thick enough to slice with a butcher knife.

■ 21 ■

THE TWO MEN CLIMBED into the cab. The driver was colored and smiling. He did not look like a US native. They wondered how good his English was.

"Quoi?" The cab driver said. "Je parle français. Uh. . .Moi. . .uh, me. . .from Guadeloupe."

Just good enough to program the GPS map and the fare, but that was it.

This suited them fine. They could talk freely.

The driver saw in the rearview mirror that the two middle-aged men resembled each other. Dark hair thinning on top. Thick lower lip, embonpoint on one, and not a lot of leanness on the other. Brothers? Cousins, maybe?

"You think he did it?" one man said.

"Clip her, you mean?" responded the other.

"It was kind of gruesome, even for him."

"You think he bumped her off with the chainsaw? Nuh! She probably got iced beforehand. Hands around the neck. Don't take long. He was good with his hands that way. Got called in for beef in the Black Book many times."

"Dude was on our ghost payroll."

"They only found the torso."

"Yeah, Venus de Fucking Milo."

"Nice touch, the drop-off in The Lake."

"And he's dead, I mean, officially. Can't accuse a dead guy of killing his wife, can ya!"

"Smart dude. But why now? She couldn't have found out he wasn't really dead, could she?"

"Don't think so. I mean, we cased the whole thing pretty good. Flowers and all the fancy shit. I mean, she was a bit upset 'bout the cremation 'n' all. She wanted to see her husband one last time, she said. We had to make up a story. A whole fucking novel, if you consider all the details we put in tryin' to convince her."

"Yeah, that's right. He'd been rubbed out by a car just as he stepped out of his Trenton gardening joint, is what we told her. Was disfigured. She wouldn't want to see the man she loved looking like squashed meat. So it was better that way. And he had wanted it that way. Said so in his will. Blah, blah, blah. You know chicks. They want a whole fucking book to tell a simple fact."

"Except here, 'twas no fact. 'Twas pure fiction."

"Good thing she bought it. She was upset about the dog, so maybe that helped."

"Poor pup."

"Yeah. Whacked it himself with pills. Dog died of an overdose. 'Magine that! 'Twas a big animal, beautiful, a Shepherd. German Shepherd."

"At least the dog got a nice place for eternal rest."

A beat.

"I wonder how she never figured out that he was, you know, connected. One of the Godfather's main buttons."

"Hey, chicks don't wanna know, you know what I'm saying?"

"Yeah, but this one was nice. Like a lady, ya know. Too good for a skipper like him."

"Yeah!"

"Yeah. But with a good business head. Legit 'n' all. That bookstore she had on 66ᵗʰ did pretty damn well. Another chick is running the business now. Says she'll probably buy it, but keep the name Open Page. My kids go there. Well, the ones among them who like to read, at least. The wife goes there too. There is a little coffee joint inside as well."

"A café."

"You been there?"

"Yeah, once or twice. To make the wife happy."

"It's a nice place."

"Yeah. Unlike my own kids, I like books."

"Yeah, true. You're the intellectual among us."

"I liked her too. She was really helpful. You'd explain what type of readin' you liked and she would show you the right books. Never missed. Didn't deserve to be knocked off like this."

"Did she know who you were?"

"Yeah, more or less."

"What duya mean?"

"She knew me from DeCallo Funerals. She just was not sure which brother I was."

"Well, didya make it specific?"

"Nah." Pause. "He should get burned. We could plan a hit. I bet we haven't lost the touch."

"Hey! Hold it! We know nothin'. We heard nothin'. You hear?"

"Okay!"

"Yeah! Plus, how are you gonna find him?"

"Well, his fake identity."

"You think he kept the same name all these years? My bet is that he changes IDs every few years. Like at every election or somethin'. If he's got dough, he can grease the right people for new driver's licenses and passports. We used to grease a member of the FBI. They're good at making fake shit look real."

"He disappeared in the first place because of a cop who was tailing him. Almost got him too. The guy had a weird name. Hercules something. Looked a bit like a Mustache Pete. Could have been one of us. A real good dresser, like the Boss. Hercules Tick."

"Leek."

"Yeah, that's right. Leek."

"He's the one investigating her hit, can ya believe it? I read about him in the papers."

"He was on TV the other night, did you see?"

"Yeah. Thinks her killer might not be in the city."

"Mm. I wonder if he suspects he is not dead. Leek is one dangerous dude."

"I'd say."

"Almost had us locked up, remember? Good thing we managed to get a judge on our side. Pinched Eliot, though. But Eliot is one stupid button. Couldn't even work for the Mickey Mouse Mafia. The idiot deserves to be in the can."

"Now the family went straight."

"A little deal here and there, and that's about it. Mostly numbers, lottery."

"Yeah. Since there's an actor among us, we've got to act legit most of the time."

"You miss the old days?"

"Eh, layin' low ain't bad. I've popped my share, but it started to get old after a while."

"So you're cool with it."

"Yeah, for the most part."

"Me, I miss the shakedowns sometimes. And the rush, you know."

"The rush? You read too much!"

■ ■

"JULIE?"

"That you, Aimé? You got something?"

"Think so."

"Can it wait? I'm beat. I'm still at the station and I really need a bath and then solid hours of snoring."

"Sorry, Julie, but I think you may want to hear this."

Julie took a deep breath, looked at her empty coffee mug, and closed her eyes. "I'm all ears, I guess. All tired ears."

"I had interesting customers in the cab tonight."

"Who?"

"DeCallos. I think two brothers of that family. And they talked about the Dorothea Sishy murder."

"Were they specific?"

"No name was mentioned, if that's what you're asking. But Dorothea's bookstore was and so was the chainsaw. There's little doubt it's our case, Julie."

"Okay. So, shoot!"

"Sishy staged his death. They used his dog ashes to do it. This means he's still alive."

"Under what name?"

"This isn't news to you?"

"There seems to be a bit of a consensus about the resurrection of that bastard. So do you have a name?"

"Not yet. The DeCallos seem to think that he changed IDs several times."

"I would, if I had become the obsession of a guy like Leek."

"Leek knew Sishy?"

"Long story. But, yes."

"Does he think Sishy is probably the murderer of his widow?"

"Yup. And I am starting to believe it too."

"So we may know who the murderer is. That's one step ahead."

"The next step is where. Where is he? But I want the next step to be zees, Aimé," said Julie. "When the hell will I get my zees?"

PART III

■ 22 ■

Crime Weapon Found in Small PA Town Backyard
BY BETH BROWN and NICHOLAS PRIEST

The chainsaw found in a backyard in Noliar, PA, on June 20 seems to be connected to the murder of Dorothea Sishy. How a crime that supposedly occurred in New York City managed to branch itself out 350 miles away from there is an additional puzzle detectives Leek and Hoffman must face.

The yard in question belongs to a Jane Dzhugashvili, a Noliar resident since 1989 and a native of the former Soviet Union. Dzhugashvili being the original name of Joseph Stalin, we wondered if aforementioned Noliar inhabitant was somehow related to the infamous Secretary of the Communist Party. The Noliarites we questioned had different opinions on the matter. Among them, about 15 percent are convinced that Jane Dzhugashvili is indeed related to Stalin; about 35 percent think that, albeit historically unfortunate, the name probably is also associated with ordinary Georgian people,

and not just famous criminals in history. The other half of
the population is either neutral or doesn't know who Joseph
Stalin was.

Who the fuck said that? He thought as he fixated his eyes on *The
New York Times* website. He had trouble handling the keyboard with
his bandaged hand. The wound had been deeper than expected. The
woman really had wolf teeth. And that stiletto heel...

But she hadn't seen his ruse. When the basement door had shut,
she had believed him when he said it was now locked from the outside, that there was no way out.

Matter of fact, he had at one point believed there was no way out
for him, either. Not because the door couldn't be opened, but because
she had his gun in her hand, pointing at him, and she seemed ready
to use it.

It would have been too dumb to die in a basement with a bleeding
Latino cunt and a couple of rats.

He had taken advantage of the nanosecond when her attention
had been derailed toward the door to suddenly jump on her, grab the
gun, and hit her on the head with it. After she had fallen unconscious,
he had made a small incision on her throat with the broken china.
And he had left her there, locked up in the basement, slowly bleeding
on the cement floor, like a pig.

Of course, he had explored other options. He could have shot
her.

That would have been that. The problem: he didn't have a silencer.
And since this was not hunting hour, the noise of a firearm would
have been noticed in the neighborhood.

He didn't want that, to be noticed.

Things had to go on as usual. He had to follow the routine. Go to the same hangouts. Chat with neighbors the friendly noncommittal and meaningless chat: "Hey, how is it goin'? Too hot. Yeah, tell me 'bout it!" Do the same-old-same-old little daily act.

He could do that. He'd done it before.

As far as letting her suffer and die a slow death, it was not so much a problem, either. Not yet anyhow.

The other option would have been to strangle her, like he did with Dorothea.

Dorothea. She had made a life for herself with her fucking bookstore. A good, successful life. He had gone there, several times, to check it out, smiling at Dorothea, always from a distance. And then getting closer and closer. And the bitch had not recognized him—at least he thought so. Until she asked him for a date.

Dorothea, asking a guy for a date!

Why?

Something had to be done.

They went to dinner first. She seemed at once lost and happy. Poor Dorothea, always confused. Well, not that confused upon reflection. She had confronted him, and she was angry—angry that he had disappeared and pretended to be dead. And he, angrier yet, that she had found out. She had observed him at Open Page, and his limp had been a clue. Not so much the limp itself, but the way he controlled it, which resulted in a funny walk. Someone else had been suspicious of that limp, Dorothea told him—someone who had actually slept with him. Someone who had recognized his voice. For Dorothea's Cuban friend had an excellent memory for voices. Limp and voice, similar height and build, too much coincidence. Dorothea had compared notes with the bitch, who had gone to New York especially for that purpose. "So now I know, you see, darling!" Dorothea had told him at the restaurant with her little voice and her mousy face and those dark eyes from where all expression had vanished. As if part of her were already dead.

How come he had forgotten that these two had been high school buddies? That they had kept in touch?

Dorothea did talk to him about a Latina girlfriend. But Dorothea was as chatty as they come, and like a good husband, he probably listened to a third of what she was saying. Not even that. And when friends came for a game of bridge, or gossip, or whatever it is women do when they meet, he had been at work. Sometimes they were there when he came back home, but he was too worn out to notice faces. Fatigue made them all look the same. That, or he didn't give a shit about his wife's chick friends. Corazon Morales, that's the name he remembered when Dorothea mentioned her Cuban friend. But he wasn't good with names. Now he knew.

Cruz Mojada. That was the name. His wife's buddy. Now in his basement.

Well, the two buddies would meet the same destiny, how was that?

A good thing he didn't clean up the chainsaw. He hid it in a spot he knew in the Jersey woods, the spot where he had taken Dorothea and done away with her. He thought about burying her there, without bothering to cut her up. But there were dogs in the neighborhood, not to mention hungry life in the wild, druggies who did their smokin', sniffin', shootin'. So one way or another, the body—parts of it—might be found. He had bought a new cordless Makita. Had never tried it on human flesh before. Everything had worked fairly smoothly. Carrying a cut up body was, frankly, a piece of cake, especially if there were trash bags at hand. A piece of cake. That was kinda funny. He chuckled.

On his way to the City, he had figured something out. He would throw Dorothea's body parts in various trash cans. This would occupy the police for a while. He even decided to be systematic about it. The head, he threw in a garbage container in the northern part of town. The left arm, in Upper West Side; the right, in Upper East Side; the right and left legs, in the southwest and southeast, respectively. He had driven through New York all night. But he knew the city well by heart. And Dorothea had loved it, every part of it. So in a way, he was paying a tribute to his late wife.

His late widow. Ha, ha!

The torso was harder to deal with. He had to wait until the following night, and by then he knew exactly where he would place it. The Lake in Central Park. He had double-bagged it, added a couple of heavy stones. There were those who dealt with sick pets that way, so why not?

In the end, he was satisfied. He had learned how to get rid of bodies with the best—the DeCallos, now retired. And with them, he took lessons about mystifying the cops. Giving them false clues, creating rock solid alibis when there were none.

When he had learned Leek was investigating his wife's death, he had almost shit in his pants at first. But after swallowing a few shots, he had laughed. Booze always helped. As smart as the guy was, he wouldn't be able to solve this one. He couldn't accuse a dead guy of killing his widow, could he?

Could he? There had been the story with Leek's niece. He didn't know who she was when he drugged her and pimped her, until it was too late. Had Leek forgotten about that? He frowned. The Mustache Guy was not the type to forget. Damn! But he was old now, and having that dyke as a partner surely wouldn't help. Although he had to admit, he had seen her on TV and the bitch looked tough.

He scratched himself between his legs with the hand that was not bandaged. It was still hurting. That stiletto heel in his balls had felt like a dagger.

He went back to reading.

The other half of the population is either neutral or doesn't know who Joseph Stalin was, he read again.

> "Jane is part of the decor, part of our lives," stated Dzhugashvili's neighbor George Mutant, a retired music teacher. "A colorful one, to be sure," added Dick Carson, another neighbor and Mutant's partner.

> When asked what Dzhugashvili did for a living, most Noliar residents responded that the source of her revenues was somewhat of a mystery to them, that for a long time she had been nicknamed "Jane Docash" because of her ability to live comfortably with no apparent salary. They assumed that she might have once been married to a wealthy man.

> We visited the Moisol, Noliar's most popular bar, and a place regularly frequented by Jane "Docash." There, a Gus Mahler and a Greg Yeany commented upon the Russian woman's reputation as a "witch." Other people present at the Moisol, including bartender Natalie "Nat" Kinders, dismissed such comments with a "Jane is just different. She's Russian." Mrs. Lara Clement, a retired USPS employee living across the street from "Docash," claims that NYPD detectives visit Jane on a fairly regular basis and is thus assuming that her neighbor is employed by the NYPD. When asked in what capacity, Clement responded, "As a psychic, of course!"

This opinion is not shared by the majority of the PA town. It is interesting to note, however, that the detectives who visit "Docash" are none other than Julie Hoffman and Hercules Leek.

Another detail that intrigued us was Dzhugashvili's current nickname: Chainsaw Jane. "It's because of the way she prunes her trees," says one neighbor, and many in Noliar concur.

Although the chainsaw found hidden under cut branches contains blood that forensics have matched up with Dorothea Sishy's DNA, most Noliar residents—with few exceptions—appear very protective of Dzhugashvili.

When part of Dzhugashvili's house burned earlier this month, it was assumed that it was an accident. But some wonder if this was not set up by the owner herself who, when the chainsaw was found, was miles away from her property. We subsequently learned that she is now living in New York City with Zoe Zimmerman, a fiction writer who was linked to the murder of a New York publisher over two years ago.

So that's where the bitch went! Not that it mattered anymore.

Noliar Police Chief Dumasky has issued an order of arrest for Jane Dzhugashvili and solicited the participation of the NYPD in the matter. He is presently facing resistance from Detectives Leek and Hoffman, who claim that, due to the lack of prints on the chainsaw, there is no proof that Dzhugashvili was involved in Sishy's murder. They also question the motive.

Other disturbing elements include the facts that Hoffman and Zimmerman, both Noliar natives, are very close to Dzhugashvili.

We asked Chief Dumasky what made him look into Dzhugashvili's backyard. "Phone call," the Chief answered. When asked if the call was anonymous, Dumasky refused to respond. We confirm here that the chainsaw was free of fingerprints, and we were offered the theory that the criminal wore gloves. But why would a murderer take such precautions on one side, leave blood on the other, and do such a poor job at hiding the weapon?

Eh, eh! Yeah, why? To confuse detectives, maybe? Leek, in particular? He thought it was a stroke of genius, if he could say so himself.

He had used a voice changer when he called the police and asked to personally talk to Chief Dumasky. That dick had never recognized him. "Who are you, ma'am? Are you sure you don't want to leave a name with the police, ma'am?" He had bought that device at Spy-Guys online, and it was fucking fantastic. His voice could be transformed into anything. In that case, he thought using a truly feminine voice with a high pitch was a nice touch. He sounded demure and innocent when he denounced that bitch Jane. And Dumasky, all cop that he was, was a sucker for ingénues. Any time a young woman who wanted out of a speeding ticket would smile a fake dumb smile, Dumasky wouldn't be able to resist it, and the girl would walk away from the station without paying a dime. And that's how he had sounded, like a fucking ingénue. An ingénue swearing that she had seen Jane hiding a big tool, a big heavy tool that kinda looked like a chainsaw, Chief. Yes, she had seen Jane hide that thing in her backyard. And no, she couldn't tell him her name. For she was so, so scared. Did she remember where in her yard, exactly? Dumasky had asked. Well, she had seen Jane move dead branches that were piled up at the far end of her yard and put her Makita there and then buried it under them.

"Well, Miss," Dumasky had declared, "I'll look into it."

Hey, hey! Now the bitch would really deserve to be called Chainsaw Jane.

Time to take care of another bitch, though. The one in the basement.

Bah, there was still time. She was dying slowly. He might not even have to finish her off.

■ 23 ■

THE EVENING SUN CAME uninvited and in a soft orange glow through the window, adding a shine to Zoe's red hair, caressing her face with its fading warmth. This usually brought a smile. Tonight she ignored it, remained seated in the living room sofa, smoking, thinking, alone.

Zieg II had had enough of the day and had retired in his deluxe quarters. Lots of corridors and tunnels and toys in his new cage. Not that it made much difference, for the rat's favorite spot was Zoe's shoulder. A plastic toy shaped like an old shoe came in second and as the place he had assigned as his bed.

Marc had locked himself in his home study for hours. He had skipped dinner. How the hell could he turn his back on Jane's cabbage rolls? Doctors didn't know the meaning of life, Zoe decided.

Aunt Jane did.

Or did she?

She acted as if nothing happened. She had acquired her fifteen minutes of fame overnight. She was the main topic on several shows on CNN last night, with a full array of self-important experts discussing the validity of her order of arrest. Leek and Julie were there too, explaining that Chief Dumasky's action was hardly legal and certainly not justified. Where was the proof that Jane Dzhugashvili was a murderer? Dumasky himself had given an interview and stated that finding a weapon linked to a murder in her own backyard was proof enough. When the issue of planted evidence was addressed, it seemed the cops avoided the question, and that included Leek and Julie.

What was going on?

Jane had watched it all with Zoe and without any reaction, and then had gone to bed. Ever since she had heard of her order of arrest, read about it, and seen her picture on TV, she had exhibited no visible reaction.

Instead, she cooked as she had done continuously for the past couple of days. Albeit worried about the fate of her waistline if this went on for too long, Zoe had enjoyed the treat. But even if the rolls, all juicy and tender, enchanted Zoe's palate, there was something bitter left in her mouth.

Worry.

Jane didn't act like Jane. She might be, understandably, in a state of denial. Still, the woman's calmness started to freak Zoe out. Something was wrong.

Definitely.

For instance, Jane no longer talked about Cruz, a topic which, up to recently, had been her obsession. When confronted with the color yellow, she made a face but hardly complained. And Julie and Leek had failed to take her with them while continuing their investigation. Their excuse: better keep a low profile under the circumstances. The people they were interrogating at this point were routine, with hardly any motive for killing Sishy. If they felt something fishy, then they would call on Jane. But hopefully, the "Jane arrest controversy," as they called it, would have faded into the background at that point.

To all this, Jane had complied without a single protest. The woman who preferred to bathe in controversy rather than shy away from it had all of a sudden turned Zen on her. Frankly, this gave Zoe the creeps.

And what about Julie and Leek?

These two didn't give a damn about whether or not they were in the midst of contention. Hell, she suspected they strove on that shit. Cops and confrontation = Coffee and donuts; that was the equation. If Julie had been somewhat tense on Fox TV with Gilda Snider, she had acquired media savvy in a jiffy. When Harold Queen had stared at her with the glance of an owl that had once again forgotten about his eye appointment, Julie had responded with twenty-twenty baby blue vision and given firm, clear answers. The bitch looked good. A young Sharon Stone—hot enough to get a date with Jodie Foster.

As for the Mustache Man, he hardly moved. In total control, totally feline. Words measured, precise. Too measured, too precise, even for him? In any case, he was the most fascinating member of the whole panel.

Zoe crushed her cigarette in the ashtray, tapped her mouth.

Still, the whole set of circumstances was strange.

Aimé, who never failed to flirt with Zoe when he saw her, appeared preoccupied.

Julie was almost polite with her. What the fuck was that? Cool Cat Leek was on the verge of rudeness. All relative, of course. Great manners, as always. Only his voice had acquired a bit of a staccato. She figured nervousness. And nervousness piercing through a steady, smooth creature made Zoe uneasy.

Zoe had counted the number of "fooks" pronounced by Jane lately. Her mouth had become a tundra as far as obscenities were concerned.

If swearwords were money, this would be total financial collapse right now.

And how long had it been since Marc had made love to her?

What the *fook* was going on?

■ ■

SHE KNOCKED ON MARC'S study door.

"I am not there, Zoe!"

"Don't give a shit. If you don't open up right now, I am going to smash your fucking door!"

"You and your 120 pounds, darling!"

"Hey, unlike you, I am eating Jane's cuisine. Gaining strength by the minute."

"Can't you wait?"

"Counting: one, two, three..."

Zoe boom-boomed the door with her fist.

No response.

She took a few steps back, ran toward the door. She was about to charge when Marc opened up. Zoe had no time to put the brakes on, continued on her course for a second or two, hit a chair, then fell on her ass. Marc started laughing.

"Ha, ha! Very funny!"

"Actually, it was, my little bull. Let me grab the matador's cape and chant 'olé'!"

Still grounded on her ass, Zoe scratched her head. "Was I? I mean, like a bull."

"Of course, sweetheart. Like Ferdinand the Bull."

Silence.

"Come on, Zoe! It's pretty funny. You're pretty funny. I'll never get bored, I'll tell you that."

Zoe hugged her knees. "You won't, will you?" She chuckled. "Help me up! My ass hurts."

"Not big enough after the consumption of Jane's rolls?"

"You want it bigger?"

"I like it just the way it is."

"Well, help me up, then! I'll let you give me a massage afterward."

"Oh, I have your permission to give you a massage?"

"You're so sexy when you're sarcastic! Now help me the fuck up!"

Marc finally bent over and lent a hand to Zoe. She grabbed it, pulled him toward her on the floor, and climbed on him. "Gotcha!"

Marc laughed again. "You're crazy."

"I just like to ride you, baby. I may be Ferdinand the Bull, but you're my stallion."

"Then don't transform the stallion into a eunuch. You're hurting me right now."

Zoe hesitated before relieving the pressure ever so slightly. "Now you're gonna tell me why the hell you keep locking yourself up and ignoring me."

Marc tried to free himself from Zoe's grasp. But he had to admit, the woman was pretty strong for her size.

"We need to talk, Marc."

Marc's lids closed halfway. After a moment of quiet, he nodded. "All right. Perhaps it's best that you know."

Zoe tussled Marc's hair. More gray coming. And a more deeply lined forehead, she observed.

■ ■

ZOE LOOKED THROUGH THE window in Marc's study. Against the black silk of the sky, a big moon was watching.

"What should I know?"

She was sitting on a Charlotte Perriand chair (one of Marc's collector's pride), facing her guy and his desk—a huge table, really. It was hard to tell it was a designer's piece at this point, as it was drowned by a zillion enlarged photographs, portraits mostly; these were roughly divided into two untidy piles: two mounds of camera-captured faces, a kaleidoscope of eyes and mouths and expressions in disarray.

So atypical of her guy, Zoe thought. Had Dr. Neatfreak gone to rehab and been replaced by a defective copy? Where was the real Marc? The real Jane? The real Julie? Where had they all gone?

It seemed the Sishy case had emptied them of their substance. Nothing was what it seemed. Everything was dislocated. Disassembled.

Just like Dorothea Sishy's body.

She felt nauseated.

She gestured toward the desk. "What's that?"

"Two things," he said.

"You might have gone to med school, but apparently they didn't teach you how to count there. I see more than two things."

"Right." Marc removed his glasses and rubbed his eyes. He picked a few photos from the pile on the left, got up, and handed them to Zoe as he sat down next to her.

Three men, one woman.

Zoe leafed through them, spending moments with each face. They looked like prom pictures. One dark-haired boy smiling shyly; another, almost as dark, but with cheeks like plumb fruit and a grin that welcomed the world. The other two, both blond, looked like brother and sister, features-wise and expression-wise. There was a lot of humor on these two open faces. A similar light shone through these four pairs of eyes: hope, hope extended, and the certitude that life would be succulent for them, at least most of the time. No hint of sadness in any of them, not even of solitude. Every face told the story of family barbecues, July 4 with Old Glory sweeping the air by the entrance door—canoe rides, fun love, and explosive laughter at silly happenings. Every face was a postcard. Every set of cheeks held a pinch of naiveté, which, in this day and age, was becoming a luxury item. That's what Zoe read, wondering what part was observation, what part was writer's imagination. She said, "What am I looking at?"

"Those were soldiers," Marc extended his arm to collect the pictures. Zoe unwittingly petted the photos before handing them to Marc. "*Were?* How about kids? They were *kids*!"

"Actually, they're still alive. They returned from the various wars we tend to have abroad."

Zoe nodded. *Better see war elsewhere than right here at home. Gangs, guns, drugs, pimps, and working girls, hey, no sweat! C'est la vie, you know. Maybe exporting death was a form of denial.*

"There's always a somewhere, isn't there? A somewhere with bombs. A somewhere to test weapons. A somewhere to occupy. Do you know we are deployed in all continents? Africa, as in Kenya? Australia? Germany? The Philippines? Portugal? Greece? Over thirty countries. I checked." Marc looked at the photos then placed them back on their stack.

Zoe stared at the pictures, flattened faces chaotically thrown on top of each other. She couldn't help comparing them to piled up bodies from concentration camps or war fields, on their way to the pauper's grave.

Identities were irrelevant well before their death.

"And sometimes these kids return home literally without a face," Marc continued.

So that was it. These photos...were just photos. And what Marc would attempt to reconstruct was remarkable, but deep down, just an abstraction. These kids didn't exist anymore. Zoe closed her eyes, swallowed. But the tears she was trying to repress rushed like a furious sea in her stomach—and then her heart, her head. She clenched her fists. She wanted to punch something. Instead, she grinded her teeth.

"You kept asking me, Zoe, why I went into cosmetic surgery. I mean, after all, not only do I help women give birth, but I treat breast and ovarian cancer as well. You always thought that was some noble task. All I can say about that is that doctors, by and large, don't get used to the loss of lives—least of all on the operating table. We say we do, but we don't. Not really. Show me a cynical physician, and I'll show you someone who can't cope with loss. Cynicism is just a hiding place."

It was a cascade of words. A dam breaking and letting the river go crazy. It was Marc fighting against fatigue. Zoe listened.

"So why this business of vanity, as you put it?" Marc put his glasses back on, forwarded a loving smile to his rebellious, now attentive, redhead.

"So that's what you were doing?" She bit her lower lip. "Trying to give faces back to these kids?"

"Yes, with Dr. Fontaine we started a free clinic. Needless to say, we're in debt." Marc looked at his desk. "I might have to sell this Le Corbusier table."

"Not the Le Corbusier. We did the deed on the Le Corbusier!"

"We've got to find money somewhere."

"How about rich donors? Fontaine got quite a few wealthy patients."

"And they're giving. But to do well, we need money to keep flowing. We're trying to get a grant from the government."

"You mean, from the people responsible for the disfigurements in the first place."

"You think we're naive?"

She shrugged. "You might get your money. Hush-hush style, though. They might have you sign papers, insinuating—using government Byzantine jargon, of course—that you're gonna get your dough if you don't show pictures of faceless kids."

"Dr. Fontaine said the same thing. He also said that this government might be suffering from double-personality disorder. Giving, saving countries in distress on one side. Killing on the other."

"Buying a conscience on one side, giving themselves permission to destroy again on the other. It's the story of the abusive significant other on a megascale."

"I hope you're wrong, Zoe."

"Me too." A beat. "Doesn't the government have cosmetic surgeons for cases like this?"

"Poorly paid, overworked. Doing approximative work. We're trying to reconstruct the identity of these kids. Their dignity."

"You're such a fucking idealist, my Médico, my little Che Guevara. I–I. . ." She started crying, then sat on Marc's lap and gave him a long, passionate kiss. Marc returned it and they remained glued together for a small eternity, pounding hearts echoing each other like tribal drums sending urgent messages.

His hands climbed underneath her T-shirt, caressed her breasts. They both rose; he pressed her against the wall, lifted her skirt, and soon, he was inside her.

It was a long, intense, sinuous breath.

It was a moment of belonging, of disappearing, when nothing mattered, when space and matter had no role to play. Just two bodies, anchored to pleasure and loving, yet oblivious to flesh. Being at once all and nothing.

And at that precise moment of being and nothingness they came.

When it was over, every object that had seemed irrelevant, non-existent, returned to its rightful place in Marc's office. All seemed tangible again.

"I thought you liked it sitting," Marc said.

"And missionary-style. And on top. My taste is eclectic. Gimme the Kama Sutra, baby."

He grinned, hugged her and kissed her hair. "I promise we will do more of that soon. Now, would you let me work for a couple of hours?"

"Let me think. Uh. . .no!"

"No?"

"No, nope, niet."

"Come on, Zoe!"

"What's in the other pile?"

"Oh, shit!"

The bell rang.

"Do you mind getting it?" said Marc.

"You think you're saved by the bell, don't you?"

The bell rang again. Zoe walked to the door. Julie stood there, cargo pants and dark cotton jacket, short-short blond hair, briefcase in hand, and stern expression on face.

Zoe let her in. "Where's Mr. Mustache?"

"Interrogating more suspects with X."

"X?"

"Exeverria. Detective-in-training. Sexist pig, but talented. Go figure."

A beat, after which Julie added, "It's awfully quiet in here. Where's Jane?"

"In her room. She's not too talkative these days. I enjoy the cook, but I miss the 'fook.'"

"Are there any of her cabbage rolls left?"

"You hungry?"

"A bit."

Zoe took Julie to the kitchen, put a couple of rolls in the microwave, and pulled out a beer from the fridge. Julie swallowed drink and food in ten minutes.

Zoe placed her hands on her hips, tapped her foot. "You do that and keep a flat stomach? You bitch!"

Julie belched.

"So that's how you do it." Zoe directed her index finger near Julie's feet. "What's with the briefcase?"

"Is Marc in his study?"

"Why you ask?"

Julie frowned. "Well, is he?"

"You need to see him?"

"Yup."

"I'm coming with you."

"It's not necessary, Zoe."

Oh, but it is! Zoe thought. She was not sure Marc knew that Julie had had a brief affair with his ex-wife, but if he did, then control management would be necessary. Granted, these two were professional. Granted, control management was not her forte.

"Oh, but it is! I really need to know what the hell is going on."

Granted, she was as curious as a chamber pot, as Aimé liked to say.

"Okay, you can come, but you'll have to shut up."

Zoe made a grand gesture and let Julie walk ahead of her. "After you, ma'am!" Julie led the way and Zoe raised her middle finger.

Without looking back, Julie responded with a similar gesture.

"**B**ROUGHT YOU NEW PHOTOS," Julie said.

Marc threw a stern glance at Julie. "I hardly had time to take a look at these," he said, shuffling through one stack of pictures. "Or the ones Detective Leek sent me. He's not with you?"

Julie shook her head. "Forget about these for now. We'll concentrate on the ones I'm bringing today." Julie removed enlarged black-and-whites from her briefcase. "And besides the hard copies, I've got this as well." She removed a chain from her neck with a sixteen mega-byte Cruzer. "There are more details in these."

Marc extended his hand. "Okay. Let's see." He picked up the Cruzer and turned his back to his visitors for a second with his rotating chair. Facing now a huge shelved-in wall inhabited by books and technology, he planted the Cruzer in one of his laptop USB ports, hit some keys, and rotated back toward Julie and Zoe. He now grabbed the hard copies, adjusted his glasses, and examined them in silence during long minutes. "These look like untouched faces," he finally said. "I'll make sure with the computer but—"

"These first two are points of reference." Julie rose slightly from her chair and pointed at the top picture Marc was holding. "This is Doug Sishy, twelve to fifteen years ago."

"It was taken at a restaurant, judging from the decor," Zoe said.

Doctor and cop turned to her.

"I thought we made a deal," Julie said. "You could stay here if you shut the hell up."

"Don't you know her better than that, Julie?" Marc bent toward the photo.

Julie shrugged. "Actually, Zoe's right. It was taken at a restaurant owned by the DeCallo family."

"How about this one?" asked Marc. "It's more recent, but the face looks the same."

"That's Walter Gother II, the son Sishy allegedly sold for a million bucks."

"Nice guy," Marc commented. "Well, the program I have will go through bone structure and the like."

"So you can figure out what transformation a face like that could have gone through," Julie said.

"Hopefully."

Julie picked a few more photos from her briefcase and handed them to Marc one by one. "And vice versa, I suppose. Your program can deconstruct a reconstructed face and go back to the original."

"Yes. Should."

The doctor was being cold, really, really cold, Zoe observed. "I need a sweater."

Doctor and cop turned to Zoe. "What?"

"Never mind."

"This here is Steve Knight," Julie resumed.

"I know the name," Marc said. "He's the famous photographer, isn't he? First impression: he doesn't look like he underwent plastic surgery. Funny, he bears a resemblance to Sishy. Not a brotherly resemblance, but he's got the same general bone structure. Smaller chin, though. Smaller eyes as well."

"Jane doesn't think he had anything to do with the murder, but we have to be thorough."

Marc lifted one eyebrow. Could cops really take mediums seriously?

"This here is Jack Teddy. Deputy Mayor for Legal Affairs. Smooth politician. Looks younger than his years. Might have had surgery."

Marc nodded. "Might. I'd say at least some Botox. Cheeks are a little full for a guy his age. And possibly a lift some years ago." He moved his fingers across the photo. "If I added a few wrinkles and caved in those cheeks, he would look a lot more like Doug Sishy."

"So you're saying that if Sishy had surgery, he might look like Jack Teddy," Julie remarked.

Marc scratched his head. "Tell me, have you checked the measurements of these guys?"

"What duya think? All these guys have approximately the same height as Sishy—give or take one inch."

"Interesting," said Zoe. "So Dorothea only fucked guys who were as tall as hubby."

"Jane said Sishy never recovered from the loss of her husband," stated Julie.

Marc took notes. "The law of compensation, you think? Trying somehow to find Sishy in other lovers?"

And never stopping her search, Julie thought. The victim had collected lovers. Consuming them one after the other, like junk food. Sometimes handling two affairs at the same time. Was it more than compensation? Revenge, maybe? A way to say "fuck you and fuck off" to a husband who had died on her—abandoned her? And put her on the verge of financial ruin, to top it all.

"It seems that Dorothea recognized her dead husband, and that's what caused her death."

"How do you know that?" Marc asked.

"Reliable sources," Julie answered.

"You mean, Jane, right? How can you believe in that stuff? You, a cop, Julie!"

"Yeah, because science has got it all so much under control, explaining it all! It is all so fucking static and stable. No theory ever collapses," Zoe declared.

"Unlike your mouth, unfortunately," Marc retorted. "What about the rotation of the earth? Is that a theory that collapses? How about Uranus taking eighty-four years to orbit around the sun?"

"Up yours, Marc!"

"What!"

"Up Uranus!"

"Will you two stop! We've got some work to do here," Julie hit Marc's desk. She got the expected result: startling the couple and keeping them quiet for a second or two. After a pause, she addressed Marc. "You've got to admit that the resemblance of the guys Dorothea dates is creepy. And the possibility that one of them could be Sishy, after all the info we ended up getting, is not that far-fetched."

Marc nodded. "In any case, you're the cops, and I'm the doc. So I apologize. I'll let you do your job, and I'll do mine." He turned toward his laptop once more, pressed a few keys. From where they sat, Zoe and Julie could see diagrams of face structures placed side-by-side with photographs. "I'll just ask this," Marc said without turning back. "How sure are you Doug Sishy is still alive?"

"I'd say seventy percent sure," Julie replied.

"Well, I am not sure you are going to like what I am going to tell you." Marc was scrutinizing his computer. "At first glance, any of these guys could be your guy."

"I thought you said Knight probably didn't have surgery."

"No surgery. *Or* top surgery. Sishy's chin's wider. To make it smaller might be the tough part here. If Sishy didn't want a better look but a slightly different face, I suppose that could be done. But why?"

"What do you mean?" Julie asked.

"If he wanted no one to recognize him, why wouldn't he change his face completely? Wouldn't that make more sense?" Marc advanced.

"Leek and I talked about it. But remember that we assume Sishy faked his own death. If people believed he was dead, he probably didn't feel the need to change his appearance that much."

"How about assuming someone else's identity?" Zoe asked. "Jack Teddy? There is a real Jack Teddy, right? Do you suppose Sishy would have killed the real Teddy and become a politician? What about his family and friends? Wouldn't they have seen the substitution?"

"You've got to admit, Julie, that's a bit far-fetched." Marc turned back to face the two women.

"But I do. Leek does as well. But we're at loss here. Plus, get this. I did research on Teddy. Leek knew him first when he was a young prosecuting attorney. What he said made me want to dig into his private life, so I did. After some lawyering first on the prosecuting side and then as a defense attorney, he left the country and married someone in Guatemala. The daughter of a wealthy hacienda owner he had met when she was a student at Columbia University. Lived there for ten years, came back to the US alone. Wife died of natural causes. Apparently she had a heart condition." Julie made a face. "And Teddy was an orphan, who went from one foster home to the next."

"Very convenient," said Marc.

Zoe turned to Julie. "So what you're trying to say is that Teddy would be a perfect target for a shit like Sishy. After so much time spent away from home, someone changes. So had Sishy decided to kill Teddy and take his place, who would have noticed."

"Especially if Teddy was a loner in the first place." Turning to Marc, Julie added, "You mentioned Botox treatment."

"Yes. Most likely."

"He could have done that in a rather ostentatious manner, for the friends who thought he looked different in the first place."

"What you mean, Julie, is that he would have added another element that was different, so that in the end, his friends would have assumed that the difference was actually due to the Botox and not anything else," Marc said.

"It's true that people mix things up. So Sishy would have bet on their selective memory," Zoe stated.

Julie nodded slowly.

"You don't sound too convinced. It's your own theory." Marc shuffled through a few more photos. "What about Knight? Would it have been possible to take his identity?"

"He travels a lot. We see the photographs, but not the photographer."

Zoe made a face. "Stealing an identity is one thing. Stealing a talent is another. How could Sishy reach the level of a pro like Knight?"

Marc surprised everyone when he declared. "Photographers display only a small percentage of their work and store the rest away."

"What he's trying to say," Julie started, "is that—"

"I know what he's trying to say. That Sishy could have used what was in storage. Stuff the public hadn't seen. He actually didn't need to take a single picture." Zoe got up, looked through the window.

"I am not sure I buy that. And what about the son? Doesn't Knight have a son?"

Julie nodded.

"Well, wouldn't the son be able to see the subterfuge? Wouldn't any son?"

Julie remembered how swift Knight had been with a needle, how fast he had given an injection to his son, and how reluctant he had been to put him in an institution. "Yes. Under normal circumstances," she told her friend who, she observed, had grown increasingly tense.

"It could be something simpler," Zoe said, her complexion now red. "Couldn't Walter Gother have killed Dorothea? After all, she sold him! Sold her own son!"

"He's one of the suspects, yes." A pause, after which Julie added, "What's with you?"

"And what's that fucking shenanigan with the chainsaw found in Aunt Jane's backyard? And all the media talking about it? And you cops acting as if it were routine?"

Zoe's hands were shaking. "Something's wrong. I can feel it. All she does is cook, smoke, drink her vodka, watch TV. She's down on her swearing. She's so withdrawn."

Julie took a breath and surveyed her surroundings. It did feel awfully silent. Too silent—a silence unquiet in its very thickness. She gave a few instructions to Marc about the photos, then rose and told Zoe, "How about we pay a little visit to Aunt Jane?"

Still trembling, Zoe smiled, nodded, and got up. Julie wrapped a protective arm around her friend and the two women went to knock on Jane's bedroom door.

■ ■

AND KNOCKED.

And knocked.

And knocked.

"Jane, hey Jane!"

"Are you sleeping? It's not your sleeping time just yet!"

"I've got Julie here. She really needs a drink of vodka! Aunt Jane!"

Silence was the only answer. Zoe made a face, opened the door. The bed was made, the room empty. "Jane's gone!"

"Maybe she went to the drugstore to get cigarettes." Julie entered the room, looked around, opened the closet. Naked hangers, vacant shelves, empty drawers. Her eyes were drawn to a white spot on the desk. "She left a note."

Zoe sat on the bed. "Well, what does it say?"

Julie read: "*Dear Zoe, I have to go. I am sorry I went without telling you, but you might have tried to stop me or to kidnap me like you did in Noliar with Aimé. Here is the reason why I must be out of here: I am worried about Cruz. I have been worried about her for a long time. But I had a bad dream about her last night. She was in a cave and bloody. I am convinced her life is in danger. And I am also eighty percent positive Dorothea Sishy's murderer is not in New York. Not 100 percent yet. That's why Julie and Detective Leek must keep on investigating right here in the city. Even mediums like me can be wrong, even if they don't make as many mistakes as, say, doctors.*"

Oh, that love story between Aunt Jane and Marc, Zoe thought.

"*Detective Leek is probably right to think that Doug Sishy is the murderer. I believe I know where he is. I hate to say this, but I feel stupid: he was right under my eyes at one point. I should never have left Noliar.*

"*I must go and try to save Cruz. If I die in the process, it's not important. I have not always lived a good life, but always an interesting one. So in case*

I don't see you again, you should know that I always thought of you as the daughter I never had. Julie too. Tell her I love her like I love you. With you two I had the opportunity to be a real mother—a true <u>mamulya</u>. So I will not sign as 'Aunt Jane' this time, but as

Mamulya Jane.

P.S. Marc is okay, I guess, specially for a doctor.

"You were out of Swiss cheese. I got some and put it in your fridge for the rat."

Julie swallowed tears.

Zoe let them run. And yet, despite being choked up by emotions, the writer in her couldn't help notice that Jane's spoken word and Jane's written word were in fact her written *world* and her spoken *world*. In that missive of hers, no article had been guillotined. Oh, Jane! Oh, Jane! And the ocean of tears that had invaded her body just rushed out now with a fury.

Julie started sobbing but grabbed a tissue from her jacket pocket and dried her face immediately. And then she hugged her buddy Zoe. For the first time in a long time, the two women hugged each other. "What the fuck, Julie, it's okay to cry. I know you're a cop, but you don't have to be a macho girl all the time!"

"No time for that now." Julie got her cell out, hit a key. "Aimé? You free? Listen, I need you to go to Noliar right now! Jane is about to do something stupid and dangerous and we've got to stop her. Call Dumasky. Here's what you do..."

■ 25 ■

INTERROGATING OTHER SUSPECTS WITH X, that had been the pretext. Julie had seemed a bit surprised at first. She assumed he would have been eager to examine the photographs of possible suspects with Dr. Trenton and, had his memory not played another trick on him, she would have been right. He was, in fact, looking forward to the doctor's diagnosis, as the Sishy investigation seemed to be stagnating. Not so much stagnating, but dancing the fandango. One step ahead, one step back, one step around. And back again.

Until it had dawned on him that it was actually about steps. About a particular step, a particular way of walking.

A limp.

And he had seen that limp not so long ago without realizing that he knew it.

It was on June 4, as he and Julie were leaving Mrs. Dzhugashvili's house and two people, a man and a woman, were having a discussion in the middle of Heritage Lane. From the rearview mirror, he had noted the woman's quick gestures as the man shrugged and then walked away with a limp.

The woman was Cruz Mojada, Mrs. Dzhugashvili's friend, who had disappeared.

The man. Well, he knew now who the man was.

■ ■

HE OPENED HIS MEDICINE cabinet where everything was alphabetically ordered and grabbed his razor and shaving cream and placed them on the right side of the bathroom sink. On the left side, a pair of small scissors was awaiting. He took hold of them, took hold of the left side of his mustache, and started cutting. When he was done with that side, he progressed to the center, then to the right. With a small Dirt Devil, he swallowed the cut hair that had fallen and spread over the floor and sink.

He filled the sink with warm water, spread shaving cream above his lip, took hold of the razor, and proceeded to remove the remains of his mustache.

He washed his face, washed the razor, washed the sink.

He adjusted the collar of his shirt, his tie.

As he left his apartment, there was his navy blue sports jacket and his hat awaiting on a hanger by the door. It was too hot to wear either one. But he never went outside without either one. He made sure there was no spot, no speck of dust on his vest as he smoothed it out over his rounded belly. The mirror was telling him he had gained a pound or two, but it didn't matter anymore. Soon it would be all over.

He made sure all the locks were in place, although he had doubts that was necessary.

That he would see his abode again was far from being a certainty.

He called for the elevator and went down.

■ ■

THE NEW OPEN PAGE owners were puzzled when they saw a funny-looking man with a hat and a three-piece suit enter the store and then grab books at random without so much as looking at them.

Dorothea Sishy would stamp the books with a "Friends of the Open Page," something most customers appreciated, and the new owners had kept the tradition.

Today, however, there was a new cashier who had yet to learn all the store customs. She had rung all the items the funny-looking customer had bought but had failed to affix them with the Open Page special seal. When she had forgotten to stamp the books, the man had smiled at her a strange, sad smile. She had noticed his large green eyes. After briefly explaining things to her, he had left with his books, among which were John Le Carre's *A Most Wanted Man*, Sartre's *Being and Nothingness*, and three copies of Ionesco's *The Bald Soprano*, all marked with "Friends of the Open Page."

"What's a bald soprano?" the cashier had asked the man with the cat's eyes.

"Oh, it's about a man and his wife who don't recognize each other," he had answered.

■ ■

NOW HE WAS ON I-80 West driving an inconspicuous old Taurus he had found at a used car rental place off 50ᵗʰ Ave. He made sure to choose a vehicle that had not been cleaned and had even stopped on the way to muddy up the plates to hide their New York registration. He needed to be as invisible as possible. And for that his own vintage

Chevy wouldn't do. Nor would an official Crown Vic. If he was on a mission, it wasn't an official one.

On a mission to Noliar, and speeding. The old Ford still had potential.

He remembered a Tarot card Mrs. Dzhugashvili had drawn for one of their cases. The Nine of Wands. So close, and yet so far away. That's what the card meant, the Russian medium had said.

So close, so far away.

He pressed on the gas pedal. Harder.

■ ■

WHEN HE SAW HERITAGE Lane, he turned off his lights. He knew that less than a quarter mile further, he would have to make a right on Drumerer Street. It wasn't even a street, but a cul-de-sac, if he remembered correctly, and it practically faced Jane Dzhugashvili's house. It would be easy to find, a dead end facing a burned house.

Miserable bastard, he thought.

There it was. Drumerer, on his right. And on his left, trees like sick columns and a house disfigured by fire. His jaws were clenched. He didn't use the turn signal, just let the Taurus glide slowly into Drumerer. He parked a hundred yards away from the house at the end of the cul-de-sac, grabbed books, closed the car door as gently as possible, and directed his steps toward the house.

This was an ideal spot, wasn't it? No immediate neighbors. And a good parcel of woods surrounding the house, a surface large enough to make shady deals—and why not smoking, or shooting, or snorting those deals—without being disturbed. Big enough to mute disturbing sounds too. It looked like he had found the perfect niche.

Well, up to now.

■ ■

IT WAS SEVEN A.M. on June 18 when Shawn Doogy's bell rang.

Who could it be? Doogy wondered as he dragged his feet to the door.

Facing him now was a man with big green eyes, a hat, and a blazer.

"Yes?" Doogy asked, his voice still sleepy.

"Selling books," said the man who was now holding a thick volume.

"Sorry, not interested." Doogy was about to close the door, but the man held it open with his foot. "Please, sir. These come from a special store. Look, look here at the stamp. See? Friends of the Open Page. Have you heard of it, sir? The Open Page? It's a fine store. Up to recently, it belonged to Dorothea Sishy. She was a fine, fine woman. But, see, she was murdered. Savagely murdered."

Doogy grew suddenly very pale. "Get the hell away from here!" He went to slam the door, but the man articulated, "I wouldn't do that if I were you. Under this copy of *Being and Nothingness* is a gun. If you don't let me in, I'll shoot."

Shaking, Doogy still managed to evaluate the situation but saw that he had no choice. "Who...who the hell are you?" he asked when the man was inside.

"You don't recognize me without my mustache? Me, I do. I recognize you. I finally do."

■ 26 ■

JANE DECIDED AGAINST FLYING or renting a car. For one thing, she didn't like driving long distances. Trucks got in the way and furthermore, they looked like gigantic, square, stupid dicks. Who needed that? She didn't care for planes, either. They tended to lose contact with the ground for one thing and then dance a funny ballet on top of clouds. And, it was a fast means of transportation only if you lived in the city. As it were, she would have to take a cab to go the airport, which would take forty-five minutes. Then she would have to wait for the next available flight to Pittsburgh. Two hours, she checked. Maybe more, as when was the last time a plane left right on time? In Pittsburgh, she would have to rent a car. Paperwork from business bureaucrap (ink-shitheads, as Zola would put it) would add at least an extra half-hour. Pittsburgh to Noliar was a two-hour drive. Under such circumstances, the bus was just as fast. Well, almost. Certainly less complicated.

And more anonymous. They were less thorough with IDs at bus stations. Thanks to CNN and Chief Dumasky, she was now famous, at least temporarily. People might be hungry for their own fooking fifteen minutes and turn her in. She figured bus travelers had less money and possibly more criminal records and, should they recognize Jane, they would see her as a special member of their family. Something like that.

And she had been right. No one seemed to recognize her or no one gave a shit, which was fine with her. Of course, dusk was setting in and faces lost their contour, just like nature. This helped too.

She had a window seat. She looked around to make sure that no one from Leek and Julie's team had followed her. She had left soon after dinner, having checked earlier in the day with Port Authority and found that there was a bus leaving for Noliar at 8:30 p.m. Marc was studying photographs in his home office; Zoe was smoking in the living room, lost in thought. Taking a French leave had been easy. Physically at least. For Jane wondered if she'd ever see Zoe again.

The cab ride from 72nd Street to 225 Park Avenue South, where Port Authority was located, had been a very brief one. A fifteen-minute walk could have taken her to the mythic Grand Central Station on 42nd and Broadway. Too bad there was no train going to Noliar.

In the bus, there was a young woman drowned with fatigue and harassed by two toddlers. There were men with features rugged up by sun, rain, wind, and manual work—road construction workers, probably. There were elderly women knitting. A few Mexicans nesting together. A good number of African-Americans. And a smell of chocolate, cookies, and cheap perfume that blended curiously with the bus defective air conditioning. Few among the bus occupants voted Republican, she would make a psychic bet on it. And an increasing number were giving up on Democrats as well. What was the difference between parties anymore? Details? Who could afford details with this economy? The government had become a two-headed monster. A nasty, stupid monster. A monster that simply didn't get it. For she saw the composite word "fed up" carved into the bottom of each pair of eyes in the bus. Even kids, even the driver—especially the driver. They were all on the same journey, different destination, but with the same certitude. None of them knew where it would end.

One needn't be a psychic to realize that their wallet was nearly empty, their bank account filled with air and promises. Thirty percent interest promises.

She had been right to come here. She felt at home amidst them, different skin, different language even, and common pain. It was like family—you spoke to some members, fought with a few, and ignored others. This here was America, with faces that spoke of hard work, of getting up again, finding a job, somewhere. Soon, soon, please! This here was tired America. Discouraged America. And to this, to the country that had saved her, she wanted to say, no, no! To these people, she wanted to say, no, no! Don't you know you've got the power? Don't you know they—the others—want you to think you don't, but you actually do? You've got the power, what *fook*! This country was built by people who were told in their respective native lands that they hadn't got the power, and look what they did. They showed the assholes! And Wall Street and the two-headed monster could be shown again.

That was what Cruz often said to Jane—at least when she was not showing her collection of tasteless miniskirts or array of sex toys. "We can get punched in the face by people getting obscenely rich on our back so many times. But wait, Jane, we'll get these shitheads someday. Mark my word: we'll get them." Jane missed the spark of her Latina friend who doubled as a bowling champion—a balls champion of sorts as well, she suspected, but that was another story. She wished Cruz could use big Wall Street guys as pins. They would all fall, rigid and silly, for Cruz, legs bent, right hand grasping, and ass in the air, never missed. The idea brought a smile—erased instantly, like steps on sand tsunamied by a wave. For Cruz was weak now, perhaps dying. Of that, she was sure. She had received signals in her last dream, a call for help. She hoped she could save her friend's life. If she couldn't, the bastard who did that to her would get it. If Cruz lived, the bastard would get it as well, for torturing her friend. And murdering the friend of her friend. "Tous les amis de mes amis sont mes amis," the French liked to say. All the friends of my friends are my friends. That's how she felt. Dorothea Sishy had come to her and become her friend. For the call for help had come from her and so had the other clues. The cave where Cruz was locked in. The dream spoke of a cave in a house. Translation: a basement.

Next to Jane sat a wiry thirty-something woman, with a white coif seated on her dark hair and a nineteenth century dress. Her hands rested on top of her lap and a serene half-smile rested on her face. Amish. Mennonite, actually. At least she wouldn't be bothered, Jane assumed. Or would she? Mennonites were polite people, but usually quiet. She would be left with her thoughts. Right now, she needed some rest.

She curled on her seat and dozed off.

■ ■

WHEN SHE WOKE UP, she almost screamed. The Mennonite woman was crocheting something yellow. That yellow she had just seen in her dream.

"Are you okay?" the Mennonite woman asked. "You were making crying sounds while you were asleep. Perhaps I should have waken you up or—"

"I had nightmare," Jane said.

"Oh, I am sorry. I *should* have woken you up."

"Would you mind removing your knitting or covering it up?"

"Oh, dear. Are you allergic to wool?"

Jane hesitated. Looking at her fellow passenger, she couldn't help connecting her to a mujik she once knew. "Something like that."

"Oh." The woman pulled out a thin cotton shawl from her shoulders and covered her knitting with it. "It's for my baby, you see. I'm expecting. I don't know if it's going to be a boy or a girl, but I do so like yellow."

Jane swallowed. "May I touch your belly?"

The woman laid her dark blue eyes on Jane. "Sure."

Jane placed one hand on the woman's abdomen. "Girl. It will be girl."

"I was hoping so. This bright yellow might be too bright for a boy. And I've got three sons already. I love bright colors. In the community they think I like them a little too much." The woman emitted a soft giggle.

Jane looked through the window. Night, a few stars and a round little moon with a know-it-all grin were doing their invasive number. A comfort zone for Jane, usually. But not tonight. She closed her eyes then looked back through the window's tinted glass, through the blur of nascent tears.

Little smiling moon. Yellow little moon. And Jane couldn't take it. She collapsed, her body bent, almost cracked, trembling through the weeping. The woman put her knitting aside and handed an embroidered handkerchief to Jane, who whispered a thank-you.

"I am a good listener. Perhaps you can tell me," said the Mennonite woman.

Jane dried her tears. "Perhaps I could. You look like nice woman. I know you're nice woman."

And then the words flooded in their little corner of the bus. "Let me tell you fairy-tale style. Once there were two little girls living in Russian countryside. They lived in small farm. This was USSR. Most farms were collective—sovkhoses or kolkhoses, as they were called. But some private farms were allowed, and little girls lived in one of these. Girls were twins, did I tell you that? It was like same person with two bodies. Two peas in pod. When one was away for five minutes, other little girl missed her. They loved to run in fields, climb trees, swim in river during summer. They had to feed chickens and milk cow before playing, of course. Go to school too. All that. Their mom and dad were good, hardworking people. Not too tough with little girls, considering farming conditions. At night, Mamulya was always knitting. Knitting, knitting. Like you. Sometimes clothes, sometimes hats or shawls. Sometimes blankets with crochet. Sometimes strange little yellow things. Little triangles. Little girls were asking about funny yellow pieces. Was Mamulya knitting triangles that she would assemble later to make beautiful bedspread or tablecloth? Mamulya didn't answer little girls, and Dad just shrugged when they turned to him. Meanwhile, little yellow wool shapes sprouted like dandelions and at one point dad had to make big chest to put them all in. Still, no blanket, no bedcover, nothing. Just shapes. Sometimes, Mamulya was crying when knitting with yellow wool, and Otets—"

"Otets?" the Mennonite interrupted.

"Yes. But listen. Pronounce: Uh-TYETS. It's Russian for 'Dad.' Well, when Mamulya was like that, Otets took her in arms, petted her hair, and then shrugged some more, like man who tried to comfort but didn't know how. Little girls hugged her too. But they didn't know what else to do. So they with their Otets just smiled at her and watched her knitting. Other times, Mamulya was very happy, though. And she played with little girls, and they danced together.

And Otets didn't shrug then; he just smiled. Happy times came when she didn't touch yellow, see."

The Mennonite woman discreetly returned her knitting into her bag.

"One day, little girls went to chest with yellow triangles and found piece of fabric there—like band with yellow triangles. One of top, the other slightly below and upside down. The two triangles were shaped like star."

"The Star of David," the Mennonite said.

"Exactly. But little girls didn't know what it was. They just saw star—not specific sign or symbol. So they took band and played with it until Otets saw them and asked, 'Where did you find that?' Little girls explained. It was their turn to ask, 'What is it?' At first Otets shrugged. 'Nothing,' he said. 'Put it back where you found it.' But sisters were stubborn and said, 'Not until you tell us what it is.' And Otets shrugged again. He was shrugging daddy, see. And he said, 'Ah, why not?' So this is story Mamulya told him.

"Mamulya was living in Paris before she met Otets and came to USSR. Her family, which was wealthy and aristocratic, had immigrated there before Russian Revolution. In the 1940s, she met history professor at Sorbonne. Laurent Lévi was name. He was specialist of tenth century Spain. That was time when Moors had emirates there and Jews, Moslems, and Christians lived together without killing each other. So this professor knew everything there was to know about Christianity, Judaism, and Islam. He probably knew everything there was to know about Mamulya too. I'll make story short. Because story of Jewish Holocaust has been told many, many times. But there have been many holocausts, right? In all five continents. How about economic holocaust, that's international; we kill working class little by little, making them work more and more and paying them less and less and creating sad life for them. That's killing spirit, see. And what are we without spirit? Oh, I should shut up. But I am tired, worried, and angry. And I see too much."

"You see too much—what do you mean?"

"Nothing. I am just old woman in need of good vodka." Jane turned to her road companion and smiled. "Think of baby. It's always best to think of baby."

"How about your story?"

"Okay, let me end story. Professor was taken to concentration camp. All that was left of him was band with Star of David and book he had written with title that went like this: *Going Forward by Going Back—How Islam Established Tolerance Ten Centuries Ago.*

"Mamulya took book and band and then left for USSR against her parents' wish, met Otets, married, and had twin girls. But she never forgot Laurent, even though she married other Jew."

"Was the name Levi too?" asked the Mennonite.

"The name was Dzhugashvili. That means 'son of Jew' in Georgian."

"Wasn't that the name of Stalin?"

"Yes. But Stalin didn't like name. That's why he changed it into Man of Steel—that's what Stalin means. Didn't treat Jews well, either. But Otets liked name. And he secretly didn't like Stalin. Because you couldn't dislike Stalin other than secretly."

The bus met a bump on the road and every passenger went through a quick and involuntary riding exercise.

"I understand why yellow is such a painful color for you," the Mennonite said after the road became even again and her body settled back on the seat.

"No you don't. Yellow was okay, even after story of Laurent Lévi, even when Mamulya knitted yellow triangles. But sister got sick, got pneumonia, was treated with bad medication, and died. I have issue with doctors too, but that's other story. And that's when I knew that Mamulya was crazy. I suspected it, but madness was mild until Nadya died."

"Nadya was your twin sister?"

"Yes. She was called after revolutionary woman Krupskaya. And Mamulya buried her with yellow triangles. First she built stars with them, then she made dress. Otets and I tried to stop her, but we couldn't. We just couldn't."

Jane shook, softly at first, then uncontrollably. The Mennonite held Jane's hand, and the night stretched and breathed and then let go of some of its darkness before the hands parted. The Mennonite woman had fallen asleep. So had Jane for a while. But now she turned on her cell phone and something made her dial Detective Leek's number. She only got Leek's answering service. Something was wrong. She could feel it from the current running through her hands. The pain was acute and continuous. She dialed again. No personal response this time, either. She closed her eyes, meditated. Again, she saw Cruz in a cave. No, a basement. Woods near that basement. A house in a cul-de-sac. So her vision was confirmed. She knew where she had to go. There was Leek in that house as well, about to get in deep shit.

Her plan had been to come and save her friend Cruz, knowing full well she might die in the process. But instead of having to face one crazy man, she would have to face two. For Leek, poised Detective Leek, had just gone crazy.

She made two additional calls, and this time she reached both destinations.

Daybreak was not there just yet, just yawning, carrying with it shapes that were still lazy, undefined; the idea of hills and valleys and forests, the stern, dignified lush that was Pennsylvania when summer was enthroned.

Noliar bus station was at the end of Main Street. In five minutes she would be there. The Mennonite woman's mouth was slightly open, her slumber quiet. Jane did not wake her up. Maybe the woman would think that the story Jane had told her was just a dream. Better that way. She touched the woman's belly, ever so gently, and then the woman's head.

She slowly ambulated toward the bus door.

■ ■

THE BUS DRIVER STEPPED down with Jane, bent toward the bus belly, opened the luggage compartment, grabbed Jane's bag, and passed it on to her. Jane thanked and tipped her.

As Jane took resolute steps into Main Street, she saw that a welcoming committee was waiting for her. A uniformed welcoming committee. She knew the two cops: Yunaw and Ayedundt.

"Jane Dzugh...Jane Docash...oh, hell, Chainsaw Jane, you're under arrest!" said Yunaw.

"Sorry, Jane," echoed Ayedundt. "I've got to say this. You have the right to remain silent. Anything you say can and will..."

Before the cop ended his Miranda Rights recitation, Jane proclaimed, "What fook!"

■ 27 ■

DUMASKY WAS WRITING AND drawing funny charts when someone boomeranged on his door. "What is it?" The Chief mumbled.

"Open up, Chief! It's...it's...it's Monkey!"

He had pulled another all-nighter. Again. To the point that the missus was wondering if he was having an affair. But after Cruz' disappearance and the work he was doing with Detective Rippon, he hardly slept anymore. And he felt they were onto something. He just didn't know what. He just had some idea. But he needed to think some more. He couldn't make a mistake, not when he was working with the fucking NYPD.

"Go away, Monkey! Some of us are working here, not getting drunk, like you!"

The boomeranging went on.

"Jeeweez!" The Chief rubbed his eyes, lifted his heavy frame, and opened the door. Monkey stood there, as wiry as ever, legs unstable, complexion scarlet, eyes bloodshot. "You need to go to detox, Monkey, is what you need!"

"I need to-to...to... tell you something...f-f-first."

Monkey entered Dumasky's office, looked at the Chief's scribbling on his desk. "What's...what's...that?" he said.

"Good, Monkey. It's called working. Notes. Working on a case. It's called none of your fucking business."

"'T'is, too, my fucking bus-business. S-s-s, sort of."

"What are you getting at?"

"I-I-I know who...did it, Chief. The guy who b-b-b-urned Jane's house, I know who that is. I-I-I saw him m-m-myself. I...I will tell you in your ear, s-s-so no one will hear."

"There's no one here!"

"Oh, b-b-but, he's d-d-dangerous! Here!"

Whoever Monkey saw or thought he saw might be dangerous, Dumasky thought, but Monkey's testimony was not reliable.

Monkey went to the Chief's ear and whispered a name.

Dumasky turned to the drunkard, squinted. "Is this about revenge, Monkey? You want to return the favor to the guy because of what he did to you?"

"Y-y-ou don't get it, Chief! What he did to me is because I knew!"

The Chief scratched his head.

Monkey fell on a chair and started snoring.

■ 28 ■

CRUZ LAY ON THE cement floor. There was some noise upstairs. Steps. That hijo de puta's steps. And someone else's. They sounded to her like gentler, more civilized steps. But maybe she was imagining things; maybe it was still that damn rat doing its fucking promenade somewhere on the beams. Steps or no steps, she had no strength to call for help. She was drained, about to leave this world. The piece of her blouse that she had tied around her neck had not entirely stopped the bleeding. She was starting to get dizzy. The burning sensation that had brought tears and screams earlier was almost gone, or she had gotten too used to the sandpaper feel inside her wound; she didn't know which. That broken piece of china he had used had really cut through. Bastard! She felt death coming to grab her. I don't want to die, she told herself. I don't want to die. She hung onto the thought, made it ring in her head like a litany. But even that was becoming too hard. If no one came, that would be the end.

■ ■

THE MAN HAD HIS gun on Doogy's back. "What's behind this door?"

"My dining room."

"Open it."

Doogy obeyed. A dark country dining table with its chairs invaded most of the room. Dishes had not been cleared, and the smell of decaying food pervaded the atmosphere. By the window stood a butcher block on wheels. While pressing his gun on Doogy's spine, the man touched the piece of furniture. "Impressive piece. Quite heavy. And appropriate, don't you think? A butcher block for a butcher."

The sound of sirens approaching.

The man lifted the window drapes. An ambulance was coming. Of course.

Doogy was standing very close to the uncleared table. Hardly moving his arms, he grabbed a knife.

■ ■

CRUZ WAS SURE HER end was near. She prayed she would die now before he could reach her.

■ ■

IT WASN'T MUCH OF a knife. A kitchen knife. But it could still do some damage. Actually, if used forcefully and precisely, it could probably kill. With a serrated blade, it would hurt quite a bit too. The man looked through the window again, gun in hand, pointed at Doogy, his other hand on the butcher block. The ambulance was almost here. He smiled. "Well, are you going to throw this knife at me or not? You better do it fast because otherwise I'll have to answer this door." The man jerked this way and that. "Well, are you?"

A bit dizzy, Doogy was about to jump on the man. Before he could do that, the man took hold of the butcher block and placed it to face Doogy.

"That won't help you, Leek," said Doogy.

"So you recognize me at last?"

"Those damn fucking eyes." Doogy positioned his knife.

"How about looking through them one last time?" Leek and the butcher block were one. With his gun he lifted the drapes one more time.

The ambulance was one block away.

"Why would I do that? You're a dead man, Leek."

"How could you say that? I've got a gun in my hand."

"You won't use it."

"Ah! You're right." Leek looked at his Glock. "I won't use it. Not yet. We've got to talk first, you and I."

"I knew it. So you're dead. This time you're dead."

"Are you scared of a dead man?" While fixating his cat's eyes on his enemy, Leek suddenly pushed the butcher block on Doogy. The piece on furniture fell on his stomach and legs, and an agonizing scream exploded out of Doogy's throat.

"Looks like these two hundred pounds of furniture have hit your bad leg. O-o-o-o-h! What can I say other than this might not improve your limp and c'est la vie. Now, if you'll excuse me, I've got a door to answer." Bending toward his victim and pointing his gun at his throat, he said, "She's in the basement, isn't she?"

■ ■

PLEASE GOD, PLEASE GOD! *Take me now! Dios, por favor!*

Cruz could hardly see, could hardly feel. She had a vague sense of floating into infinite space. This wasn't so bad. Death might not be bad.

■ ■

"WE GOT A CALL from Chainsaw...uh...Jane. She said Cruz Mojada was here, badly wounded," said the Noliar ambulance woman. Two nurses and a stretcher were behind her.

"In the basement," said Leek as he nervously showed his NYPD badge. "Hurry!"

■ ■

LEEK HAD FOUND DUCT tape in a cupboard, and used it on Doogy's mouth and joined his wrists. After removing the butcher block from his body, he had forced the man up, then down on a chair. He had then taped the man's ankles to each other and to the legs of the chair. He himself sat at the dining table across from Doogy, his Glock by his side.

"Now we are ready to talk," he said. "So how have you been, Sishy, since I last saw you? I should call you by your real name, don't you think? Not that it matters. In a few minutes you will be dead. This time dead for good.

"You're wondering how I managed to find out that you're still alive. I must admit, the DeCallos had organized your death to perfection. You probably laughed in a corner when you saw me go to your funeral. Knowing you, you probably still do after all these years. Well, what do you know, he who laughs last laughs best. When was that? A decade ago or so? No one like the mafia to do a funeral.

Especially when they own funeral parlors themselves. Little did I know, little did your "widow" know, that we were actually burying your dog instead. No open casket, of course.

"What brought your resurrection was, ironically, your wife's murder. None of the suspects fit the bill. That is, if the suspects were actually who they said they were. For indeed we played with the possibility that they might not be. Even your son was one of the suspects. The son you forced your wife to sell, remember?

"But what is that to you? You were up to your ear in the commerce of drugs, death, and prostitution. My niece, remember? My only family. You sold her drugs, then you had her sell her body." Leek bit his lips. "And then she killed herself.

"I almost got you. But you organized your death before I could do that.

"In any case, it was over. My niece was gone, but you were six feet under as well. So I could somehow go on.

"Until the Dorothea Sishy case." A pause. "She found out, didn't she?

"I told myself. Who would want to murder a successful bookstore owner like her? Of course, there are plenty of pathological cases in New York City. But this murder had a signature. A DeCallo and associates signature.

"Well, DeCallos are retired now. One of them is an actor. So they aspire to a certain degree of respectability.

"Then there were a couple of incidents that I consider mistakes. Your mistakes. First, the disappearance of Cruz Mojada. Incidentally, I saw her on the stretcher—what you did to her. Cut her throat? What were you planning to do? Have her die slowly, like they do with pigs in some places? You are a sick man, Doug Sishy."

Leek played with the Glock on the table, gliding it slightly one way and another, grabbing it, pointing it at the man who had been known by Noliarites as Shawn Doogy, the tree guy, wondering if he should pull the trigger now, then all of a sudden abandoning the idea.

Sishy's tied-up body was shaking like a willow under a windstorm.

Hatted, jacketed, and tied, Leek was smiling.

"The thing is, we eventually found out that Cruz Mojada and your wife were born in Newark. Then we learned they were good friends. Now, you did change your looks somewhat, but Ms. Mojada must have somehow recognized you and contacted your wife. You're shaking your head. Well, I might be wrong about some details.

"Maybe you were curious about her bookstore, and so you went. Ah, I see that's it. And she did recognize you, and you had to kill her.

"And when Ms. Mojada learned about her friend's horrific death, she started to think." Leek plunged his gaze into Sishy's and didn't utter a word for lengthy seconds. "You were going out with her, weren't you? It amused you to go out with a friend of your wife and not be recognized? Of course, you were supposedly dead. And you were the landscape man in Noliar. Everyone knew you. Everyone hired you to cut their branches. Maybe put up a new shrubbery. It seems like such an innocent occupation. You always managed to get good covers, didn't you? Mm. The real business is drugs here too, isn't it? Drugs are rampant in rural America. The Noliar chief of police is suspecting a drug mafia of sorts. He doesn't know the mafia is you, does he? And you? Do you know Dumasky is working with the NYPD on this case? Surprised, Sishy?"

Sishy's trembling made his chair wobble.

"Ah, but I digress. Somehow Ms. Mojada managed to find out who you were. My guess for her first clue: the limp. She's a librarian, isn't she. Therefore, she reads. A reader notices details. She's not unlike a cop that way. I saw you with her on Heritage Lane on June 4. That day, Julie and I had come to consult Mrs. Dzhugashvili. I saw you as we were leaving in my rearview mirror. There was some animated discussion. Lots of gesturing. A prelude to the boudoir, all this theater. Some lovers need their stage, and the street is the oldest stage in the world. That's what I thought when I saw the scene unrolling in my rearview mirror.

"But then a detail came to haunt me again. The limp. I knew that limp. Or rather the walk of someone who was trying to hide his limp."

Leek got up, went to the kitchen and returned with a glass of water.

"All this talk is making me thirsty. Incidentally, you should do your dishes a little more often, Sishy. It stinks in here."

Leek took a sip of water.

"The second mistake was the burning of Mrs. Dzhugashvili's house. Really, a faux pas, Sishy. Especially so quickly after the disappearance of Ms. Mojada, her best friend. So, tell me, were you trying to scare her? Or kill her too?

"It's a good thing we needed Mrs. Dzhugashvili in the city right about that time. She's very set in her ways, you know. We had to use a whole stratagem, pretending there had been an anonymous phone call about her life being in danger. Well, little did we know that it was true—her life really was in danger. We somehow out-mediumed the great medium with our little ruse. Unwittingly so, but we did. To your chagrin, I assume, Sishy."

Leek took another swallow of water, ran his fingers above his mouth. There was no mustache to adjust. It felt odd. But it didn't matter anymore. Soon it would all end.

"Now, speaking of anonymous phone calls. Here's your third mistake. A major one. The one that was too much. Entirely de trop. There was one, a real one this time, about a chainsaw buried in Mrs. Dzhugashvili's yard. It was a woman's voice, Chief Dumasky reported. Or the pretense of a woman's voice, he added when he contacted us. Could be a voice changer, he said. And we asked him why. He was troubled by the fact that she mentioned a Makita, a very specific chainsaw. How could she know? Granted, women use chainsaws these days—at least some of them. But she said she had seen Mrs. Dzhugashvili hide her 'Makita' in her yard from a distance. How could she have known from a distance the chainsaw was a Makita?

"I bet it won't take me long until I find that voice changer. But first, I must kill you. Bury you for good this time."

■ 29 ■

"**I** NEED TO TALK TO Chief Dumasky right away!"

They had placed Jane in the only cell there was at the police station. A redbrick building with a turret and dented walls, oddly evocative of some medieval fortified castle, imposed its shape in the middle of the room's window. The Noliar County Jail. It basically told the inexperienced delinquent, "Here's where you might end if you don't get your shit together." Jane faced the window, faced the building, killed two birds with one stone by giving them both the finger, and started shouting again. "It's fooking urgent! Someone is going to die if fooking Chief doesn't do something about it."

Officers Yunaw and Ayedundt had tried to ignore the Russian woman, as instructed. But it was a hard task. The woman had screamed her lungs out since her arrest.

Speaking of her arrest, they had trouble believing Jane was capable of committing any type of violent crime. Besides amputating her trees, that is.

The Makita that had been found in her yard had little to do with the basic chainsaw that had been found in her garage. Even simple minds like Yunaw and Ayedundt figured out that there was foul play somewhere. But the Chief had ordered Jane's arrest nonetheless. "It's for her own good," he had said. "Put her in the room with a view. 'T'will calm her down."

And so they had obeyed the Chief. But the Chief had been dead wrong. The office with the prison panorama had done everything but keep Jane quiet.

And now they both had a headache.

Yunaw rose, went to knock on the Chief's door, came back a minute later, and went to Jane. "Listen, the Chief is with that New York detective. They're about to get out. Rippoff's the name, or something."

"*Rippon*, you fooking moron! Let me out! I need to talk to both of them!"

Ayedundt intervened. "He said you would say that. But we can't let you out just now."

"What you are doing is fooking illegal! But that's not important. Not right now. Right now, two lives are in danger. Life of bastard— that one, who cares. But life of nice guy as well. Nice guy who has gone crazy."

"How would you know that, Jane?" Yunaw had his arms crossed on his nascent beer belly.

"LET ME FOOK OUT YOU FOOKING ASSHOLES!"

Ayedundt and Yunaw thought that Jane could actually get arrested for *that*.

■ ■

"THAT'S WHAT MONKEY SAID? Mm. I see." Aimé told Dumasky as both cops stood in the Chief's office.

"Yup. The guy is a drunkard, but I never saw him tell anything other than the truth."

"The guy fired Monkey, right?"

"For a reason."

"So there's no time to waste."

■ ■

"LET ME FOOK OUT!"

"Enough already!" Yunaw faced Jane.

"I've taken four Advil since you've been here, damn it!" Ayedundt yelled at the Russian woman. "I'd rather have addicts and thieves in here than you."

At the moment the large frames of Aimé Rippon and Chief Dumasky stepped in and shadowed the scene.

"Can't you tell we're trying to protect you, Jane? If we had let you do what you intended to do, chances are you'd be dead right now." Aimé exclaimed. "You've got to stop this. You're not helping!"

"Let's go!" Dumasky said.

"You don't know situation!" Jane was pulling her hair. "Two men are about to die! Two! And one is Detective Leek!"

Aimé jumped. "What? Leek is here?"

Dumasky's cell rang. "Noliar Police. Dumasky talking..." He walked a few steps back to take the call. "Mm...I see...Yeah...Will do... Okay" was heard by the others. He walked back to face Aimé. "That was the Noliar Hospital Ambulance Service."

A brief pause, during which the Chief scratched his throat. "A helicopter is taking Cruz Mojada to the Pittsburgh Allegheny Hospital—"

Dumasky saw that Jane had turned very pale. "If Cruz's life is saved, it will be because of you, Jane. Because you knew before we did where she was and because you called when you did. But I am sorry,

Jane, we have to leave right now!" He now turned to Aimé. "The other thing the ambulance service said was about the guy who opened Doogy's door. Showed a police badge all right, but very quickly. Said they'd never seen the guy before and wanted to know if I hired someone new. Were surprised, though, 'cause the man looked kinda old for a new hire."

"Let's go!" Aimé said.

"I'm going with you, whether you fooking like it or not!" Jane cried out.

The detective and the Chief looked at each other, quickly grimaced their concern, then simultaneously nodded.

■ ■

"IF YOU BELIEVE IN some god, it's time to say your prayers, Sishy. For I am going to pull the trigger in a few seconds. Thirty seconds, that's the time I'm giving you to do your act of contrition."

Sishy's complexion had gone gray, and his eyes were filled with fear and pain.

"And then what, Leek?" said a familiar voice behind him. Leek jumped on his seat. He turned back and saw Aimé, followed by Chief Dumasky who closed the dining room door behind him. Both cops were holding their Glocks.

"You should leave, gentlemen, and let me finish my business."

"We can't let you do that, Leek. That's not the way it is done."

"Not professional, you mean? Oh, I know that. It's personal now. Personal business. That is why I have to ask you to leave. Otherwise, I'll be forced to use my gun on you. And I certainly don't want to. At least not on you two."

"But you want to use it on Doogy, 'that it?" said Dumasky.

"His name is Doug Sishy," said Leek. "That's a bad, bad name."

"Let our justice system handle it." Aimé stepped closer to Leek.

Leek produced a sardonic laugh. "I prefer my own, gentlemen. My own justice system. It makes more sense. This man is a pimp, a drug dealer, and a butcher, and his life needs to end now."

Sishy and the chair he was taped to were shaking. It led to some impromptu drumming on the hardwood floor.

"Suppose you kill this piece of shit. I mean, I don't disagree with you. Guys like this are a waste. We need to put them away, clean up our system. But there are places for that. Prisons." Aimé was tempted to sit down and try to bring reason back to his colleague. He had an enormous respect for Leek. But what he was facing now was not a reasonable man, but a tenuous situation at best. He had to be a cop first. Not a colleague. Not a friend. Just a cop. And so he stood, his Glock ready if needed.

"Prison is too good for someone like that, Detective Rippon."

"We have witnesses," said Dumasky. "One who saw Doogy, I mean, Sishy, set the fire at Jane's house. His name is Ed Reed. We call him 'Monkey' 'round here. Obviously because he can climb trees. I mean, really climb. And that night when he saw something weird happening, he went up a tree to have a better view and saw it all. And I suppose, Monkey, who's never sober, must have made remarks to Doogy, I mean, Sishy." The Chief turned to the tied-up man with an angry smile. "Ain't that right, Shawn?" Then, he sternly turned toward Leek. "So Monkey got fired 'cause of that. I'm sure if you hadn't stopped the guy, Monkey would have been found dead someday. So we want to thank you for your help, Detective. But since we got the guy, why take the justice into your own hands?"

"And why not?"

"Suppose you kill this bastard," stated Aimé. "Now what happens to you? We'll have to arrest you. I get it: what you just killed is not much of a human being, but you just committed a murder nonetheless. So we would have to put the handcuffs on you all the same. It's the law."

"But, gentlemen, you won't have to do that. See, after I am done with him, I'll take care of myself."

"What does that mean?" Dumasky asked.

"It means he's going to fooking kill himself." In a most Napoleonic way, Jane had opened the dining room door and entered the battlefield.

"I told you to stay behind, Jane." Aimé stood straight and tense, and with his left hand he tried to gesture Jane away.

"I think Detective Rippon is right, Mrs. Dzhugashvili. You shouldn't be here. None of you should be here. Leave Sishy and me alone. It will soon be over."

Silence struck the room, and the breathing of all present thickened it rather than broke it. Sishy, who was forced into nasal respiration, gave it an unnerving, whistling cadence.

"Over my ass!" Jane finally yelled. She went and sat by Leek. "Detective Leek, what fook is going on? You are brainiest detective in New York. You catch worst criminals with those eyes and those gray cells. And you choose this time to go fooking berserk."

"I've had a good career, Madame, it's true."

"And you think killing someone is good way to honor career?"

"It's a good way to avenge my niece. She was my only family." Leek pointed to Sishy with his chin. "And he took her away from me. And besides that, he did many horrible things. So do you really think killing him is an act of folly in this case?"

"Maybe not act of folly, but of stupidity."

"How so, Madame?"

"Well, you kill him, and that's it. He doesn't suffer. He's just dead. But if you let police arrest him, he will rot in prison for life. He will have to face shitty cell, shitty companions, shitty conscience, and shitty orange clothes."

"Frankly, I can't see you in orange clothes, Leek. Besides, what would I do without my partner? And his mustache? Hey, what happened to the mustache? Hey, have you thought of that?" Julie, armed and out of breath, had rushed into the room.

"About fooking time," Jane mumbled.

Julie rushed to her partner. "It's over, Leek. Do you know I had to take a helicopter to come here, and I hate those things? Just for you. Threw up three times. Now, give me your gun, Leek." She gently touched his armed hand. "Give it to me. Please."

■ ■

"I'VE GOT TO OFFICIALLY arrest him," Dumasky said.

"I know you do. But it was temporary insanity. It never happened to Leek before. Can't you just let it pass? You've got the credit for Sishy's arrest," Aimé answered.

They were in the Chief's office.

"I don't know, Rippon."

"He going to undergo serious counseling. We've got some good pros at the NYPD. And you don't know Julie."

"Matter of fact, I do."

"That's right, I forgot. You were her boss once. So you know she's a tough cookie. She's gonna harass Leek. I wouldn't be surprised if she took him to counseling herself. These two have a bond, man."

Dumasky nodded. "She's probably the only one he listens to, eh?"

"He listens to Jane too. But Julie's the partner."

"A bit like a daughter, looks like to me." Dumasky dragged his steps to the window.

"So how about it?"

"Dunno."

"Come on, Dumasky, you owe me one."

"How duya figure that one?"

"Remember when I first came to see you? You served me the shittiest brain juice in the world. Don't you think I saw you had an espresso machine?"

■ 30 ■

FLOWERS. FLOWERS EVERYWHERE. IN large vases, in small vases. In bright colors, in muted colors. Against walls, in the middle of the room. A regiment of bouquets on a large table. Individual arrangements on small tables. One on the window sill. Orchids, roses, carnations, gladiolas, sunflowers, lavender. A symphony of blues, mauves, pinks, fuchsias, reds.

"And fooking yellows. They couldn't have avoided fooking yellows."

A small sofa and a couple of armchairs had been pulled into the room to welcome guests. Courtesy of Dr. Selavee from the Allegheny General Hospital in Pittsburgh.

"I like yellow, Jane," said Cruz, who was propped up on her pillows. "Although I must admit with all these flowers, the room looks like a funeral parlor."

"All your fooking admirers. And I mean that literally."

Cruz touched her neck. "I don't know if I'll ever go out with a guy anymore."

Jane rolled her eyes. "Like I believe you. But just in case."

"Just in case," Zoe hammered in as she entered the hospital room. "Jane and I got you something." Zoe was holding a brightly colored bouquet.

"More flowers. How nice." Cruz pouted.

"Look closer, you bitch!" said Jane.

As Zoe handed her the arrangement, Cruz realized that it wasn't floral.

"Oh, how wonderful. Dildos! And in all colors! I didn't know they had them in acid green! Oh, thank you, gracias, gracias, amigas mías!"

Someone quickly knocked on the door, then got in the room. Dr. Selavee. A tall woman in her late fifties, handsome in a disheveled way, with pale skin, high cheekbones, and a resolute expression in her almond-shaped eyes, she had been married many times, once to a Paul Trenton. Of that unsuccessful union came what she considered her most successful achievement: her son, Marc. She looked at Cruz' chart. On her way to her patient, she quickly patted Zoe's head, then examined Cruz' neck and checked her vitals. "Well, looks like you're about ready to go. About time too. Was a long visit, wasn't it? Almost two weeks. Of course, you almost went to the other side—whatever that other side might be. So this explains that. You're a tough cookie, my dear. You were dead on the operating table for a couple of minutes, but you came back. So what do you say? Pack your bags and say good-bye to this damn hospital."

The doctor saw the non-floral arrangement by the bedside. "Dildos! How great! Can I have one?"

"Sure," said Cruz. "Take what color you like. Except the acid green."

"Take yellow," said Jane.

"Mother!" cried Marc who had just entered the room at the moment Dr. Selavee had grabbed the yellow dildo. "What, darling? These things are reliable, you know." She went to kiss her son. "Well, maybe you don't. But I do. And I bet the majority of the company here does too."

All the women in the room nodded, including a nurse aid who had come to remove Cruz' food platter.

"Can't replace love." Marc addressed a sore look to Zoe, who answered with a fatalistic shrug and a smile.

Dr. Selavee wrapped her arm around her son. "Ah, sweetheart, if you had been fucked up by men the way I have, you would have divorced them too! And I don't mean 'fucked up' in the good sense— as in the boudoir. They were okay in there. Except for one. That was Spaghetti land, I am afraid. And he wasn't even Italian."

"Maybe you should get a collection like me. With all this variety, doctor, I tell you, I am going to renounce men," said Cruz.

"Address of the nearest convent, please!" Jane exclaimed.

Dr. Selavee felt her patient's neck again. "You will have to renounce men, dear. At least for a while. A month, I'd say."

"Oh, Dios mío, one full month! How about two weeks? Like if I am really, really careful and only practice the missionary position. Doctor?"

EPILOGUE ■ One Year Later

DRAPES AND CURTAINS WERE lifting from discreet corners in the houses on Heritage Lane. Gossips were at their post, en garde with binoculars. It was a hot June day, and most of these faux bird-watchers had good air conditioning. A car was coming, the type of car that no one saw anymore. A couple of foolhardy Heritage inhabitants deciding to defy the heat, stepped out and grabbed their brooms to sweep their impeccable porches. They needed poise. Mostly, they needed a better view.

Gossip-in-Chief Lara Clement came out and swept.

Old couple Dick Carson and George Mutant came out and swept, each with his own personal broom. They just had a fight, and they didn't want the other's dirty paws to touch their sweeping device. But they had been together thirty-three years, and in a couple of hours it would end the way it always ended—with the two brooms so close together one could not tell them apart.

Cruz Mojada came out and swept. When her beau du jour attempted to draw her back inside, she kicked him with the broom, saying, "Mi amór, this is important sweeping." Her beau's hesitant reply of "But, but—" was immediately retorted with "Butt for later!"

And so they swept.

The car was registered in New York State, yet it was a far cry from the Crown Vic they had come used to for the past couple of years, and from which Julie and that funny older man with the mustache would come out and visit Jane every few months. Actually, they had not seen the funny man for a while. It seemed Julie had a new partner, a black guy, young and very good looking, smiling all the time. He was the one who had come this past year with Julie and visited Jane.

The sweepers had momentarily stopped their redundant sweeping as they finally were able to identify the sedan that was slowly approaching. Most of them were kids when the car had first come out, some of them teens, but by golly, if this wasn't a 1952 Cadillac, then they had never made out with pretty girls and pretty boys in backseats, either!

Who would drive such a car?

She was no spring chicken, but a thing of beauty nonetheless: forest green and shiny and with gold wing ornaments right under the headlights, just like it was back then. That was what one sweeper told his next door sweeper just now as the '52 Cadillac turning signal flashed on as the car finally glided into Jane's alley.

Who would come out of such a car?

Someone with money, or nostalgia. Or a passion for vintage cars.

Someone who didn't give a shit about new vehicles with all the damn technology, that's for sure.

Someone very meticulous about cleaning.

Someone who was taking his jolly time. Or her jolly time.

Well, come out of the freaking car already! How much more sweeping would go on until a face would finally be revealed?

Finally, the door opened, 't'was about time, but no face was seen. Only a hat, a three-piece navy suit. Black shoes almost as shiny as the Cadillac.

And a thick mustache.

Well, if it isn't that funny man from New York again. They'll be darned!

The sweepers and drape lifters and binoculars holders were waiting for the passenger door to open, but no movement came from that end.

The Mustache Man was alone.

He walked rhythmically toward Jane's door. Neither in a hurry nor dragging his feet. Here was a man who measured his efforts. Efficient, not without grace.

True, some cats looked funny. But they all had grace.

And, of course, a mustache.

■ ■

WITH THE HELP OF a good fire insurance and the Noliar BS (short for BuiltSolid) Company, Jane's house now looked fresh and clean.

And her backyard seemed fairly normal. The formerly amputated branches had resumed their twist and turn little acts—and this with a vengeance. The veggie garden was well-tended, unlike the grass which, unmowed and happy, was dancing in the humid breeze.

"You're looking at my lawn, Detective?" Jane smiled. "Actually, it's not lawn anymore. It's wild grass. I like it that way. At least on backyard."

They were seated on Jane's shaded patio, well-protected from the sun and from sweepers.

"Indeed you would. It's like a witch's domain. I bet you have some special herbs growing amidst this grass."

Jane didn't answer.

"I see that the branches on your trees have grown as well, Madame."

"Ah, Detective Leek, it looks like I have grown allergic to chainsaws. Go figure."

Leek chuckled. "Go figure," he echoed. "But you have a toolshed. I don't think I noticed a toolshed before."

"That. It's for squirrels. We have arrangement. Instead of going to attic, they sleep there during winter. I provide them with supplies. Nuts, peanuts, walnuts. And I have oak trees, so they pick their own fooking acorns. Sometimes they come right here on patio and I feed them carrots. Those things aren't shy. I bought shed shortly after you—" Jane hesitated.

"You can say it. After I went into treatment."

Jane observed Leek. "Yes, and apparently, it helped. You look good. And mustache is back. I never thought I would fooking say that. But am I glad to see that mustache!"

"You know I came for a reading, right?"

Jane nodded. "Personal, right?"

"Can you get in touch with my niece?"

Jane eyed Leek for stretchy seconds.

"I have something that was hers," he said, handing Jane a small circular stone engraved with a spider's web. "Actually, it was a gift from her. She said the web reminded her of me."

"Because of your job. And because of who you are. Very complicated, mysterious man," Jane responded as she took the stone.

"Give me your hands now, Detective. We'll meditate for minute."

Leek did as he was asked.

Holding the object and closing her eyes, she then proceeded to give Leek a reading. She talked nonstop for about half an hour and Leek listened. Finally, he couldn't help it. A notebook landed on his hands as if by magic. Cop instinct, despite a year spent away from the force.

"So my niece is fine," Leek said in the end.

"She's very happy, yes." Jane opened her eyes, saw the notebook. "I could feel it while I was reading. But it's all right. Good sign. You're ready to go back to work. That's what fooking notebook means."

"Is she—uh—in another dimension? Or has she somehow...hm... reincarnated?"

"What you want to know, Detective, is if Julie is your niece."

Leek's complexion reddened.

"Why can't you love Julie for who she is? Your partner, the cop who saved your life. The person who belongs to present, not past. Stop living in fooking past, Detective Leek!"

Leek nodded, and then exploded into laughter. "You know, Chainsaw Jane is a name that suits you perfectly."

"And why is that?"

"Why, Mrs. Dzhugashvili, you cut through the crap like no one else."

www.ingramcontent.com/pod-product-compliance
Lightning Source LLC
Chambersburg PA
CBHW020343180626
46812CB00001B/316